all fall down

all

A NOVEL BY

fall down

**JAMES
LEO
HERLIHY**

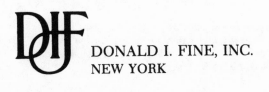
DONALD I. FINE, INC.
NEW YORK

Library of Congress Cataloging-in-Publication Data
Herlihy, James Leo.
    All fall down / by James Leo Herlihy.
      p.   cm.
    ISBN 1-55611-192-4
    I. Title.
PS3515.E6325A78   1990
813'.54—dc20   90-55086
                                                        CIP

Manufactured in the United States of America

10 9 8 7 6 5 4 3 2 1

The line from Dardanella used by permission of the copyright owners, Fred Fisher Music Company, Inc. Written by
Johnny S. Block, Fred Fisher, and Felix Bernard.

The lines from The Darktown Strutters' Ball used by permission of the copyright proprietor. Words and music by
Shelton Brooks. © Copyright 1917 / Copyright renewal
1945 Leo Feist Inc., New York, N.Y.

for Dick Duane
for his help

Introduction

We 20th-century men are learning, because we
simply must in order to survive, that brotherhood
is not an ideal but a necessity. We really are inter-
dependent. We are one. One organism. It's no
poem, either. It's a fact of ecology. In our har-
mony, in our genuine deep caring for one another,
lies our survival.

—James Leo Herlihy in an essay from the book,
Sexual Latitude

"Ama et fac quod vis." St. Augustine advised some
fifteen centuries ago, "Love and do as you will." If one
agrees that, in the work of all truly laudable writers, there
pervades an ambience that binds the artist in some
unique and compelling way to a group of persons with
whom he has had little or no direct contact, the syllogism
between Augustine's words and Herlihy's is not only apparent, but profound. Both the Augustinian adage and
the body of Herlihy's work convey the same compacted
truth and insight; both recognize the redemptive power
of love and the awesome freedom implicit in that power.
If Augustine is saying, in a phrase, that the essence of
being human and the worth of human activity derives
from the will to care for and empathize with others, Herlihy, through his books, translates this moral principle
into terms of contemporary experience. In so doing, he
demonstrates that the human phenomenon is predicated
upon a greater intangibility, the phenomenon of love.

Purely defined, love is an involved sharing of oneself
with others; of all human emotions, love is pervasive and

1

unique. As the fundamental precept of Western moral thought, it has had a more profound impact upon the fate of our race than any other factor. Although we have killed, plundered, and desecrated in the name of the love of God or humanity, love has consistently maintained itself as a constructive impulse. The most positive and creative forces instigated in any realm of endeavor can be readily traced to the overwhelming need of human beings to communicate emotionally with their fellows. In our peculiarly psychological age, this need for communication has acquired a more highly personalized aspect; love has become the means—perhaps the only effective means—of salvation from the anonymity of contemporary existence. This search for salvation, which could be defined as the ability to recognize one's face both in the mirror *and* in the crowd, is the hallmark of twentieth century man. The dissection and illumination of this condition is the particular province of the contemporary artist.

Because he is very much a product of our "Anonymous Age" and yet affirms and transmits a belief in the efficacy of love, Herlihy deserves an analysis and an appreciation that he has yet to be fully accorded. More than most writers of note, he perceives the multidimensional nature of love; he recognizes not only that love is the motivating power for artistic pursuit, but he acknowledges the more basic premise that the correlative of love is creativity and that, from creative endeavors, man derives all enjoyment of beauty and all pleasure. Believing that the result of love is liberation, Herlihy refuses to function in the rarefied atmosphere of artistic detachment; rather, he *participates* in being and, through his art, urges others toward the same sense of involvement.

Like a number of other writers of a first-rate and consistent quality, Herlihy has been victimized somewhat by an elitist and academic approach to our literature. As a body, we tend to admire and honor most those writers who most conspicuously detach themselves from their native environment; the hallucinogenic and satirical imagination tends to provoke the greatest attention. Happily, however, America always has bred a strain of writers whose primary concern and impetus has been a direct involvement with the immediacy of the human condition. Theirs is not a world of empirical rationalism or pure fancy (both of which may be ingredients of the American environment but are not truly indigenous to the American zone); rather, they are nurtured by the more formidable nebulae of feeling, by an intuition in which the dichotomy of being is seen as a vague chaos made liveable by the resolve of an interior being.

Herlihy's works are filled with the subtleties of a brilliant perception in which the inherent comedy and sadness of simply being are conveyed without pretense; he is aware of the inexorable melancholy of life, but never surrenders to it. His writing is sparked by an imagination that feeds upon his concern for people, and by a love of life which never allows the candid imagination to degenerate into artifice. Herlihy's books brim with delightful specifics so ideally suited to their subject and so convincingly presented that they seem to come out of one's own memory. The interaction of characters who come alive through the humane nuances of Herlihy's language create in the reader a sense of loss and depletion, a feeling of true catharsis; upon finishing one of his books, one is both saddened and, in a strange way, invigorated. Invariably, the source of this catharsis is Herlihy's perception

3

of love. His books all relate the durability of love and its ramifications both privately (as sexual response) and socially (as reflections of the political order). The loss or misuse of love is a haunting theme in all of his works, as is the regenerative power of a consistent love; each of his major works reiterates the penetrating forcefulness of genuine caring, without which there is only emptiness and loneliness.

Herlihy belongs to a distinguished line of American writers who may be termed "native" because their artistic sustenance depends upon their native and physical environment. Through his perception of life as the poetry of being and his use of language less as explication than as a vehicle to express the continuum of emotion, he is a *de facto* heir of the tradition of Walt Whitman, Hart Crane, Sinclair Lewis and Tennessee Williams. Having been spawned by the contemporary American scene, Herlihy's work flows from and returns to the same source: the consciousness that defines and nurtures the national entity. In many ways, he is the prototype of that writer, peculiar to the American tableau, who functions outside a literary establishment or hierarchy, and whose work becomes a mirror of the communal soul; he is a writer who captures from his own experience a significant and abiding moment in the experience of his race. This is not to say that Herlihy's work is preponderantly autobiographical. Rather than relying upon incidents from his personal past, his writing is a testament to his preoccupation with, and his sensitivity toward, the experience of others. Herlihy does not simply re-create reality; he illumines it through the free working of the imagination. "Every character I've ever written has come out of my imagination," he has said privately. While reflecting a personal strength and resourcefulness, this premise relates a state of mind that is not entirely unambivalent.

"There is a mystery involved in the writing impulse—there's a compulsiveness about it," he explained in a recent interview. "It's like trying to discover what sex is. You can't do it . . . For me, I know that a book has to be written when one character, one specific being, has moved into my head and unpacked and doesn't show any sign of leaving.

The backdrop for Herlihy's work is the psychological landscape of America. In eight plays, two collections of short stories and, most especially, in his three novels, *All Fall Down* (1960), *Midnight Cowboy* (1965), and *The Season of the Witch* (1971), Herlihy has peopled the American continent with an array of characters who are, in essence, the spiritual aborigines of a latter-day Atlantis, a continent struggling under the burden of its own genius to postpone, if not indeed alter, its fate. His novels each convey a sense of the overwhelming bigness of this country; the journeys which their protagonists take across it are not only wanderings in the physical sense, used as a means of developing a particular story line, but they are also allegories of self-growth and spiritual maturation. More particularly, these journeys correspond to the emotional odyssey of adolescence. One can hardly overstress the significance of the adolescent experience in Herlihy's work. For Herlihy, adolescence reflects a keener sense of being, a more spontaneous response to physical and emotional stimuli, a closer connection with the nuances of the imagination, and a greater willingness to share the core of one's self, than is generally associated with the adult world. For this reason, the major protagonists of Herlihy's novels are either adolescents themselves (Clinton in *All Fall Down,* for example) or they are

5

closely related to the adolescent experience (Echo O'-Brien in *All Fall Down*). Adolescence is seen by Herlihy as the acceptance of the full nature of the self; it is the mating of sensuality and innocence, which the inhibitions of adulthood sadly diminish.

Herlihy's adults either suffer from a loss of youth that is synonymous with the loss of innocence (Annabel and the drunken Ralph in *All Fall Down*), or they prove themselves capable of transforming the essence of youth—an expansive and benevolent expression of self-hood—into a motivating life principle (the socialist-idealist aspect of Ralph in *All Fall Down*). Young or old, his characters all suffer from the American dilemma that places physical youth at a premium while denigrating the moral idealism of the young; they are all victimized by a mythical history in which the pursuit of materialism has been substituted for the pursuit of happiness.

The major protagonists of Herlihy's novels all share two primary attributes: a hypersensitivity to their own being that translates to their perception of the world around them, and an abiding desire to realize themselves not only as individuals but as part of the general environment. There is a naiveté about the compulsiveness of their relationship to the mystery of being, in their enthusiasm for life, in their celebration of innocence, but their convictions are so pristine, so near to our innate understanding of truth, that we as readers must celebrate with them. We accept their naiveté and mourn its loss. We see through these characters how thoroughly Herlihy is a believer in love as a preternatural instinct; he believes in the predilection of human beings for good. Indifference, cruelty, loneliness, these are true perversions and are viewed as outgrowths of a lack of love. Though his characters are often victims of this lack, the enduring strength

6

that resides within them results not only in their ability to overcome it, but in their compulsion to do so; by loving, they reaffirm the basis of life. They do this without pretense, often without knowing that they *are* doing it. While the characters of these books stand very firmly on their own as individuals and are in no way mere prototypes, they do serve to substantiate a premise larger than themselves: the novels all reflect the psychic potence of sexuality and the power of love as both a political and a social force.

More than most writers of note, James Leo Herlihy has recognized the uniquely pervasive potency of love in the lives of human beings. He has succeeded in conveying this insight not in the fatuous terms of the sentimentalist or in the bloodless epistemology of the professional moralist, but simply as a man of intense feeling who happens also to be a disciplined artist. His prose is both virile and intuitive, and he possesses the one essential attribute of the first-rate writer: the power to translate, through the language of reality, the intangible poetry of emotion. Few writers stand as entirely unembarrassed before the *fact* of love, which is, after all, an overwhelming fact; few writers maintain a more abiding faith in the conviction that men live in a symbiotic relationship to each other. This belief in the purity and ubiquity of love is the mainstay of Herlihy's work; it provides the central motivation for his characters, and is the source of his power to affect and appreciative readership. For Herlihy, writing is itself an act of love.

—Jeffrey Bailey
Casablanca, Morocco
June 1990

. . . There was the truth of virginity and the truth of passion, the truth of wealth and of poverty, of thrift and of profligacy, of carelessness and abandon. Hundreds and hundreds were the truths and they were all beautiful.

And then the people came along. Each as he appeared snatched up one of the truths and some who were quite strong snatched up a dozen of them.

It was the truths that made the people grotesques. . . . The moment one of the people took one of the truths to himself . . . and tried to live his life by it, he became a grotesque and the truth he embraced became a falsehood.

—Sherwood Anderson,
in Winesburg, Ohio

all fall down

part 1

IT IS KNOWN that in every neighborhood in the United States there is at least one house that is special. Special because it is haunted, or because of an act of violence that took place there. Or there are thought to be crazy persons living in it. Or Communists. Or someone in it is known to have served a jail term. All children, good and bad, know these stories and help to circulate them. Go to any small child on the block and ask him where such a house is located: he will know. And if you question him on Seminary Street in Cleveland, Ohio, chances are he will lead you to the house the Williamses live in.

A sign on the front door says:

LICENSED REAL ESTATE DEALER
AND
NOTARY PUBLIC

But since outsiders are seldom seen going through that door, the sign is believed to be a cover-up for some unholy activity, very likely of a seditious nature.

The Williams house is big. It is made of wood. No architect had anything to do with the designing of it. Some big development organization in the Twenties turned out more than a hundred just like it; so there is nothing unusual about the place. —But if you were to believe a fraction of the stories that are told, the house might take on a peculiar look, even the bushes out front would seem different: children claim they bear poison flowers in the spring.

They may even tell you about a lamp that often burns long into the night in one of the basement windows. Although curtains cover every possible peephole, these youngsters claim to know just what that grinning old man,

11

the father, does down there. The stories do vary to some extent: one child will swear to you that in the Williams cellar is a small but powerful radio station on which he receives messages from some subversive organization; another maintains that Mr. Williams prepares pamphlets and speeches designed to agitate against the government; still another prefers to believe that secret meetings are held there, and that entrance and egress is achieved only through underground tunnels. Whatever clashes there may be in these childish imaginings, one belief is shared by all: the old man represents some real threat to the American form of government and what's more, he does not believe in God. This much is *known;* because Mr. Williams, on a number of occasions, perhaps rendered incautious by alcohol, had, himself, in a public saloon, not only admitted to but *announced* certain political and religious views, which were then interpreted by his listeners and disseminated on the street.

The old man had two sons. One of them, the older, was called Berry-berry.

Berry-berry was known in the neighborhood to be a wild person, with narrow eyes and a cleft chin, who traveled around getting arrested in Covington, Kentucky; Biloxi, Mississippi, and other strange places. The Williamses' arrival on Seminary Street took place just a month after Berry-berry's twenty-first birthday, and it was at this age that he began his travels. A bedroom was prepared for him in the new house, but the young man had not even slept in it. His Western Stories were placed on his bookshelf, and his locked cedar chest full of childhood belongings, mostly weapons and tools, was placed at the foot of his bed. But the books were never again opened and the cedar chest was never unlocked. Since the move he had paid certain irregular and surprise visits to Cleveland, and it was

12

on these occasions that the neighbors caught their brief glimpses of him: once, he was seen standing at a second-story window of the house, peeing on the porch roof; and he was known to be responsible for a good deal of door slamming at odd hours of the night. During one particular summer he was often observed arriving and departing in a blue Ford pickup truck; this vehicle might have aroused less speculation had it not been for the fact that, parked right behind it, was a 1929 Dodge touring car, painted a flawless shiny black, with a FOREIGN CONSUL sticker on the windshield. Berry-berry was often seen with the "ambassador" herself, a beautiful woman who wore a variety of large and expensive hats. Actual clues to the nature of his association with this woman were meager, but a number of full-blown tales grew up around them.

In plain fact, the owner of this car was not an ambassador or any other kind of important personage. Her name was Echo O'Brien, she was a receptionist for an insurance company in Toledo, Ohio, and the FOREIGN CONSUL sticker happened to be on the windshield when she first bought the Dodge in a used-car lot. Her part in the story of the Williamses will be told in its proper place. The point is simply this:

There was often a wide and ridiculous difference between what took place in the Williams house and what the people of Seminary Street believed.

Now, the younger son was Clinton.

Clinton Williams was not yet a full-fledged person. He was a small boy with big quick eyes. Angular in body and in manner, uncertain of himself and puzzled by others, he was as graceless as a new bird.

Although these qualities are not unusual in a young person, Clinton was nonetheless the recipient of many deferential smiles on the street; they said he was not quite *right*,

13

and showed their sympathy by these extra kindnesses. He was of high-school age, but attended no high school or any other school: the boy simply stayed home. As he did not seem to lack intelligence, his truancy was generally held to be a sign of some more sinister defect, perhaps a serious nervous disorder. It was known, for instance, that he occupied himself with the keeping of little notebooks in which he wrote down every word that was said to him or spoken within his hearing. This "nervous habit" became known because such a notebook, marked Number 142 (indicating the existence of at least 141 others), was found at the Aloha Sweet Shop on Mound Road and read by the manager, both clerks, and several customers before Clinton came back the next morning to claim it. He maintained to the manager that it was all part of a "fictitious" book he was writing, but since the manager had found his own name in it, and many of the things he himself had said, the story did not seem to hold water. —From then on, when Clinton passed the Aloha Sweet Shop, he walked on the other side of the street.

The fourth Williams was the mother of these two boys.

Annabel Williams was generally believed to be a sane and law-abiding person, and no unusual stories of her behavior were circulated. Her head rested on her shoulders at a deliberate and sensible angle. Annabel was thin and pretty for a woman who must be nearly fifty years old, and her hair-dos and dresses were all of the sort worn only by sensible and law-abiding women. She was never seen on the street without a full make-up; and she was a church-goer. Therefore, if Annabel Williams was discussed at all unfavorably it was only by reason of her marriage to a man who would, some said, overthrow the United States government by force, and gladly; with one wild son whose whereabouts and doings were as a rule unknown or

14

unsavory; with one odd son who had nervous habits like
writing everything down and might one day go berserk;
and with an intermittent visitor, the strangely beautiful
driver of the 1929 Dodge touring car, who was the consul
for God alone knew which foreign power.

At any rate, Mrs. Williams' slate was clean—except for
one trivial event that took place the day they moved in:

A flock of children gathered around the Seminary Street
place to watch the Italians unload furniture from the van.
Annabel hunted through a kitchen barrel, as yet unpacked,
and found in it a box of marshmallows. She tried to make
friends with these new children by passing out the marshmallows to them. But as she did so, something happened
in the truck: a bird cage got smashed. It was a cage made
by Berry-berry in an eighth-grade woodcrafting class, a
fragile thing to begin with, and not large enough to be
comfortably lived in by any bird. But Annabel scolded the
workmen in such a way that the children withdrew and
widened their circle. And then some bold child, a boy of
eight, came forward and held out his hand: "Ma'am, I
didn't get a marshmallow!" Annabel turned to him in irri-
tation. "Here!" she said sharply, "take the whole package!"
But what she handed the child was the broken cage.
Frightened, he dropped it at her feet and withdrew
quickly to hide behind the other children. Annabel instantly realized her mistake and tried to make reparations.
But the children backed off. One by one, and in small
groups, they disappeared into driveways and behind
parked cars. From where they watched, the children knew
she was crying as she called to them: "There's lots more
left, there's a whole bottom layer. Doesn't anybody like
marshmallows any more?" But children are suspicious of
grownups who weep; and chances are, word got around

15

that very morning that something was wrong with the new lady.

Seminary Street had hold of half the truth, and this was the half that made it wary of the entire Williams family. You could not say it was unfriendly to them. Most of the grown-up people made a point of smiling at any Williams they met on the street or in a store or gas station; and though certain older children might, on a dare, run up on the porch and try to peep into a window at night, not even the boldest of them would ever make an out-and-out nuisance of himself on their property, or repeat to any Williams the tales that went around.

As a result of all this politeness, only Clinton, of the Williamses, had any hint of the fact that he and his family lived under this special scrutiny. And he was too concerned with internal affairs to give much thought to outside opinion. Besides, Clinton always regarded it as the New Neighborhood and did not even try to make friends in it. Outside his own family, the only people of importance to him were a small handful of Old Neighbors from Amelia Street where he was born. At first, he set out to make regular Saturday trips on the streetcar to visit these Old Neighbors; but as he began to suspect that in certain of those kitchens his visits were regarded as a nuisance, the trips soon petered out and stopped altogether.

Here are some sample pages from one of Clinton's notebooks; they were written on a certain November day during the Williamses' first year on Seminary Street:

[*Clinton's Notebook*]

    "I see you've pulled your blankets out again."
    I pretend to be asleep. She raised the blind.
    "I suppose you think you're getting away with this.

Sleep till noon, make a servant of your mother. Lord, I wish I knew how anyone could sleep with the blankets pulled out. I couldn't sleep a wink if I thought my feet were . . . ! —You're awake, mister, I can tell by your breathing. I'm looking at your eyelids right this minute, now see if you can keep them from fluttering!"

I opened my eyes and faced her.

"Do you think your father's going to sit by and let you get away with this?" She got busy with the blankets.

I said, "I don't think he cares whether or not I sleep with them tucked in." I knew she wasn't talking about the blankets, but I had some impulse to throw her a curve.

"Smart."

"What time is it?"

"Ten o'clock."

"I thought you said noon."

"There! I *knew* you weren't asleep! I can always tell by your breath when you play possum. I always know when you boys are lying. Now why don't you just own up, and tell me where you spent all those days? If it was perfectly honorable and decent, why so secret? Do you think I won't find out? Do you think it won't come home to roost? There's something else I want to know. We're going to have less secrecy around here. Are you in secret communication with Berry-berry?"

"No."

"Clinton. Do you love your family?"

"Yes."

"So does Berry-berry, loves us to pieces. I don't doubt that by an eyelash. Are you getting up or not?"

"I can't while you're standing there."

She started walking toward the door. "Berry-berry always slept without his bottoms, too. I don't know why. I couldn't sleep a wink if I thought my . . ."

"If you thought your what?"

"Smart!"

"You want me to get up?"

"Look here, mister star boarder. You haven't gotten away with a thing. You've got some questions to answer, so don't think you can rest on your laurels."

She left the room. I put on my clothes and went down to the kitchen. She was sitting at the table with her coffee cup, looking pretty good what with the vaseline on her eyelashes and the sun coming in through the orange curtains. I poured myself some coffee.

"Clinton."

Beware. Soft voice. She may decide to weep.

"Yes, Annabel."

"Why is it I have never got used to being called Annabel by you boys? You'd think after years and years—but it was never *my* idea, this first-name thing with this family. It's all part of your father's contempt for the family unit. He thinks Mother is a dirty word."

"That's because some mothers blackmail their kids about the birth trauma and all that. It makes good sense."

"That's right. If you've got a weak board," she said, "then by all means burn the house down, Heil Hitler, and away we go. Ooooh! (A noise of distaste; very hard to spell.) —I hope you don't believe every word your father says is gospel!"

"I don't."

"But on the other hand, you should respect him for what he was."

I looked at her.

"Don't think you can poo-poo your father, or be condescending to him. Not by a long shot, mister fourteen-years-old-and-don't-forget-it."

"I *wasn't!*"

"Because he was as brilliant a man as I'd ever met— before he started committing suicide. Sweetheart, I wouldn't lean on that stove in those nice trousers; it's impossible to keep it *that* clean, clean enough to just lie down and go to *sleep* on."

I moved over to the cupboard and leaned against it. "What did you mean about suicide?"

"It's no secret. Your father's been committing systematic suicide for the last thirty years. Bourbon. Ever hear of it?"

"That must not be a very effective method of killing yourself. I mean if it takes *that* long. Now if he really wanted to do the job . . . !"

"Whoah! Just whoah!" She took a big drag on her cigarette. I love the way Annabel smokes, she always fills up her whole body with the stuff. I had a sudden very strong urge to light up about a dozen of them and smoke myself blue.

"I realize," she said, "you're educated to the point where it's no longer necessary for you to attend the tenth grade. Oh heavens yes, there's very little you couldn't teach any college professor. But it happens that the literature I have read on alcoholism was *written* by a college professor."

"Has he met Ralph?"

"He doesn't need to."

"Has this college professor ever seen Ralph passed out drunk? Because I never have."

"Clinton," she said quietly, "I have a new word for you. It's 'contrary.' Now listen, how often have you *admitted* to me that your father makes more sense when he's not drinking? Just answer."

"*More* sense, but that doesn't mean the minute he takes a drink he's gone nuts or killing himself."

"Thank you. I have canvassed the family attitude and found myself as usual a very lonely minority."

I started out of the room. This cigarette thing has gotten hold of me; sometimes I just have to have one.

"Clinton." Soft voice again. "Clinton, listen a minute. Families must not quarrel among themselves. I was *wrong* about your pulling the blankets out. That was just nervousness on my part. *I* happen to be more comfortable with my feet safe, but it's individual preference. Now will you sit down here for a minute. I want to ask you something, just two friends, no umbilical cords. Ooh! What a disgusting word!" I sat down at the table. "Clinton, do you honestly think all I care about is Mother's Day presents?" She laughed. "Oh golly, how little we understand each other. But listen, little baby, we have love, don't we? And that surpasseth all. Now tell me what you did all those days?"

I considered telling her.

"Fifty-seven days, Clinton. And it's not just a matter of playing a little hookey, you didn't even go to register. Did you?"

"No."

"In other words, you have never once set foot inside of John J. Pershing High School?"

"No."

"Where did you get those books you carry?"

"They're last year's."

She did various things with her face, lip-biting, eye work, etc. Then she said, "If you prefer the Old Neighborhood so much, would you like to commute every day and take up again at Central? You can get student fares on the streetcar, and I'll pack your lunch."

"They won't let you. You have to live in a certain district."

"You mean you've tried?"

"Yeah. And then I got to hanging around over there and pretty soon a lot of time had passed and . . ."

"Fifty-seven *days?*"

"No, I stopped going over there about a month ago."

"And are you going to tell me you've spent the last four weeks sitting in the Aloha Sweet Shop on Mound Road?"

"More or less."

"But, Clinton, doing *what?* It doesn't make sense!"

I thought for a minute, then I decided to blurt it out.

"I've done about twenty-five more notebooks."

Her mouth fell open, then she leaned back, closed her eyes, and as her breath came out, she sort of intoned it. Gradually she pulled herself together again and sat forward, touching my wrist with her fingertips. "Thank you for telling me the truth. We won't talk any more just now, but thank you."

I started into the bedroom with my coffee.

"Clinton?" I stopped walking. She talked to my back. "Are you going in there now and shut your door?" I nodded. "I see. And get everything all caught up to date? Is that it?"

I said, "Can I go now?"

"Yes. And make sure you don't leave anything out."

I don't think I have. There was some more about the blankets, but it was repetitious.

Later there were a couple of telephone calls, too. The first one from the Gas Company. Talk not very interesting. Annabel had sent Water Board check to Gas Company and vice versa.

The second call was from Willidene Gibbs, wife of an old lawyer and former partner of Ralph's. Annabel picked it up on the first ring.

"Helloah? (Pause) No, I don't. Look, I can't guess, so I think you better tell me. (Pause) Willidene! Oooh! (Fake pleasure, not too convincing.) If you had a dollar for every time I've thought of you, you could travel all over the world on it. Look, I've got cookies in the oven (lie), so I may have to be abrupt. Oatmeal cookies, that's the only kind they'll touch. How's mister? —Well, make him understand that carrying all that weight is a drain on the heart, look at Laird Cregar! (Pause) Oh, Ralph never changes, you know Ralph. (Implication: Ralph is my cross.) You wouldn't know these boys, talk about big and handsome. Berry-berry's traveling now, you know. Just seeing the country and we couldn't be happier about it (lie), footloose and twenty-one, writes regularly (lie), says the Grand Canyon is breathtaking (lie), and I don't know *where* all he's been (true). Did you know if you throw a penny down it, you'll never have arthritis? The Grand Canyon. I didn't either, but that's the saying. (Pause) Oooh! That little snotnose (me), do you know what he did? Quit school and didn't say a word to either of us. We're looking around for something private for him, more advanced; it's so hard for him to drag behind with the slowpokes, I don't blame him a bit. Do you know what I wish we could afford? An old-fashioned tutor! I may do it myself, you know, three hours a day, classes in the kitchen, we could make a game of it."

There followed a series of seven yesses and two wonderfuls. But I don't think Annabel was listening to Willidene Gibbs. The "cookies" started to burn, and she hung up.

Tonight there was a conversation between Annabel and Ralph in the basement.

Ralph uses the basement all the time now. He has his card table set up in front of the furnace. When the new stoker was put in, he went down there every few minutes to make sure it was operating right and to sneak a drink of Old Grandad, which he's got bottles of hidden all over hell. Then finally he set up a card table and started working jigsaw puzzles and just stayed there. I think it makes him feel more like a Socialist to sit in a basement. Because upstairs Annabel's got all kinds of Venetian blinds and knickknacks and it's hard to think about proletarians, etc. Anyway he hates it up there. So do I. There's something creepy about those two bedrooms going to waste, Berryberry's and the guest room. For a while Ralph tried to get Annabel to take in refugees so they wouldn't be empty any more, but she put thumbs down on the whole idea. So now when Ralph sits in the basement it's kind of like pouting. Sometimes I sit there with him and help him with the puzzles. But we don't talk much because Annabel has got the basement tapped. Not exactly tapped. She uses the laundry chute. You open a little door in the bathroom and put your head inside, and you can hear everything that goes on in the basement. This does not bother me any. I understand the impulse. But it slows Ralph down some. However, when he is in a certain mood, he likes the idea that she's listening and says some things especially for her benefit. For instance, before the refugee question simmered down, he had these regular broadcasts about how all women are fascists at heart, etc. For a while it was pretty nerve-racking.

This evening, Annabel went down there after the dishes were put away, and I took her place on the edge of the bathtub with my head in the clothes chute. It is none too comfortable. Sometimes in fact, when the conversation drags, it hardly seems worth the effort.

The beginning was very slow. Much fussing with laundry, putting away of empty bottles, etc., and a few feeble openers like, "If that's *The Grand Canal of Venice,* I believe there's a piece missing."

No answer from Ralph. It is well known in this family that *The Grand Canal* has got a piece missing in the sky part.

(Hello, notebook. Sometimes when I'm putting stuff down in here, I like to stop and kiss the page. I don't know why. It just makes me feel good for some reason.)

A moment passed, and then Annabel said: "When they're not interlocking, it drives me crazy."

"*The Grand Canal of Venice,*" said Ralph, "is interlocking."

"No it's not, sweetheart. Look. See? If it was interlocking these pieces would just hang together in the air."

No answer from Ralph.

Then she said, "Have you talked with Clinton yet?"

"Nope."

"Do you have any intention of so doing?"

"If he comes to me of his own free will."

"Oh, but you don't *believe* in free will," she said.

"That's right."

"End of conversation!" After a few seconds, she said: "I'd like to have one of your cigarettes, please. Will you light it for me?" He probably handed her the matches. I could tell by her tone when she said, "*Thank* you."

This clothes chute is a lot better than the radio. They always spell it all out for you on the radio, but with this thing, you have to fill in with your imagination.

Annabel said, "I respect the fact that you have nothing to say, but I *do.* I intend to send him to a— some kind of a psych—some sort of counselor."

"Send who to a *what?*"

"That's what I want to dis*cuss.* As his father, it occurs to me you should have some say-so."

"You bet your ass . . . !"

"Ralph!"

". . . I've got some say-so!"

"Do you forbid it?"

"Yes. I forbid it."

"What about his own free will? You just said . . . !"

"Aaaannnnabelll." He dragged it out for about ten seconds. This dragging out of a person's name has got about three uses. Ralph says it makes a person reconsider what they've said, it lets them know how foolish it sounded, and it's a good stall. When he went on, his voice seemed to be addressing some little kid. "The

25

free will in which I disbelieve is the Catholic kind that's got to do with committing sins. I say if a man beats up his poor old grandmaw, free will's got nothing to do with it. His glands, his environment, and all the powers of the universe since time began have conspired to force that man to take a clip at her."

"A nasty old woman to begin with." This was Ralph's usual line, but Annabel slipped it in.

"Right! Now, to the subject at hand. If Clinton wants to speak to me, I want it to be his glands, his environment, et cetera, and not because his mother shoved him down the stairs feet first. Ditto when it comes to going to a psychiatrist."

"Are you proud," Annabel said, "that your thinking on the subject is forty years behind? Are you proud of your open mind?"

"Oh, keep still." A pause. "I *have* got an open mind."

"This cigarette is *bone* dry."

"What's wrong with Clinton?" Ralph said.

"Point A, as you well know, he quit school. Blithely."

"Well, if you're gonna do a thing, you might as well do it blithely."

"I assume you do not care that he's quit school."

"Doesn't faze me."

"Without your permission?"

"All the better, show's independence. What's point B?"

"Point B. Now listen, Ralph, this is very serious and very difficult to put over. You'll have to meet me halfway. I know that's a *strain*, but . . . Ralph, listen, all those days he wasn't in school he was sitting in the Aloha Sweet Shop."

"Where's that?"

"On Mound Road, but that's not the point. The point is, he was doing conversations. He filled twenty-five notebooks. Now don't say anything silly, because Ralph, this is serious. You remember those very intelligent kids that used to be on the radio? Well, one of them grew up to be insane. He went around memorizing streetcar transfers and they finally put him away. No, Ralph, this isn't just normal or anything like that. Say he wanted to be a newspaper reporter and was practicing; well, it's not like that at all. It's more like a very very terrible form of nail-biting and he can't help himself. When he was in the sixth grade, I thought he was going through a *stage*, but those teachers at John Marshall were driven *crazy*. Ralph, last year at Central he failed every single subject except shorthand. Normal? I should say not!"

"I thought he'd quit that notebook business."

"Ha-ha, he quit doing it *in front of us*, that's all. What do you think he did this morning? I said something about blankets, some trivial thing, and he couldn't *wait* to get it into his notebook."

"Listen, Annabel," Ralph spoke quietly. "How do you suppose Upton Sinclair spent his boyhood, looking at a blackboard? And listening to a gang of old maids?"

"Ralph, how do we know that Upton Sinclair was *sane?*"

This was the first time I'd ever heard Ralph let somebody take a jab at Upton Sinclair without defending him. He wrote all about immigrant labor being oppressed in the Chicago stockyards, and so Ralph used to give away copies as presents to people. Usually, in a case like this, he'd raise his voice and say that *The Jungle* was the finest book ever written in

27

the English language. But I suppose he thought Annabel was hopeless.

"Then Victor Hugo. Do you suppose he didn't take an interest in the things people said to each other?"

"Can't I make you understand? This is a—an *obsession!*"

"Balls."

"Thank you. Point C. I don't know why I bother— but I might as well finish. —Ralph?"

A long silence. Maybe she was lighting another one of his bone-dry cigarettes.

"Ralph, he has no friends. At all. And he misses his brother."

Neither one of them talked for a long time. I wondered what was going on. Then I heard Ralph.

"I think we did wrong to move in here. It's a barn, all those rooms. If Berry-berry'd given us some hint he wasn't gonna make the move with us, we could've . . . It's almost spooky up there. All you can hear is the clock and that goddamned refrigerator." (A pause) "If he'd just said, 'Now look here, Ralph, I may not make the move with you to Seminary Street, I may just fly the coop instead,'—Christ knows I wouldn't of sit on him. Hell, with all those rooms, I feel like a Boston billionaire. And what am I worth, I'm not worthy fifty thousand dollars. But I hate an empty room. Did you throw away *The Painted Desert* when we moved?"

"No," Annabel said. "It's in your closet. Do you want it? It's not interlocking either, but if you want it, I'll get it."

"No, I just wanted to make sure we still had it."

A moment passed, and then Ralph said, "No postcards, no nothin', huh?"

"No."

"Well, he's too damn busy and more power to him. You can bet your (pause) bottom dollar, I didn't sit around writing postcards when *I* was on the bum."

"*Don't* say 'on the bum'! It was a lecture tour, and you know it. —Clinton! Are you in that bathroom?"

I moved away from the laundry chute.

"Yes, why?"

"Listening?"

"Listening to what?"

"Never mind," she said. That was the end of the talk between Ralph and Annabel. She is now at the kitchen table writing a letter to Bernice O'Brien. I hope she asks me to mail it for her.

While Annabel Williams wrote her letter that evening, Clinton sat in the basement helping his father with the jigsaw puzzle. There was no conversation between them. Clinton knew the old man's mind was not on the puzzle: once, for instance, he had hold of the very piece he was looking for, but instead of putting it in, he went to his hiding place behind the furnace and poured himself some bourbon.

These puzzles had been in the family for more than twenty years so that by now the pieces were as familiar to Ralph as his own memories. Some days they would fall together almost without any effort at all on his part; at other times the cardboard fragments seemed so capricious it would have been a relief to learn that some devil had actually reshaped them, carved new notches into some and, into others, totally irreconcilable curves. His rememberings followed a similar pattern. Therefore, whenever he came upon one of these snags in the puzzle, his thoughts would turn inevitably to his old days on the road.

In his youth Ralph Williams had spent fifteen years in public speaking. Times were bad then and he had gone about the country as a tramp, penniless, riding boxcars, giving speeches on Socialism in parks and along railroad sidings. He wrote many of these speeches himself. They were made up of statistics he had found in pamphlets and library books, vivid anecdotes he had collected in his travels or filched from other speakers. It was during this public activity that he perfected certain theatrical devices for holding the interest of his audience. For example: at a moment of flagging attention he might lower his head to one side, cock an eyebrow and stand for a long moment utterly motionless and silent; soon the crowd was under this hushed spell, and when next Ralph spoke it would be in a quiet and simple fashion that brought cheers to almost anything he chose to say. Ralph never abandoned these devices. In his routine daily encounters with people, even his own family, he still employed these old charms and tricks, left over from the days of his public life, used them with all the pride and assurance of an aged belle who continues to show her ankles and her shoulders, as if by habit, long after they have ceased to be objects of beauty.

Ralph Williams believed if he had not let himself get soft, he could have survived that life forever because of his sense of humor: this was his ace in the hole. He could always laugh in hot weather or cold, feast or famine, and make a joke of whatever bad straits he happened to be in. If he now questioned the absolute validity of certain doctrines he had preached, they still seemed to him a part of the grand humor of his life on the bum. He had entertained thousands of jobless people in those days, people gathered together in public places sharing their idleness with others.

When times improved, he went to work at the Ford plant in Detroit and saved every penny he could. After

30

two years he took his savings and moved to Cleveland where he set himself up as a real estate dealer. He did so well in real estate that it began to bother his conscience; because, even in those days, he could see no humor in a man's loss of his ideals. One day he mentioned these misgivings to the girl who worked in his office. He told her what his ideals were and asked her if she believed his success in business made him technically a capitalist. After all, if a man bought a loaf of bread for a nickel and sold it for a dime, that margin of profit was pure theft: so he had always preached. But the girl reassured him that he was still a liberal, though perhaps not a Socialist. She told him of a movement called Munocracy—a contraction of municipal (or munificent? He couldn't remember) and democracy—that was gathering momentum right there in Cleveland, a movement founded on the belief that a good liberal could also be a shrewd and successful businessman.

He took a keen interest in this secretary. Her name was Annabel Holznagel. They began attending Munocracy meetings together, and one night, after a few months' acquaintance, he talked her into sleeping in his bed. He made it a challenge to her intelligence. She accepted. Ralph admired her for it and soon they were married. The first year, they moved into the house on Amelia Street in what they now called the Old Neighborhood. The second year, Berry-berry was born. And by the third year there was no longer any talk of Munocracy in the house. The movement had ceased to exist. On several occasions Ralph halfheartedly urged Annabel to think about Socialism. The first time she smiled at him indulgently, but on all subsequent occasions she looked at him blankly, as if she had not heard a word he said. But Ralph continued to need someone with whom he could discuss these urgent and

31

radical matters. He took to spending many of his free hours in neighborhood speakeasies talking about his beliefs. But when a successful businessman talks about sharing the wealth, he sets himself up for a certain amount of ridicule. Ralph at first defended himself on the basis that if a tiger lives in a jungle, he has to obey its laws, but gradually he switched over to atheism, another radical idea that had less to do with a man's pocketbook. The men respected Ralph Williams and they liked to listen and to try to argue with him. But his long practice gave him the edge in a discussion, and when these cronies grew tired of defeat they began to avoid him. He would then take his patronage to some new place, and before long he had an entire round of places where he was known and could visit them like stops on a vaudeville tour.

He soon became known affectionately to the men in these bars as The Tiger of Amelia Street. They looked forward to his coming because he had charm and humor; and as the years passed by, he no longer felt the need to talk with them exclusively of urgent and radical matters. He even discovered that an occasional change of topic was needed to hold their interest and esteem. And a man with his genius for persuasion and good fellowship could as easily stiffen the ears of a group of men by recounting to them the wild doings of his son, as by telling over and over again of his profane beliefs.

Berry-berry became his favorite topic, and he was shrewd enough to parcel out these stories with the discretion of an old trouper trained in judging the attention span of his audience. The first such story was of Berry-berry's name, which needed an explanation because some men claimed it was a disease. The flat truth is that it came from some foolishness of Annabel's: as a baby, the boy's cheeks were astonishingly red; as she plucked them in quick succession she would say *berry berry berry*, to make the child giggle. But Ralph's story was this: he claimed that in the Belgian Congo there is a tribe known as the Galbralians. Now, when the king of this tribe gathers all of his sons together, after the youngest has matured, he puts them through a long series of rigid competitions. The victor among them from that day forward is known as Berry-berry, which, in the Galbralian language invented by Ralph Williams, means *Son of the Tiger.*

When the old man told these stories, he did not always know the details of them until he heard them from his own lips. Like many good talkers and taletellers, he relied on inspiration. His tongue was like a pump hooked up to some deep well of secrets, and when he got it primed the tales he spewed up were as astonishing to him as to any man in the room. He sometimes wondered at the source of them.

Now, on this November night in the basement, Ralph gave some thought to his second son for whom no Galbralian name had ever been invented. Clinton was good company, not talkative himself, but a perfect listener, and though he was not wild he had a lot to him in a quiet way.

Ralph's head was inclined over the puzzle. He stole a glance at this tame son and felt a sudden flush of guilt that he had never given him a nickname. He drank his liquor and busied himself with the puzzle. A moment later, he mumbled, "It's a *tribe* of Galbralians." Clinton laughed in a quiet, agreeable way, and Ralph said: "Don't you snicker. You're just as bad as that other one. You're *both* Galbralians. You want a drink of liquor?" Clinton said, "Yes, please," and took a small swallow from the bottle. The two of them laughed together over nothing in particular, and pretty soon the old man felt better about the whole matter.

Clinton did not place the letter in the first mailbox he passed. He went first to a White Tower hamburger place and ordered a cup of coffee. He often stopped at this place during his late evening walks. You could not always count on interesting talk here, but on occasions it had been lively enough. There was a public telephone on the wall, not encased by a booth, and you could often get half of a conversation.

The counter man was a thin person of indeterminate age and faded eyes. He spoke with a machine-gun hillbilly speed and, though usually laconic, Clinton found his little scraps of talk worth listening to: for instance, when he spoke his name, Melvin, you could not hear the "l"; and he talked of Tennessee as if it were Paradise. Clinton always thought of him as Mevvin from Heaven. He also admired Mevvin's efficiency behind the counter. The man could take care of eight stools, work the grill, serve, and ring up cash without ever getting confused or flustered. Clinton had long ago entered all of these facts, along with samples of Mevvin's talk, in his notebook.

Now Clinton sat at the counter and removed various articles of equipment from his pocket and placed them before him: his notebook, a ball-point pen with his name on it in gold (received through the mail from a crippled war veteran along with a letter inviting him to become a ball-point pen salesman in his neighborhood; he gave it some thought, but never followed through on it), a package of king-sized cigarettes in a plastic container, book matches, a roll of transparent tape, a key ring with a metal tag on it that read: I HAVE BEEN TELEVISED AT THE NEW YORK WORLD'S FAIR; from this key ring depended a large number of useless keys and a single-bladed knife given him by a Red Cross Shoes salesman.

Then he took from his shirt the envelope addressed to Mrs. W. B. O'Brien in Toledo, Ohio. Though his mother wrote with great speed and you had to study certain words to know what they were, she had a graceful hand and wrote in even, well-spaced lines. At the bottom of the page the writing would get smaller and smaller and creep up the sides, as if she limited herself to a certain number of sheets.

This correspondent, Bernice O'Brien, was his mother's special confidante. Perhaps because they so seldom met face to face, Annabel felt she could write the truth to Bernice. The woman had been her closest friend in high school, and later married a tire salesman. When Annabel attended a class reunion in Toledo, some years ago, she found that Bernice had become fat and arthritic and was confined to a wheel chair. Her misery was constant, and even though she had taken up metaphysical studies to help her cope with it, the pain was at times so intense she needed drugs to subdue it. Because of this sad condition, Bernice's only child, a daughter named Echo O'Brien, now almost thirty years old, had never married and still lived at home. Annabel had met this daughter at the time of the class reunion, and always spoke of her as a "beautiful thing, but very silent, the poor creature."

Because Annabel wrote the truth in these letters, Clinton always counted himself lucky to get hold of one of them, and took great pleasure in copying them into his notebooks. He knew that this theft of her privacy was a kind of crime. But he could commit it without any feeling

35

of guilt. If his fingers shook as he slit the envelope, it was from an excess of eagerness to enjoy the secrets it might contain.

He smoked a cigarette as he read:

1129 SEMINARY ST.
CLEVELAND, O.—WED. EVE.

DEAREST FRIEND, DEAREST BERNICE,

I'm afraid you find me at a low ebb as I have been fighting the blues something awful. Isnt it interesting in the sense of ironical that I have no one to turn to but you for consolation my dearest friend whose burdens are so much heavier than anybody elses? But thats life and it is such a comfort to me. I dont know why you dont write back and say Dear Annabel! I have troubles of my own. Ha. God bless you and I do pray for you every single day. And how is lovely Echo doing?

Still no word from Berry-berry. I would appreciate it if you would meditate about this as he is the type to get into trouble. If anything comes to you, no matter how awful it is, I know you would pass it on to me, as some word of any kind is better than just worrying myself sick. I have still not yet gotten over how it all came to you about Gladys Huntsinger's pregnancy at 38 long after she'd given up hope—not to mention the death of poor Carole Lombard 12 hours prior to the radio—*and the downfall of Japan was nothing to sneeze at!!* I still urge you to get some of these things notarized showing the dates, and then just watch the doubting Thomases. Do pray for Berry-berry. I'm afraid he is a chip off the old block but he gets his height and broad shoulders and good eyesight from my side of the family. Remember how tall and straight my father stood, and stood out in a crowd? Taking nothing away from Ralph, a good-looking man B.P. (Before Prohibition. Ha.) but was never tall and his hair is gone as well. Even so, if you could see him, dear Bernice, a small man but strong with the constitution of a horse, and you wouldn't believe he was sixty-one these days but the calendar doesnt lie. I'm

36

afraid Berry-berry is a chip off the old block, but thank heaven he does not preach C-ism. Ralph was never an out-and-out C either. He just likes being different. For instance if everybody went atheist, I am certain he would become a priest. Ha. Because lately he says he is an agnostic and just loves sitting in the basement doing jigsaw puzzles. But I knew when I married a man dogs years older I would have to pay the piper so this is no complaint. However Bernice dont laugh at me but do you ever have dreams? Bernice there is not a living soul I would breathe this to, but I dream quite a bit lately about Arch Roper. *Very romantic dreams.* Arch Roper is not in the Yearbook as he was taken out of school by his father but you remember him well I'm sure. So you see I am an old middle-aged woman who still has dreams of taking walks and dating and everything. I feel silly telling all this, and dont know how you can read it without getting mad at me. Oh, Bernice, I just love you to pieces.

Our new trouble is Clinton who it now comes out has quit school fifty-seven days ago in a row and would not go back on pain of death. If he had some kind of job to occupy him I wouldn't mind so much, but he is doing conversations again and am now considering your advice of two years ago about getting professional counsel because I cant get through to him and Ralph *will* not. Would you advise us to move out of this house? I shiver every time I go past Berry-berry's room, which he never once slept in. It's as if he was dead even though going around the country is a common thing in young men. Ralph put it very well, he has a turn of phrase, he said the clock ticks louder here, which is very fitting because sometimes I think I'm going crazy. Ha. Bernice, it's like we have got all our things arranged but none of us is moved in yet, can you understand that and we've been here almost a year? However we will all get settled soon and I dont want you to worry about us. Because I feel better already, dearest friend, so write soon and *if there is anything I can do please let me know* and I will drop everything! Give my love to Echo, she is pretty as a picture.

Lovingly,
ANNABEL

Clinton read the letter a second time. Then he lit another cigarette and, sipping his coffee, copied the letter into his notebook. When he had finished, he repaired the envelope with transparent tape, hoping that Bernice would not notice its condition or make any comment on it in her answer. He placed his belongings in his pockets—except for the notebook which always rode on his belly, tucked under his shirt and secured by the belt of his trousers.

Apart from his pleasure in partaking of its secrets, Annabel's letter had touched him in some other way that was also in itself a secret. It was this extra mystery that he pondered on the way home. Out of her presence, if he ever tried to conjure up a picture of Annabel, her fragments always seemed to float in air and never would stand still for him. There seemed to be no part of her or her life that was whole, without gaps. Her conversations had this quality, too. Whenever she took hold of a subject, it sprang a leak and all the facts dribbled away from her. Or a person: if she reached out to a person, it seemed that the part she got hold of ceased to exist, and she was left holding the ghost of an arm, the ghost of a hand or a chin or a cheek, the ghost of someone's heart. These letters that went to Toledo, Ohio, were the most solid communications of her life; and they went to a crippled lady, half-drugged and in pain, who seldom sent back answers of any length except on rare occasions when her fingers could manipulate the fountain pen. Annabel was like some unhappy Midas whose touch was liquid; whatever she reached out for dissolved, floated away from her. Clinton's thinking

about these matters was of a similar character. The sadness
of it would not stand still for him either, but floated away.
He could not even gather up one strong firm thought to
put down in his notebook.

After he had placed the letter in the slot, he tipped back
the iron pan once again to make certain the envelope had
slid down into the box. He never took this kind of thing
for granted, and if he failed to double-check, the matter
would worry him. For a moment, Clinton was aware of
this New Neighborhood he was walking through. The
houses were plain and undistinguished, most of them
frame, well cared for, with neat lawns and modest
splotches of shrubbery outlining the porches and some of
the driveways and paths. He knew the street only as any
passer-by would know it at first glance; it was not familiar
to him in any personal sense at all, and he knew it never
would be. It seemed impossible to him that any neighborhood could have any flavor to it unless Berry-berry lived
in it.

Now this thought captured him. Berry-berry had always
this power over him, to move in, even in the form of a
thought, and take over his imagination, no matter what
else might be pressing in on it for attention. The reason
was this: his brother was the center of Clinton's most important dream: that one day when he was considered old
enough, perhaps at seventeen, Berry-berry would send for
him to go traveling with him. What made the dream important was not only that he wanted it to come true—but
that he was certain it never would. It was therefore impossible to get rid of, and had tormented him for a long time.

Before Berry-berry went away, Clinton gave him a piece
of paper with a certain address on it where he could always be reached without the letter becoming a matter of
general knowledge to the family. It was the address of a

girl named Mildred Murphy, who lived in the Old Neighborhood. She had agreed to act as a secret post office for any messages between the brothers. But after Berry-berry left the house, Clinton had found the piece of paper with the address on it in a pair of trousers that were left behind. This made it fairly certain that Berry-berry had no intention of sending for him.

Besides, he had to admit that his brother had never truly let him in on any important secrets. Even in the Amelia Street days, Berry-berry had kept the meanings of his comings and goings strictly to himself. The old man was careful never to question him on the nature of his absences, whether for an hour or a day or a group of days, and Berry-berry never volunteered anything. Annabel, on the other hand, made it a point to question him closely, and as a result gleaned even less information than anyone else.

Therefore, since Clinton did not have hold of any facts, he was careful not to commit himself to any hard and fast conclusions; but appearances were that Berry-berry Williams had engaged in every kind of debauch ever heard of or imagined. For instance, one night in the old house, the young man, returning from some escapade, had climbed in Clinton's window at 4:00 A.M. (Because the front door of the place was kept locked, and Berry-berry had never been furnished with a key, he often used Clinton's window as a means of entrance.) Clinton would wake up and sometimes they would have a conversation. On this particular night that Clinton was remembering, Berry-berry came in giggling from the wine he had drunk, and between his teeth he carried an inflated balloon of great size. He tossed an empty box on the bed, and Clinton saw that the balloon was in fact a blown-up contraceptive. Clinton was twelve then, and naturally had never made use of one of these devices himself; but he knew they came three in a box, and he was eager to know what had become of the other two. But on close questioning of this sort, Berry-berry would only laugh. He dropped his trousers, peed out the window, and sang some crazy song.

Clinton did not know what to believe; he knew there were two schools of thought on the subject of fornication: either it was a widespread custom that took place almost constantly in every parked car and hotel room in the world, or a rare event that almost never occurred—and if it did you were likely to end up in jail or with your name in the paper. In the Old Neighborhood, he had for some time hung around in the back room of a chain grocery store where a friend of his was employed putting potatoes in paper sacks. Conversations among the older male clerks seemed to indicate that the main purpose of life was fornication; whereas, the manager himself, a grown-up married man, had got into the discussion one day and maintained hotly that it was all talk, the only single people who ever engaged in such activities were underprivileged nincompoops and basically non compos mentis, and furthermore, people who handled groceries to be eaten by the general public had no business even thinking about such subjects. Clinton suspected even then that the truth might lie somewhere between these extremes, but he would have liked to get hold of some authoritative information that would settle the matter.

Whether or not Berry-berry had actually been out fornicating that night was a matter of small importance to him. *Some,* perhaps, but in itself it was not the mystery that tormented his imagination. Clinton felt that no matter what Berry-berry did, whether away from the house or in it, he was Living. It was something that took place even when he slept, hidden in his body and under his eyelids; it was always going on, and none of the ten thousand questions he asked ever brought an answer that touched in any way the source of this deep wonder. Therefore, when Clinton began to suspect that Berry-berry intended to leave home, he grew more and more anxious about these matters until, by the time his brother actually announced his plans, his panic was so great that the thought of being left behind made him vomit.

It was at this time that he conceived the Mildred Murphy plan, whereby his brother could secretly send for him. But when he found the address had been left behind, a belief took shape in him that he could not himself have put into words. It was this: that Life had conspired to avoid him altogether. For a while he halfheartedly hoped to find some sign of Life in the Old Neighborhood, but after snooping around over there for more than a month, he gave up that hope. Life was a thing that took place out of his presence: it went on in a room just before he entered it and took up again after he left; it was on the other end of a telephone wire, in envelopes he could not get hold of that were delivered to other houses, in all books except those he could lay hands on himself; and surely it moved along with Berry-berry, inside of him on that vague and dimly lighted, hard-to-imagine road he traveled.

This, then, was his private terror: that these mysteries would never unfold. He would not be sent for. It is a sad fact that the futility of a desire will not wipe it out; and so, this longing that had come to being in him, that had taken to parading around inside him, mostly in his chest, would have to be dealt with in some private way. He believed that the thing had begun to nibble at his heart, at his sanity. The symptoms alarmed him: at fourteen he had no nails left to bite and had set to work on the cuticles, he smoked regularly, did conversations, and the very thought

42

of sitting in a schoolroom caused him physical anguish. It occurred to him that poor Annabel might have good grounds for her worries. If privately he believed there could be no letup in his bad behavior, he could not admit it to her. She would never understand that it all had to do with Berry-berry, and the thing that pranced around inside him.

Annabel had said to Ralph: "He misses his brother," and the enormity of this understatement, spoken in those soft, cooing tones, had made him want to beat his head against the laundry chute until his brain was raw. But now, with the burden of all her talk and the letter resting in his notebook, he again felt sympathy for her. By the time he arrived home, he had made a decision.

He found Annabel in a highly agitated state: "Don't speak! Keep still! Shut up!" she cried. "I've got to hear this."

She was looking at television. There had been talk of the possibility of a colossal new war; Clinton wondered if its beginning was now being announced. But what he saw on the screen was a familiar master of ceremonies, nearly as overcome with emotion as his mother. He was reading song titles into a microphone. After a moment, Annabel exclaimed, "I would have won!" She was near tears.

Clinton said, "Won what?"

"I had all three! It's World War I song titles. *Give My Regards to Broadway, Hello, Central, Give Me No Man's Land,* and *Indianola.* Of course, *any* fool could have got the first one, but the others were real toughies! How many people today know *Indianola?* 'Ta-te-ta-te-ta-da, I love your harem eyes.'"

Clinton said, "I thought I'd go out tomorrow and get some kind of a job."

"Imagine," Annabel said, "I had the envelope all ad-

43

dressed, everything. The only difference between me and that lady in Milwaukee is, she *mailed* hers." And then, "What?"

"I thought just some kind of a job for a while, to keep occupied."

"Why, that's a grand idea, maybe part time at the post office. Just for the Christmas rush. Then next semester, who knows? Will you come and kiss me?"

Clinton kissed his mother on the forehead. Her eyes were damp, filled with emotion—but whether for himself or for the lady in Milwaukee, he could not be certain.

"Clinton, you'll think I've lost my mind, but do you know I've got *Indianola* all mixed up with *Dardanella?*" She turned to the television. "I *wish* they'd play it again."

Clinton went to his bedroom and brought the notebook up-to-date.

Now, this day in the Williams house had been like many that had passed before and many that were yet to come. Similar late morning scenes took place in Clinton's bedroom and in the kitchen and basement, and the issues at stake shifted only slightly. Clinton did not find work. Annabel laid this failure to the fact that only early birds caught worms: no one had ever been hired for any kind of job after twelve o'clock noon; you had to be there wearing a starched shirt when the place opened its doors at 9:00 A.M. Then they knew you meant *business*.

But the actual reason for Clinton's continued unemployment was the fact that, even though he appeared at many places in starched shirts, he failed to tell anyone he wanted to be hired. He could not believe that anyone would take his request for a job seriously: a person with nervous habits who needed professional counsel could hardly ex-

44

pect anyone to pay him for his services. They might even laugh at him.

But he did spend five afternoons a week away from the house. Every now and then on a clear day he would go downtown on the streetcar and sit on the steps of the City Hall where old men fed pigeons, or out in front of the Public Library where groups of college students huddled together in the winter sunshine smoking cigarettes and looking wiser than the rest of the world. On colder days or when it snowed, Clinton did not venture far from home. He found a number of places where he could sit indoors without being too conspicuous. Afternoons were slow at the Aloha Sweet Shop, and so long as the visit did not extend itself for more than, say, a half-hour, the manager seemed to enjoy his company.

One day, at another of his stops, Voitek's Dependable Pharmacy, he did a favor for Mr. Voitek: the floor was covered with melting slush that had fallen in cakes from the customers' galoshes; Clinton took the broom from the old druggist and swept the mess out the front door for him. For a while the performance of this task gave the boy an almost proprietary feeling about the place, and at the soda fountain he often used the end stool, the same one that Mr. Voitek himself sat on when he rested. But one day Clinton went too far. Mr. Voitek had been out in back filling a prescription, when a second customer walked in and stood at the cigarette counter. Clinton had a sudden impulse to wait on him: in this way he might demonstrate to Voitek his value as a possible employee. The man wanted a cigar. Clinton, with all the appearance of boldness, though his heart beat heavy under his shirt, went behind the counter and brought out the box of cigars. The customer made his selection and left the correct number of coins on the counter. When the druggist came back up front, Clinton handed him the money and described the transaction to him. Mr. Voitek frowned and he did not look Clinton in the eyes when he said: "I thank you, but I don't like a customer behind my counter. And you not a customer, you don't buy nothing. And you not work here eeder. I thank you." He rang the cash register and deposited the coins. He did not sit down at the fountain as usual, but made himself appear very busy at the cigarette counter. Clinton moved slowly toward the door, whistling in his effort to appear casual. He did not want Mr. Voitek to think he was leaving because of what had taken place between them. But once outside, he quickened his pace and hurried through the cold gray slush like a fugitive. When he stopped for a traffic light, his head whirled dizzily, his body was hot and moist, and he felt so weak he wanted to sit down right there on the curbstone.

But aside from the Aloha and Voitek's Dependable Pharmacy, Clinton had several other stops: two chain drugstores, a chili-con-carne place, a magazine store, and the White Tower. Mevvin from Heaven was always glad to see him, but Clinton knew he was in danger of wearing out his welcome and so he timed these visits accordingly.

He rarely returned to the Old Neighborhood any more. Perhaps once in two or three weeks he would go there to wait for Mildred Murphy on the corner where he knew she caught her bus when school let out. Mildred Murphy was usually good for an hour's conversation, but there were never any letters from Berry-berry.

On the first day of December, Annabel received an answer to her letter to Bernice O'Brien. Clinton managed to get hold of it within a few hours after its arrival: when Annabel took her afternoon bath, he saw his opportunity and seized it. He could see, in the penmanship itself,

46

sprawling and childlike, all the pain in the hand that had written it.

Nov. 27

DEAREST ANNABEL,

Your letter big event for me. Excuse writing, hard to manage pen, but pain not bad now. Thanksgiving lovely, Echo cooked with all trimmings, so devoted I worry she may miss out on life of own. We play cards, she does my hair each Saturday, sits with me evenings, tries to read to me but is hard for her as has no literary bent. But is getting to be good mechanic, put new motor in her Dodge all by self, and so feminine never even gets clothes or hands dirty. Whod ever guess she's strong as mule. Make good wife some day but meets nobody. Loves her mother and so patient with useless old woman. At night in bed with eyes closed I study you and family. Don't worry, everything works out, law of nature. Your dream of old days makes me cry, you sweet thing. But smile and pray, everything okay in end. Forgive shortness, hand tired. Write soon to your loving friend

B—

P.S. I see your older boy and X-mas tree in same picture. Holiday visitor may surprise you. So smile and pray.

Christmas preparations began at once. Clinton knew that this postscript in Bernice O'Brien's letter had lighted a fuse in Annabel. Though she scarcely mentioned Berryberry at all, he knew she had accepted Bernice's prophecy as fact. Clinton was afraid to share this belief himself. His experience had taught him that if you wanted a thing *too* much, you would not get it. You would only be doomed to wanting it all the more and your longing would be more painful than ever. He therefore worried about Annabel, who devoted all her powers to preparations. When she spoke of the holiday, he felt he saw an invisible jaw squared as she led her invisible armies across the days of

December. "By heaven, we're going to have a Christmas," she said repeatedly, and each time with renewed intensity until the word "Christmas" contained all the guttural determination of a war cry. Indeed, "Christmas" had become the name of the archenemy that marched toward them. It would strike on the 25th of the month, and by all the gods of dime stores, mail-order catalogues and cookbooks, the Williamses—her actions seemed to serve notice on the enemy—the Williamses would have their larders stocked, their tree would blaze in the window like a torch. She brought out greeting cards received in other years and glued the prettiest hundred of them to the doorframes. She shopped each day and baked long into the nights. No other subject was worthy of discussion: "I have no *time* for that, don't you *see?*" And pausing only long enough to retie an apron or to check her many "lists," she pressed tirelessly forward in her strategy of cookies and candles and ornaments. Higher and higher grew the bulwarks of mincemeat, gift wrappings and holly, as Bing Crosby on the radio inspired the resistance forces with musical promises of snow. The newspapers each day kept the count in a front-page box: Twelve more shopping days till Christmas! it threatened; and then nine, eight, seven; the number diminished ominously. For a time things began to go haywire, a cake fell, a package refused to arrive, or the weatherman did not foresee snow. The footsteps of Christmas echoed in the distance, and there was every possibility that with some mistake in timing they would be unprepared for it.

Ralph merely tended the stoker and sipped his bourbon in the basement. His pacifism galled her, but Annabel's efforts increased in intensity. She glutted the mails with greeting cards and handkerchiefs and mufflers. She prepared envelopes with two-dollar tokens for the mailman, the milkman, the breadman, and the newsboy. The newsboy's nose was always running that winter: Annabel noticed this and included in his envelope a box of Four-Way Cold Tablets and a note:

DEAR LITTLE BOY,
Season's Greetings. Take these *faithfully* and that head will clear right up. Best wishes.

MRS. WILLIAMS

She packed Berry-berry's share of fruitcake and cookies and gifts in a large cardboard box. When it was all wrapped and tied and ready for the post office, she placed it under the tree with the address sticker left blank. But Clinton knew that she believed privately the box would never be posted: Berry-berry would be there in person to open it in the Williams living room.

Now, in a Christian country not even a professed atheist can be totally indifferent to the advent of Christmas; and Ralph Williams was to make his own peculiar contribution to the holiday. It had been a month of bitter cold, and through many of these long evenings, in which he listened to the cruel winds that beat upon his basement windows, the old man was besieged with memories of his own earlier Decembers. He told Clinton of a Christmas Eve he had spent in Grand Island, Nebraska, hungry and cold, in the back seat of a parked car whose owner had left it unlocked; another, in a Salvation Army place in Cincinnati, Ohio; and one year he and two companions broke into a tomb in a Dearborn, Michigan, graveyard, where they passed a sleepless Christmas night huddled together against its marble walls. These thoughts of his own hard times, now long past, caused him to ponder the present situation of millions of others. He told Clinton of the hungry Chinese,

49

the Eskimos, the Navajo Indians, the Negroes, the homeless refugees everywhere, and of all the wanderers of the world.

"But you know what we are?" At this, he raised his voice and projected it toward the laundry chute: "We're the fat-asses of the world. We just sit here and think about it, and stuff all the cupboards full of fruitcake!" In his heart, he laid all the blame for the world's wretchedness upon Annabel's indifference to it. The more she baked and laid by for the stomachs of the Williamses, the deeper his bitterness grew.

But suddenly, on the morning of the day before Christmas, this sullenness disappeared, mysteriously to Annabel, altogether. Indeed, Ralph became so remarkably cheerful that she looked for an opportunity to sniff his breath: there was bourbon on it, but since she couldn't remember a time when there had not been, the clue was useless to her. When he left the house in mid-afternoon, with spirits so exalted that he kissed her on the mouth, Annabel was forced to conclude that by some miracle Ralph had been so touched by the contagion of her own Christmas zeal that he had actually gone out to buy a present for her. If this were true, she might even hope that another miracle would see him standing next to her in church, flanked by his sons, on Christmas morning.

When he failed to return for supper, other possible explanations crept quietly into the corners of her imagination, but none of them were ugly enough to subdue her own high spirits. She served Clinton a simple meal in the kitchen—the real gorging did not begin, traditionally, until Christmas itself—but her own appetite was small. A taste of soup and half a slice of bread was all she could manage.

When dishes were out of the way, Annabel took a long hot bath. Then, as if she were dressing for a lover, she spent forty minutes applying make-up and removing curlers from her hair. She put on a new dress, a dark blue one with a full skirt that rustled when she moved; matching earrings and necklace, set with false sapphires; and her high-heeled shoes.

It was not until she made her appearance in the living room and, with an elaborate crinkling and whooshing of her skirts, arranged herself on a pouf at the foot of the Christmas tree, that she admitted to herself the existence of some doubt as to Berry-berry's returning for the holiday. If she had thought by her elaborate preparations to exclude from her mind this painful possibility, Annabel's error was great. But if her private wish had been to set up a vivid backdrop against which to play her Christmas Eve drama of the mother who sits in her chair, waiting, candle in the window, for the return of the prodigal who never arrives, then her labors had not gone unrewarded. For the garish carnival trappings of the holiday seemed only to call attention to the emptiness of all of his places in the house. Who can say for sure which of these ends she had envisioned? perhaps both. For a woman's heart is known to be a battleground of conflicting sentiments, and her deepest wishes are often a mystery even to herself.

At any rate, Annabel wept inconsolably. When Clinton entered the living room he found her in the last stages of her sorrow, blowing her nose. She smiled brightly: "Merry Christmas, precious."

Clinton sensed something of insincerity in both her gaiety and her tears. "What's wrong?" he said.

"Oh, it's just I'm so happy. Mothers are crazy creatures, you know that. —Isn't the tree perfect? It's beautifully shaped. We always have such well-shaped trees, I lose my mind deciding which part to face to the wall. And

51

my favorite ornament is still that lovely angel. What time is it?"

"Ten o'clock."

"Oh, *just* ten o'clock? That's the shank of the evening. Now, which is your favorite?"

"Favorite what?"

"Ornament."

"I guess the angel," Clinton said, without considering the matter at all. Then he glanced at the top of the tree: a haggard old doll with misshapen wings perched there in the branches, smiling benignly upon the room. It was like the image of a dilapidated chorus girl who had gone mad and fled to the top of the tree to escape her keepers.

Clinton handed his mother a small package. "Here. Merry Christmas."

Annabel praised the wrappings, and then, holding the box to her ears, she shook it, acting out a pantomime of curiosity over its contents. All of this she performed with a little girl's sense of wonder that was unbecoming to her; in repose, her face was pretty enough, but this posturing seemed to sharpen and distort her small features. "Dare I open it?" she said. "As a rule I wouldn't open a stick of gum till Christmas morning, but I just don't think I can wait. Shall I do it?"

"I don't care."

"All right then, here goes!"

The box contained six ball-point pens, purchased through the mail from the crippled war veteran in North Dakota. Each pen was of a different color and each had ANNABEL WILLIAMS stamped on it in gold.

"Why, what are they?" she said.

"Ball-point *pens!*"

"*Ball*-point? The kind that slides off the paper?"

Clinton said, "Yeah, but they've got your name stamped on 'em in gold."

"And they're lovely. But my tenth anniversary pen is still good as new. —Awwh, bless your heart, lover, that's very sweet. But you know how everyone admires my handwriting, how graceful it is, and six of them, my heaven, won't they look pretty on my desk? That's what I'll do, I'll put them on my desk. What ever made you get six?"

"They're different colors, and I thought, like say, if you wore a blue dress, then . . ."

"Oh! For different *outfits*! Well, you've got the biggest darned heart of anybody. Here, I'll leave the box open so people can see."

The sight of these pens, sitting at the base of the tree where she placed them, caused in Clinton a sudden wave of hatred for himself and for Annabel and, more than ever before, for this house they lived in. Its barnlike proportions were suddenly dwarfed, and he felt that its walls pressed in on them like those of a tiny jail cell.

"You know, Annabel, I think all this crap in here's gonna make everybody feel lousy."

"All of what 'crap'?"

"I don't mean crap exactly, but this Christmas stuff. I mean, I think this family's got to the point where Christmas'd be better if we didn't make such a big do over it."

Annabel's hand went to her chin. "I can't believe my ears," she said.

"Okay, excuse me, maybe I'm wrong, that's all."

"Clinton, just answer me something: do you think I went to all this agony for my*self*?"

"Look, please just forget I said anything. All of a sudden I just got kind of nervous is all."

At this moment, the front door opened. Ralph Williams entered. "Just a moment, gentlemen," he said to whomever the people were who waited for him on the porch. "Just one moment."

He closed the door softly and approached the pouf where Annabel sat, her face distorted by an equal mixture of pain and puzzlement.

"Now listen to me, Annabel." Ralph lowered his head and pinned her to silence with his eyes. "On our front porch there stand three children of God, orphans of misfortune, whom I have invited to spend this night and tomorrow under my roof. Shut up."

She had scarcely opened her mouth.

He continued: "You're gonna stuff their gullets with about half that food you got stashed away in there, then we'll put 'em to bed with a bottle o' whisky apiece. Keep still. In the morning, I want you to give 'em some of that junk under the tree there. And if you betray by an eyelash that they're anything less than welcome in Ralph Williams' house, I'll beat your rear end till it's black and blue."

Annabel assumed a profound stillness of body and face. But Ralph, as he returned to the front door, seemed to have shed a dozen years. There was spring in his step and color in his cheeks. He swung the door open wide.

"Gentlemen," he said, with a full gesture of the arm, "the pleasures of my humble house." To Clinton and Annabel, he said: "These three kings will pause here tonight. Tomorrow they will continue the journey to Bethlehem."

Now three peculiar men entered the room. Their appearances made it immediately apparent that Ralph had found them on that part of Euclid Avenue known as skid row. The first to enter was a tiny man of perhaps thirty-five; he clutched his hat in both hands and with a few quick and nervous movements of his birdlike eyes, studied the room suspiciously. The second, middle-aged, round-shouldered, seemed to retreat even as he advanced; he

54

seemed intent on pleasing everyone, and bowed obsequiously in all directions. These two were followed by a jolly old wreckage of seventy, white stubble on his chin, a bright red baseball cap tucked under his arm; one leg seemed shorter than the other as he rolled vigorously into the room, hand outstretched, approaching Annabel. His toothless mouth agape with merriment, he had the air of some crazy politician campaigning in a ghost town. But his speech was impossible to understand: there were no teeth and too much spittle.

Annabel stood stiff as a board as the merry old gentleman smothered her hand in both of his own, and paid his gibberish compliments to the house and to its mistress. Her face was a terrible thing to behold: she smiled graciously, but in a frozen manner that would turn blood into ice.

"Ah bow t'de gwowne, putty wady, for dis kiness of de warmf of y'housh an' harf." He made a regular speech, gesturing about the room as he spoke. One could only guess at what he might be saying, but he had all the confidence of a golden-throated orator. "Ah shank you, fom de bottom mishole," he concluded. Then he stepped back and folded his hands, resting them on his protruding stomach.

Annabel's voice was not her own when she said: "Won't you be seated, gentlemen?" It was the voice of some animal, pained and stricken, who could manage only one note. "Ralph? Would you excuse yourself? And help me prepare a drink for your friends?"

Annabel left the room. Then Ralph excused himself and followed her into the kitchen. Clinton remained in the living room until the two younger men had seated themselves uncomfortably on the edge of the couch. He glanced at the old politician, who had settled himself happily in an overstuffed chair. When their eyes met, the old man giggled wickedly and winked at him; it was as if they were all gathered here, Clinton included, to partake in some forbidden bacchanalian rites.

When Clinton heard voices in the kitchen, he had to excuse himself; he went to the dining room to listen at the door, behind which his parents whispered hoarsely at each other:

"Has it never occurred to you," Annabel was saying, "that your son might wish to use his own bed on Christmas Eve, and how many diseases do you suppose these men are carrying around with them?"

"Berry-berry's not gonna use that bed tonight or any other night and . . ."

"How do you know that at this very moment he is not racing toward this house at sixty miles an hour?"

". . . and when a man is jobless that doesn't mean he's got diseases. They check 'em over at the mission house before they let 'em in, so . . ."

"I'm sure he'd love to walk in and find those filthy . . ."

"Before you make up any more excuses that make you sound like an ignoramus, why don't you drink a glass of water and think about what it says in the Bible?"

"Thank you, Ralph, you don't have to waste your time telling me what you think of my mind. It has long ago been conceded that the brains . . . ! Can you *dare* quote the Bible to me! Ralph, that is one area, I serve you warning, there are sacred matters that . . ."

" 'There was no room at the inn.' "

"You have an absolute contempt for the Bible and yet you dare . . ."

"I do not have contempt for the Bible. I have never in my life . . ."

". . . you have the gall to hide behind Jesus Christ, just for the sake of those persons in the living room! Jobless,

56

my big toe; why, do you know what they are? I'll tell you what they are!"

"The Bible is one thing and religion is another. Now, you can take every religion in the world and you can wrap them all up in one big hairy package, and then you can take 'em and . . ."

"Ralph, I warn you! You can have your Communism and your atheism and every other absurdism you can find, and I'll leave you perfectly at peace with them, but I promise you . . ."

"You know goddam well what I think of Russia!"

"Ralph Williams, you don't fool me one bit, you don't care about those three tramps. If you did you'd give them some money and leave them alone. Do you know what it costs to fumigate a house?"

"They don't want money. They want to spend the night in a warm house, in a good comfortable bed, and they want to eat some good food and drink some good liquor. So get some sheets and blankets on those beds and keep still."

As Clinton heard the clinking of glasses he moved swiftly away from the door. Ralph passed him on his way to the living room. "Forgot all about you, Clint," he said. "Go fetch yourself a glass."

Clinton went to the kitchen. As he took a glass from the shelf, his mother stopped weeping and glared at him in horror. "I forbid you to drink liquor." But Clinton instinctively allied himself with Ralph. He took the glass and left Annabel in the kitchen. "Et tu, Brute?" she said, as the door swung closed.

In the living room, Ralph poured four generous helpings of bourbon from the pint in his pocket, and one smaller share in the glass Clinton held out to him. He distributed the glasses among his guests, then, raising his own, he said,

57

in a voice colored with emotion that Clinton knew to be utterly sincere:

"Honored guests, I would like to propose a toast in honor of the greatest man that ever drew breath. As you all know, tonight's his birthday. So let's all drink to him, to Jesus Christ—the *founder* of the Socialist Party!"

Clinton saw Annabel in the doorway. She raised her eyes to heaven as if begging forgiveness for this blasphemy. But Clinton drank with the others. When the liquor went down, he drew a deep breath and tensed the muscles of his throat. The burning was furious but not overwhelming, and he felt immediately drunk.

Annabel entered the room carrying her pocketbook, and accompanied by the dry swooshing of her skirts. Her manner was animated and gay, but her eyes shone with a cold, impenetrable glaze that demanded attention.

"Well! Surrounded by one-two-three-four-five handsome men! Aren't *I* a lucky stiff? Now listen, gentlemen, it's Christmas!" She perched herself brightly on the pouf. "And Christmas is the nicest time of all," she continued, without a hint of malice. Then, addressing herself to the strangers: "We have one more son that you haven't met yet, our Clinton's older brother." Clinton stood next to her. She took his hand, kissed it lightly, then went on holding it. "My husband and all of us miss him very much, especially at Christmastime." The toothless old man at this point put in some incomprehensible remark. Annabel smiled appreciatively, and continued: "And we have this big old empty house just going to waste. So we'd just love to have you all stay the night and enjoy Christmas dinner with us. But only if you'd enjoy it, too. Isn't that so, Ralph?"

Ralph looked at her, but he remained silent: there was no way of knowing how the wind blew. Annabel opened her pocketbook. "I'm almost sure I have here three crisp new ten-dollar bills."

Clinton looked at the strangers: the eyes of each of them were fixed hungrily on Annabel's pocketbook.

"So you can have your choice," she concluded, rising from the pouf and holding the bills in her hand. The visitors rose too, their eyes on the money. The older man glanced briefly at his companions; then he stepped forward like the chairman of a committee and once again engulfed Annabel's hand in both of his own. When he had finished a speech of considerable length, the three bills were in his pocket and he had retreated to the front door. The other men followed him out.

Annabel closed the door. Ralph sank heavily into the easy chair vacated by the merry old tramp. Clinton looked through the front window at the three departing kings who huddled together on the lawn redistributing their wealth.

Annabel was more timid now. She approached her husband uncertainly, and spoke softly: "Ralph, it's never my intention to go against your wishes, but there *are* times when . . ."

"Keep still," he said, not even looking at her.

"All right, sulk if you have to."

"Keep still."

The telephone rang. Annabel hugged her own elbows: could it be Christmas? Had Christmas arrived? Was it Berry-berry? "Dear God in Heaven!" she said aloud, half prayer, half exclamation.

Clinton picked up the telephone in the dining room.

"Hello? —Yeah, just a minute. —Ralph, it's for you. Long distance. Covington, Kentucky!"

Ralph rose quickly to his feet. "*Cov*ington?" He went to

the phone. Annabel and Clinton formed a cluster at his elbow.

Clinton said, "Does Ralph know somebody in Covington, Kentucky?"

"It's Berry-berry," said Annabel. "He's on his way home and calling to tell us."

"Keep still," Ralph said. "I can't hear a goddam thing." Then, into the telephone: "Talk up, will you? —Yes, I'm Ralph Williams, who wants me, who wants to talk to Ralph Williams?" After a moment, he shouted impatiently: "Well, *put him on!* Naturally I'll pay for it, he's my son!" Annabel made a deep sound of delight. Ralph looked at her. "Now you keep still, I want to hear what this is all about." He squeezed the instrument with both hands, as if it were an empty water pouch and he was dying of thirst. "Hello, you big sonofabitch!" he shouted at last.

Annabel grimaced. "Oh, that language is so *cute!* So cute on Christmas Eve, I could *vomit!*"

"I can't hear you," Ralph said, "your mother's here puttin' on a show for us, she's squawkin' her head off and doin' a fanny dance. I'll see if I can talk her into shutting her goddam mouth."

Ralph glanced at her. She glared back at him coldly.

"Now, what the hell's this all about?" Ralph shouted good-naturedly into the mouthpiece. "You're where? In the Covington *what?* Well, good for you, I knew you'd make the grade, you little shitass. Go on, tell me the rest of it."

The next pause seemed interminable to Clinton. He had even lighted a cigarette before he realized that he never smoked in Annabel's presence. Then he put it out.

Annabel held her silence for a long while. Finally, she whispered, "Doesn't he want to talk to me?"

"Yeah, go on," Ralph said, into the phone.

"*Self*ishness!" Annabel breathed. "Self, self, self!"

"Well, I don't blame you one iota," Ralph put in. "I wish *I'd* been there." Another pause followed.

Annabel made no further effort at restraining herself. "Give me that phone," she demanded. "He wants to talk to his mother!"

"Hold on a minute, boy," Ralph said. Then, covering the mouthpiece with his hand, he turned to Annabel and said, very distinctly, "He can't talk to you because he's in jail." He watched the stunned silence fall about her like a shroud, then returned to the phone. "Go on, kid, I got rid of the interference."

It seemed to Clinton that the old man was not entirely unhappy about this situation. Nor was he himself. After all, the idea of Berry-berry's being in jail was not without its virtues: maybe he could get down to Covington before they released him and . . .

"Where do I send it?" The old man turned to Clinton: "Get me a pencil." Clinton gave him paper and a pencil, and Ralph wrote down an address.

Annabel said: "Maybe the State of Kentucky doesn't *realize* it yet, but this country has a Bill of Rights and a Constitution! This is *not* a police state! Ralph. Tell Berry-berry this is not a police state and he should demand . . ."

"Son?" Ralph said. "Your mother wants to say Merry Christmas. Now hold on a minute. Can you hold on?" He handed the receiver to Annabel. "Just say Merry Christmas, will you; he doesn't want to hear about the Constitution."

"Berry-berry, listen," Annabel began, "I *knew* you'd call, I had this truly amazing letter from Bernice O'Brien. —What? —Oh, all right, Merry Christmas, and don't *worry*. If we have to, we'll mortgage this house so fast . . . ! All right, all right! —Clinton? A quick Merry Christmas to your brother; they're breathing down his neck, so hurry!"

Clinton took the phone: "Berry-berry?"

There was a pause. Annabel said, "What's he *saying?*"

Bewildered, Clinton placed the receiver in its cradle. "Nothing. He— He wasn't *there*. I grabbed the phone and I said 'Berry-berry,' and he was just—he wasn't there any more."

Ralph was studying a blank space on the wall. Annabel moved quickly into his line of vision. "Will you please *speak?*" she said.

Ralph forced his mind to return from some great distance. "Oh, it's nothin'. I'm to go to the Western Union and wire him fifty dollars, that's all. It's for bail."

"Bail? What for? What are they holding him for?"

"Annabel, these things happen all the time. It's just a matter of—well, they call it vagrancy. He got in a scrape in some bar, and one thing led to another . . ."

"Ralph. I'm going to insist, I have a right!"

"The connection wasn't any good and you kept squawking all the time, so . . ."

"You heard plenty."

"All right, he was sitting there, and somebody come up and started to bother him. So he took a poke at this—person. There's not gonna be any pressing of charges, but there was *some* damage to the pinball machine, and the bird that operates this place got sore and I don't know what-all. Give me my coat."

"Are you holding back something dreadful?"

"Listen, if I was holding back something dreadful, the bail'd be one helluva lot worse than fifty smackers, so don't get your hopes up." He studied the scrap of paper: "Prob'ly a bail bondsman or some shyster lawyer. Anyway, I'm to send it to this bozo, and I'm to send it right away by

Western Union. —Come on, Clint, you ride downtown with me."

Clinton was delighted to be a part of this emergency. In a matter of seconds, he was in his winter coat and standing at the front door.

"Ralph," Annabel said, as she handed him his car keys and opened the door for them, "I'm going to say something and I don't want any filthy answer: I've always worshiped you for the way you are in a crisis. Always the complete master, and that's a very *Christian* way to be. Now go ahead, say I'm silly."

"Come on, let's go," Ralph said. He took hold of Clinton's arm.

As they crossed the porch and descended the icy steps, Clinton felt that in a way the old man was leaning on him for support. He even felt, for that moment and during the ride downtown, that he was a necessary person, not just some nail-biting nuisance who was always underfoot.

"I got a load on my mind, boy," Ralph said to him. They stopped for a red light and the two of them lighted cigarettes. "You know what that Galbralian did? You know who he took a poke at? You know what it was that big-assed brother o' yours took and swung on? It was a *woman*, is what it was. That's what he took a swing at, some woman."

A horn sounded behind them. They moved forward. "Boy, he don't fool, that big-assed Galbralian brother o' yours, no-sir-goddam*ree!*" He whistled like a man gravely impressed by the doings of another.

Then, his eyes on the traffic, he said, "What about you, Clint, you still hangin' on to your cherry?"

Clinton went stiff with embarrassment and shame, but he did not like to tell lies. "Yes, sir, I am," he said. "I've still got it."

"Well, there's nothin' wrong with that," Ralph consoled him, with more gentleness than his words themselves could convey. "You just hang onto it for a while if you want to. It won't hurt you. What are you, fourteen years old? —Well, *I* say there's too goddam much song-and-dance about the whole matter anyway. You know they's lots of women would like to have a man believe they got some priceless sonofabitch of an heirloom tucked away down there, but that's not the *case*. That's not the case atoll. It's not *platinum* either, and it's not some priceless goddam heirloom. If you want to know what it is, *I*'ll tell you. It's a crack, is what it is. And I'm not knockin' it either, it has a perfectly scientific function, and the world'd be in one sorry spot without it. But what I'm gettin' at is that big six-footer of a Galbralian of a brother of yours—he's out of his goddam *head* on the subject."

Ralph leaned forward in his seat. "Now I'll just reconstruct this whole Covington, Kentucky, mess right now for you. What he did, he got hold of some bar-fly and he took her upstairs and he *planked* her. He planked her, and from then on she wouldn't keep away from him, just kept suckin' around at his elbow till he let her have it."

"Is that what he said?" Clinton asked.

"No, no. That's what *I* say. *I*'m doing the reconstructing. I'm reconstructing this whole thing, and there it is. —Course, she wasn't no fiddling good, prob'ly a drunk to boot, and maybe even some kind of a maniac in the bargain. But you see, that Berry-berry, he can't keep away from her in the first place, can he. O-*hooo* no! And it's the old man that carries the gold down to Western Union!"

They drove in silence for a long time. Clinton pictured in his mind a dimly lighted tavern in the hills of Kentucky, Berry-berry flipping a coin at the bar while sloe-eyed, long-haired, smooth-skinned women cloaked their desire

64

in cigarette smoke, tapped in time to the jukebox with
high-heeled slippers; and waited, waited, waited. In his
mind, everybody tapped out the time, nervously, even the
bartender and the faceless men who sat against the walls
watching, waiting; but Clinton, as the author of this picture, could not really get the thing moving; he could never
see Berry-berry in operation, only this throbbing frieze of
tension and desire.

"But I'm bettin' on him," Ralph said, as if there had been
no pause. "He's just foolin' around, sampling. He's *sampling*." He seemed to like that word: "Sampling life and all
of its riches. —But when he buckles down, look out!"

"What's he going to do then?" Clinton wanted to know.

"Just watch. And I'm bettin' on him to win. I didn't say
I was bettin' on him to show or to place. I'm bettin' on
him to *win!*"

When Ralph Williams laughed, he did not as a rule use
his vocal chords at all. He blew out air that passed first
through pockets of spittle in his cheeks. So the sound was
more than anything else like an escape of steam. This is
how he laughed now; and it signified his complete confidence in Berry-berry's prospects.

Now Clinton, during this ride downtown, was experiencing something that he did not at the time think about
by name: for the minute a happy person names his condition there is at that moment a chink in it: he has turned the
coin over and studied it too closely. But on this trip downtown, every part of Clinton Williams had got inside of the
moment that was then taking place: his eyes saw the
Christmas Eve movements of people and automobiles
through the frosted windshield and his own white breath;
he smelled the cold, and the car, and his father, and the
tobacco they burned between them; his ears were filled
with Ralph's theories and reconstructions; and his own

65

imagination was alive, enriching each word the old man spoke.

And as the car rolled across Cleveland toward the Western Union office, Clinton knew, again without naming what he knew, that he himself was moving across some stretch of time and ignorance, covering, so to speak, some of the ground that lay between him and his brother.

part **2**

CLINTON stood at the cash register paying for his coffee. As the woman made change, Clinton asked her to tell him the name of the town they were now in. Every hour or two the bus would stop to give the passengers a chance to stretch their legs and attend to personal comforts. And at each of these stops Clinton made it a point to find out where he was. Then when he got back on the bus he would make a note of it: "Malted milk in Leesburg, Tennessee. Jukebox playing *The Wheel of Fortune*. Waitress with pretty eyes and bad teeth tried to sing along with it. I'll bet she'd like to get on the bus and go someplace. Maybe not, though, because she had on a wedding ring. But even so, who knows?" Just a brief note was all he would need, later on, to remind him of the places he had been. However, Leesburg had been last night. Since then, while he slept, they'd passed another state line into Georgia. Now it was high noon on the fifth day of June, and another long blue-sky afternoon of sitting on the bus lay before him, an afternoon of a dozen more new places drifting past the window.

"This is Micah, G.A., sonny boy," she said, and her eyes seemed to add, "Don't you forget it." Clinton had noticed that all the waitresses in southern places were either hostile or friendly; none of them seemed to want to be caught without an attitude. He made a mental note of this lady's category, hostile, and the name of the town, Micah, and then walked to the screen door of the place. Before going through it, however, he counted his belongings: duffel bag, notebook, money belt, and a pocketful of assorted small possessions. Other passengers left their bags on the bus when they made a stop, but Clinton did not want his

69

trip spoiled by the loss or theft of any of these articles.
Aside from the clothes he had on his back—blue jeans
and a T-shirt, shoes and socks—his duffel bag contained a
pair of sneakers, a sweater, two shirts, extra socks, a supply
of pencils, and various toilet articles. These toilet articles
did not include a razor because even now, at sixteen, he
did not have use for one. In his determination to travel
light, free, ready for a quick move, he wore no underwear,
nor did he carry any. It was summer anyway: if later on he
and Berry-berry went off to some cold-weather place,
Clinton figured it would be a simple matter to purchase
such objects on the spot. Meanwhile, there would be no
heaviness of belongings to weigh down the vagabond
whims that would stir them.

The notebook he carried was large and thick, but after
long habit it encumbered him little more than his own
arms and legs. And because it had been nearly as vital to
him as these other members, he now handled it and made
use of it with an unconscious ease similar to that of walking or feeding oneself.

Clinton often touched his middle section to assure himself that his money belt still rode there, safe on his belly.
The money belt contained almost three hundred dollars,
which was about half of what he had saved in a year of
waiting on customers at the White Tower in Cleveland.
One of the small economies which enabled him to accumu-
late this money was in the matter of clothing: he was able
to make do with old ones because he had not grown
any, not one inch in all that time. Annabel attributed this
to the early use of cigarettes. But Clinton's own belief was
this: that the power of normal adolescent growth in him
had distributed itself in all the parts of his body, with
nothing left over for height. Indeed, through no special
efforts of his own, his slight body had developed a fine

young network of muscle. The surprise appearance of biceps caused him no little pride: every now and then he would flex them, glance down at himself, and look up reassured. In fact, he wore all these new qualities of body—hard stomach, sturdy legs, breadth of shoulder and strength of neck—with all the self-conscious pleasure of a dandy who has just purchased himself a shimmering new silk suit. Though Clinton was no athlete and did not exercise himself, the movements of his body had begun to offer him this new pleasure: a sense of its own normal powers.

Now, if you were a passenger on the back seat of this bus, and you happened to look at Clinton Williams, happened to watch him move down the aisle toward his seat, small, strong, clear of skin, determination in his aspect, you would not know for certain if he were fourteen or twenty. His skin was of an ivory color made incandescent by youth, and over all was that vague wash of blue one finds on the faces of habitual dreamers. In this fair setting, surrounded by their dark brown lashes, his quick eyes took on a quality of deep wonder, of perpetual surprise. But in spite of this innocence of feature, it was a disturbing face: for intense seriousness, in one so young, can be an awesome thing to look upon.

Clinton had wished, ever since he got on board yesterday in Cleveland, that some fellow passenger would ask him where he was bound for. Then he would hear himself say it out loud: Key Bonita. To his ear it sounded like the most faraway place in this country: Key Bonita. He wondered what reaction this name would get from a person who was on his way to some ordinary place like Pensacola or Tampa. They would look at him for a moment, impressed, and then ask him where such a place was located. "Oh, it's just an island off the coast of Florida," he would explain it in an offhand way—"an old pirate hangout. My brother got in a jam down there, and he sent for me to help him out."

Clinton at certain moments found himself believing that Berry-berry had actually sent for him. Whereas, what he had sent for was two hundred dollars; and the request had come not to him, Clinton, but to Ralph. On this occasion the old man had said he wanted Berry-berry to deal with his predicament without any assistance from him. Since the Covington, Kentucky, episode, there had been half a dozen of these urgent requests in eighteen months: twice he had asked for money to get out of jail, and the other pleas had been for relief from an assortment of crises: in Norfolk, Virginia, he had demolished someone's car and was being held for damages; in San Pedro, California, he wanted to ship out with the Merchant Marine and needed money for seaman's papers; apparently he had not shipped out after all, because the next S.O.S. had come from Biloxi, Mississippi, where he had smashed the window of a department store and caused considerable damage to its Christmas display. There had been no other communications from Berry-berry, only these messages of distress, and they never came twice from the same town. Clinton had kept a map, following in this way Berry-berry's zigzag progress to Key Bonita.

Clinton had been working the late shift at the White Tower, taking over the job from Mevvin who had gone back to his heaven in Tennessee. Ralph Williams often walked over to the place in the evenings and sat with his son during the slack hour between eleven and midnight. Just three nights ago, as Ralph sidled up to the counter, he handed Clinton the telegram that had just been delivered to him from Key Bonita:

72

DEAR RALPH HAVE FINE OPPORTUNITY TO BUY INTO SHRIMP-
ING BUSINESS. OWNER OF BOAT DESPERATE FOR CASH, WILL
GIVE ME GENEROUS SHARE EXCHANGE FOR FUEL MONEY. WE
MAKE FIVE-DAY TRIPS. PROFIT AVERAGES THOUSAND DOLLARS
A TRIP. PLEASE RUSH TWO HUNDRED, WILL RETURN SAME IN
TEN DAYS. LOVE.

> BERRY-BERRY WILLIAMS
> TIN POT ARMS HOTEL
> KEY BONITA FLORIDA

Clinton read it four times. As his eye lingered on the
address, he knew with a sudden and overwhelming certainty that he himself, within a very short time, would be
standing in the lobby of the Tin Pot Arms Hotel. He had
never before heard of the place, but its name was inexplicably familiar; it was as if it existed in his past rather
than in his future. But he did not question it. His excitement was sharp and pleasurable and, in an effort to hide it
from his father, he busied himself with wiping all the
catsup dispensers.

"You gonna send the two hundred?" he asked.

"Listen, are you kiddin'?" Ralph rested his hands on the
counter, entwined his fingers, twiddled his thumbs. "Give
me a—what you got there, root beer? Give me a root beer.
Listen, are you kiddin'?"

"I just wondered. Large or small?"

"Large."

"'Cause I wouldn't blame you if you didn't," Clinton
said. "I just wondered. Where *is* Key Bonita anyway?" He
placed a large glass of root beer on the counter.

"You know where Key West is? Well, this Key Bonita is
nowheres near there, not even in the same chain of islands.
I looked it up in the atlas. —Say, this stuff is awful sweet."

73

"I thought you'd like it that way. I pulled the handle down twice; that way you get two loads of syrup."

"Oh," Ralph said. "Well, it's got a real nice flavor of root beer to it." He took another sip.

"It's too sweet, I can give you another one."

But Ralph would not let go of the glass. "Now, Key West is one thing, but this Key Bonita is another kettle of fish. It hangs down off the Florida west coast, and it's not a coral key. See, they got coral keys like Key West and then they got this other kind. I never went down there myself. I was never crazy about the water."

"Berry-berry is," said Clinton. "He's nuts about the water. Everyplace he goes, it's got water."

Ralph agreed to this: "San Pedro, Biloxi, Norfolk; you're right, goddamit, he's just a nut on the subject of water. I never thought about that before."

"I wonder," Clinton said, "if he ever actually went out on the ocean."

"Listen, are you kiddin'?" Ralph said. "Why the hell should *I* send that bozo two hundred dollars? Does he think I'm made of money, just go out in the yard and pluck it off a tree?"

"I don't know."

"I b'lieve the worst thing I could do would be send him two hundred dollars. Shrimp! I'd like to *see* all that shrimp, a thousand dollars in five days. Listen, *my* mother didn't raise any foolish children! —And it's not the money either, I care about. Do him good to get off his buns, raise two hundred himself. He's got it in his head the only way to raise money is at the Western Union. He's got it in his head the Western Union is some kind of a bank. He just goes in there, scribbles out some cock-'n'-bull story, and out comes two hundred dollars. Listen, are you kiddin'?"

"Well, I just wondered."

74

"Hey." Ralph caught Clinton's eye and held it. Then he said, quietly: "What d'*you* think I ought to do? I'll leave it up to you."

"Gee, Ralph, I just don't know."

"Well, *I* do. Listen, my old man knew the value of a buck. He was a blacksmith, strong as an ox. You want me tell you what a blacksmith would do, he got a wire like this?"

"What would he do?"

"Wouldn't even answer it."

"W-What're *you* gonna do?" Clinton said.

"Not even gonna answer it."

"Well, can I have it then?"

"What, this telegram? What do you want with it?"

"I thought I'd just keep it."

"What for?"

"Oh, it doesn't make any difference," Clinton said, "I don't care. —*You* keep it."

"Naw," Ralph said, "that's all right, you can have it. Hell, I don't want the thing." He pushed the telegram across the counter. Clinton picked it up and started to fold it.

"What're you gonna do with it?" Ralph said.

"Just keep it."

"Tell you the truth," Ralph said, "I guess I'd better hang on to it m'self. Yeah. Second thought, you better let me keep it."

Clinton handed it back to him, and Ralph put it in his pocket. Then he put a dime on the counter for his root beer, which he had only tasted, and got up from the stool.

"Well," Clinton said, "you gonna send Berry-berry the two hundred?"

Ralph put his hat on and said: "Listen, I've washed my

75

hands. I wouldn't send that jailbird two hundred jelly-beans."

"I just wondered."

"Be the worst thing I could do," Ralph said, and as he went out the door he was shaking his head vigorously.

Clinton took a pencil from the cash register and wrote Berry-berry's address on a scrap of paper.

The door opened. He put the address in his pocket and looked up. Ralph had returned. He walked over to the counter and leaned on it, but he did not sit down.

"Listen, I'm gonna tell you something else," Ralph said. "It wouldn't hurt that big sonofabitch to sit down and write a post card to Annabel either. Mean a lot to that woman to get a penny post card in the mail. I personally don't give a damn and I'd never ask *any*body to spend all their time hangin' around post offices, don't believe in it." He tapped the counter several times to make his point: "But that woman Annabel has got a weak nervous system, is *famous* in this family for a weak nervous system. And you think he gives two farts in hell? Why, even a China-man would have better sense than go a thousand years without writin' a penny post card to a woman like that. I'm off of him. I am. I'm off of him for good."

He went to the door and opened it. Then he turned to Clinton once more, his head cocked to one side, fixing him with his eye. "I'll tell you what that bird is good at, he's an expert at sendin' telegrams. Berry-berry Williams is a colossal expert at the Western Union, and for my money, he can . . ." A customer, entering the place, was trying to get past Ralph. Ralph stepped back, bowing and smiling: "I beg your pardon, gentle sir." Then, as he went out the door, Ralph called over his shoulder, "See you at the house, boy."

That night, when Clinton arrived home at a few minutes

76

past midnight, he went to his room and closed the door. Two hours later, he had made his plans.

[*Clinton's Notebook*]

Get up at eight A.M.

Go to downtown office and tell them Saturday's your last day at the White Tower.

Go to bank and draw out all money. $601.07.

Go to Greyhound Station and get bus ticket.

Go to Western Union office, send $200, with this message:

URGENT GOT TO GET AWAY FROM HERE. ARRIVING TUESDAY WITH MORE MONEY. PLEASE INCLUDE ME ON THE SHRIMP BOAT. VERY IMPORTANT.

CLINT WILLIAMS

Go to Army-Navy Store and buy that duffel bag and money belt.

IMPORTANT. Do not say anything to Annabel until bus ticket has already been bought.

Do not let on about sending money to Berry-berry.

On Saturday, when he had carried out this plan, Clinton made another entry in his notebook:

[*Clinton's Notebook*]

My last night at White Tower. It's now 2 A.M. I got home at midnight and did a very smart thing. But I don't actually feel so hot about it. I got Annabel and Ralph together in her bedroom and told them both at once. My psychology was that Annabel would lose

77

any argument that came up. Namely, Ralph would have to be on my side, because he always lectures about how families should be disbanded when the offspring get through puberty, say at about fourteen. So, with me being sixteen, my psychology was that if I announced a mere trip, he'd have to back me up. As far as Annabel goes, I figured she would raise a stink about it even if I was two hundred years old, because of her having the change of life, etc.

Well, actually everything's okay now, but was it ever a weird thing to go through. To begin with, Ralph was the one that started making up all kinds of objections, and Annabel acts like she *wants* me to go. She acts like I'm going to spend a weekend with Aunt Imelda in Tecumseh or to Boy Scout camp or some damn place. Whereas, Ralph said it was a screwball idea and how did I know what kind of a mess I'd run into down there. So I had to bring up the families being disbanded business myself. He didn't put his foot down of course, or pull any parents and children crap, because he knew I had the goods on him. Besides, it would kill him to do anything real cheap like pulling his rank, etc., so he just left the room and that was that.

Then I had this very peculiar talk with Annabel. She can't *wait* for me to get on that bus! Which is completely out of character and I don't know what to think. Is she having her goddam menopause or isn't she?

This book by Doctor Wilhelm Levi explains all the weird things women get wrong with them, like frigidity and menstruation and jealousy about not having a penis, and so on. For a long time I've been positive Annabel fitted into the part about change of

78

life. But she is not at all thrown about me going to Key Bonita, which is absolutely nuts.

I tried to stop using those words, nuts and insane and crazy, because I thought I was too intelligent, but I may go back to it and give up psychology altogether. For a long time I used to think everybody in the world was insane and I was scared to death on account of it and had nightmares about all these maniacs being on the loose everyplace. But now that I know better I just get depressed. Because they still act like they're crazy.

Anyway this whole Aunt Imelda attitude about my trip threw me for a loop. She started right off by saying she was tickled pink, and now I can't even remember what all she said. (Another crazy thing, because usually I remember every word.) Also, she gave me this photograph she had taken in the dime store and made me promise I'd give it to Berry-berry. She must have moved her head when the shutter clicked, because it came out very blurry and makes her look like Mary Astor with little lights in her eyes and all.

Enough of that.

Now I've got to put something down that I hate. I don't even want to think about it. But my whole theory is that if a thing is true or actually happened or got said by somebody, then I've got to put it down or else go crazy. I'm a firm believer in the principle if you admit a thing to yourself, no matter how terrible it is, you're better off. The Bible backs me up a hundred per cent. It says the truth shall make ye free. Ralph says the Bible is fairy tales. Maybe so, but Shakespeare is also on my side in this thing, and so is Upton Sinclair.

Now the thing I have to put down is this. I'm afraid. I'm afraid of the bus ride all alone through the mountains of Tennessee. I'm afraid of all the strange people I'll meet all the way down there. I'm afraid of Key Bonita. I wish I had a real mean face with scars all over it and everybody was scared of me.

But the point is I know it's a mistake to go down to Key Bonita. And I know something terrible is going to happen there, but I can't stop myself from going. Naturally I *could* stop myself, because only a real nut gets driven to do things and go places he doesn't want to go. But—

I just now cried. I picked up this notebook and held it like a little baby holds a Teddy bear and I cried. Now I feel better. But boy did I cry there for a while. Now I'm kind of laughing. I feel sorry for all the people who do not have a really close friend like this notebook. It's only imitation leather, but if it got hurt or burned or anything, I'd bury it and say prayers just the same as if it was my own brother. Or any person I trusted enough to tell everything to.

I can't wait to get on the bus.

Resolutions for trip. If you get really scared, write it all down, no matter how dumb it sounds. Then if somebody clubs you to death or you drown, or something even worse, it won't make so much difference.

And if some really mean son of a bitch comes at you just because you've got a baby face, and starts screwing around and you haven't got time to write it down—don't let him know you're scared. Just squint your eyes down to where they're narrow as hell, talk real deep and snarl if you have to, and fight to kill. They call it a fishing town, okay, but these waterfront crooks are just the same as pirates and are sanguinary.

80

This means they like bloodshed and prefer killing to any other amusement. I don't happen to believe this just because it's common knowledge either. It happens to be the God's truth, I just know it.

Maybe going on this trip is not a mistake after all. Ever since I made up my mind to go I have not once masturbated or even considered it. Which is fabulous because there for a while it got so bad I was afraid of getting pimples. At my age, if you get pimples, everybody knows you've got this dirty habit, and it's a big mess. So no matter how black it all looks at times, I'm really lucky as hell about certain things.

In twenty hours, I'll be getting on the bus. I'm still afraid but it doesn't make any difference because I'd rather die than not go where Berry-berry is. Even some awful death like toothpicks pushed under my fingernails and branding irons in my eyeballs. Do I really mean this?

Yes, I do.

See, in your mind, the west coast of Florida on the Gulf of Mexico. Picture a chain of seven islands, linked together by bridges. This chain curves gently to form an S. The top of the S is attached, by another bridge, to the mainland, a few miles south of Naples. The bottom point of the S is an island called Key Bonita.

A bus called Tamiami will bring you as far down the coast as Naples, but from there a traveler to Key Bonita has to choose between a number of inconvenient alternatives. An Everglades bus would leave him four miles from that first bridge, and continue its journey east; there is a local bus line that would take him directly to Key Bonita, but it sends a bus down that way only once in two days.

The third choice is hitchhiking; but motorists are few in the Everglades, and these few are nervous and drive fast: this is desolate swampland, and a lone figure on the highway arouses suspicion. Therefore, the hitchhiker's chances are slim, and he may end up with a long mean walk before him.

But this was the method Clinton Williams chose. At first his luck ran high. A cheerful man in a long black car brought him to the fork, the very point at which the swamp bus turns off into the Everglades on its way to the east coast. But from there, the going was hard.

After an hour, in which darkness had begun to fall and only six cars had turned off in the direction of the bridge, he set out to walk the four miles. The road was straight and dreary, lined with mangroves and scrubby seagrape trees. Serpents lived there, camouflaged in the mangroves' twisted roots, and on the surface of the dead-still waters, mosquitoes in their millions bred millions more. These bloodthirsty nuisances raised welts on Clinton's skin. After a few minutes he gave up slapping at them or even scratching the places they had bitten. Scuffling lizards made nightmare noises, and frogs croaked in their hiding places. For a while, the boy sang any song that came into his head, just to drown out their sounds. But after a time, when he gave up resisting any of these miseries, they became strangely pleasurable. The full moon, like some demon skilled in chiaroscuro, made awful shadow creatures to hide imperfectly in the foliage. Clinton wondered why he was not afraid of them: it was as if he had died and gone to hell and found it curiously to his taste. He tingled with the excitement of this terrible place. If one of the moon's monsters had come forward, he might have reached out to it eagerly, hugged it to his itching, perspiration-drenched body, and begged it to make love to him.

82

For he had become, to himself, one of its miserable creatures, a shape of evil, ready to surrender.

Who knows how long he trudged forward on this road, absorbed by these feelings a hot country can engender in a stranger? Perhaps an hour or two, or more. And then he reached the bridge, the bridge that was the top of the chain of islands that ended in Key Bonita.

Perhaps two hundred yards long, built on pilings without a superstructure, the bridge was an overseas continuation of the swamp road. Clinton walked out to the center of this bridge. He wanted to have the feeling of being over the water, away from the swamps. Then he sat on the concrete railing and lighted a cigarette. Before he had smoked even half of it, a motorcycle roared past him, the first vehicle of any kind that he had seen since nightfall. The motorcycle did not slow down for him; it continued in the direction of Key Bonita. But Clinton knew it would come back and give him a lift. He did not know how he knew, but he was certain.

He put out his cigarette, picked up his duffel bag, and waited. Then he heard the slow return of the motorcycle. As it passed him this second time, at low speed, its driver studied Clinton's appearance, stopped ten yards from him, and turned around.

The rider was in his twenties, dark, solidly built. Like Clinton, he wore Levis, a T-shirt. He removed his goggles. His voice was deep, husky. "You want a ride?"

"Yes, sir."

"Come here."

Clinton walked quickly to his side.

"Where you goin'?" the man said.

"Key Bonita."

"You live there?"

"No, but my brother does. He's waiting there for me. His name is Berry-berry Williams."

"Berry-berry?" The stranger's interest quickened.

"You know him?"

No answer. The man said, "How old are you?"

"Sixteen."

"You got a knife?"

"Yeah. You want to use it?"

"Let's see it."

Clinton reached into his pocket and withdrew his key ring from which depended the small knife given him by the Red Cross Shoes salesman. "It's just a little one," he said, "for cutting string. You know, and fingernails."

The man took the knife, glanced at it quickly, then handed it back with a derisive little laugh. He strapped the duffel bag to a bar under the seat. Clinton put his notebook in his trousers, under the belt.

"Hop on," the man said. Clinton got on. "You ever ride a buddy seat before? Keep your feet on those bars. And hang onto me, around my belly. We're gonna travel."

At the first island, there was a sharp increase in speed. The hot and heavy night was transformed by an endless rush of wind in Clinton's face, against his legs. Even the landscape changed: the mangroves on the left became an insignificant strip of black, and on the right lay the Gulf of Mexico. With his chest against the back of the cyclist, and his arms encircling him, the motorcycle itself seemed to come to life and breathe as it roared forward from island to island and bridge to bridge. These last miles of his journey to meet Berry-berry had taken on the proportions of a myth. Out of the swamp-hell had come this wild animal of the night, and on its back he now raced across a world so transformed that the change seemed to have been worked by magic. Each mile had in it not only its

84

own swift beauty, this heaven of speed, but the knowledge, as well, that it drew him closer and closer to the true
beginning of his life. If anything marred his pleasure, it
was his desire to get all these experiences into his notebook; but even that diminished as he began to hope that,
having passed, on this very night, some invisible threshold
into the life of his dreams, the need for a record might
have fallen away and his friendship with the notebook
terminated. It was still there, though. He could feel it
under his belt, the imitation-leather binding pressed
against his belly, the only part of him that continued to
perspire.

Once you have crossed the bridge onto Key Bonita, you
see a lot of coconut trees. They line the highway along the
Gulf. If you look through these palms and past the bight,
you see a few lights from the town itself: streetlamps, the
windows of fishing lodges, the neon of taverns, hamburger
places and tourist courts. The foliage is dense and it makes
these lights seem to twinkle like lightning bugs. Along the
boardwalk at the edge of the bight, moored to the many
piers that extend from it, there are hundreds of boats:
shrimp boats and barges, boats for pleasure and for every
kind of fishing. You will even see a houseboat with laundry
hanging on her decks and potted palms on her window-
sills.

Go along for another mile, pass a traffic light, turn to
the right, and you are on the main street of the town, Gasparilla Street, named for a buccaneer who made his
headquarters here in the darker days of blood and treasure. The houses are old, made of wood, most of them white
but a number of them gray from neglect and in bad repair.
Many of the yards are unkempt and have turned to jungle:
thick clumps of banana trees send up leaves taller than
men to reach into the fern-like branches of poincianas;

the giant philodendron vines are like serpents in fancy dress, they climb every wall and fence and suck the knotted trunks of banyan trees; there are breaks in the sidewalks where rubber-tree roots have gone berserk; and enormous cactus plants lean on houses, like monsters with tiny brains they threaten the lacework of tired Victorian porches.

You see people on the streets all night long. Sailors alone and in twos and threes, Latin dandies in pleated shirts, black-haired women at their elbows, drunken shrimpers clinging to parking meters for support. And all the solitary persons. Men and women young and old lean on storefronts and streetlamps, wander in and out of taverns, all of them seeming to take part in the same slow and indifferent search. And for every person you see, you will feel as sharply the presence of several invisible souls. For the town is plainly haunted. Lazy ghosts of old inhabitants rock forever on all the empty porches, and others watch over the street from shutters at second-story windows. If you do not believe in ghosts, the town will make you nervous: give up your disbelief or you will wonder forever at the sources of certain inexplicable sounds.

A number of young men in their late teens and early twenties leaned against the green plaster front of a hamburger place called Pepito's. Others congregated in its doorway.

Most of these young men watched the arrival of the motorcycle, watched with a kind of boldness of eye that would disturb any stranger.

Clinton climbed off and started to untie his duffel bag, but the owner of the bike stopped him gruffly. "Here! I'll do that!"

Then he tossed the bag into Clinton's arms. "Okay. Now you want something else?"

"No. I just wanted to thank you because—well, thanks. That's all."

The man said nothing.

"You know where the Tin Pot Arms Hotel is?" Clinton asked.

"The end of the street. On the water."

The other young men had moved in closer. They seemed to want to know everything that took place in front of Pepito's. Clinton glanced quickly at them, and then his eyes returned to the dark man who had given him the ride.

"You want somethin' else now?" the man challenged him.

"No, but thanks for the ride."

"Okay. Move."

Clinton wanted to walk away, but he had been made to feel there was some challenge he had not accepted. "Look," he said, "you give me a ride for about twenty miles or maybe even thirty, and now you act like you're sore about something. How come?"

The man did not answer. And suddenly Clinton knew that he could not. For he belonged to this group of loiterers, and one of their unspoken rules called for strict hostility to strangers. Something in the man's eyes had told him this; then he shrugged a shoulder and walked into Pepito's. Clinton watched him enter the place, and a few of the men followed him inside. After one slow glance at the remaining young men, a glance that he hoped would convey, "Don't mess with me, I'm mean as hell," Clinton turned and walked toward the end of the street, feeling that he had dealt with his first band of pirates.

He did not hurry. He wanted to savor every step of the hundred yards that lay between himself and the Tin Pot

Arms Hotel. He had thought a good deal on the bus from Cleveland—and written much in his notebook—about what this last few minutes of the trip would be. Now he tried to force the reality of it into his head, but for some reason, perhaps fatigue, his eyes saw the place without making any real contact with it. It was an enormous three-story frame building that had not been painted for a long time. There was a widow's walk at the peak of the roof; and through the jungle garden that separated it from the street, Clinton caught brief glimpses of the once-elegant old galleries that surrounded its two lower floors. Hanging over the front steps of the place was a large tin cutout of its symbol. But there was no lettering on it, just this rusty old silhouette of a tin pot.

Now Clinton stopped walking altogether. He had studied the advisability of certain attitudes he might adopt when he actually walked into Berry-berry's room. He had thought up ways of impressing him with the necessity for including him in the shrimp-boat partnership, certain unanswerable arguments in favor of their traveling together. In fact, he had experienced this meeting so often in his imagination that he was now at a loss as to how to manage it.

He entered the hotel and approached the desk. The clerk bore a startling resemblance to Ralph Williams, though older and more decrepit.

Clinton said, "I'm looking for Berry-berry Williams."

"Not here," the old man said, his eyes on a magazine.

"When does he generally get back?" The old man did not seem to hear this question. Clinton said, "Can I use his room to wait for him in? I'm his brother."

The clerk looked at him quickly. "He ain't got a room here n'more. He give it up."

"Well, where'd he move to?"

88

The clerk shrugged his shoulders. Then he looked into a dime-store ledger that served as a register. "Left on Friday," he said. "Just paid up and left."

"You mean—*town?* He left town?"

"That'd be my guess. But I don't know one way or the other."

"Then why would that be your guess, that he left town?"

The clerk leaned over and took off a shoe. He put his hand inside of it, felt it with his fingers. " 'Cause if I'd been him, I woulda."

"Why?"

The clerk, still exploring the inside of his shoe, glanced at Clinton through narrowed eyes. "You say you're his brother?"

"I *am* his brother." Clinton was ready to defend this point, if necessary.

"What you do," asked the clerk, "come down here from up North?"

Clinton nodded. "Cleveland."

"Just to see *him?*"

"What's wrong with that?"

"Nothin'. 'Cept he idden here. That's all."

"Look, it's very important, I got to find him."

The clerk placed the shoe on the floor in front of him. "I'd try the jail," he said.

"The *jail?*" Clinton stood there for a moment, watching as the clerk tied his shoe. "So you think maybe he's in jail, huh?"

"Tell you what you do, go to the fellow at the desk. Name's Ramírez. He's the lieutenant. You go to Ramírez and ask him where Berry-berry is." The clerk enjoyed giving these directions. "Don't even have to give his last name, just say Berry-berry. They all know him over there."

The Key Bonita jail is on a short lane called Hawthorne Alley, two and a half blocks from the Tin Pot Arms Hotel. It is a one-story affair, made of stone, old, run-down, illuminated by fluorescent lights. Three young policemen, in short-sleeved summer uniforms open at the throat, lounged on benches inside the front door. A somewhat older man, swarthy and black-haired, with a thin, suave mustache, was seated at a desk in the far corner of the room.

When Clinton entered the place, the three younger men did not look at him, but he knew they were aware of him. He walked up to the desk, where the mustached officer was shouting into a telephone. The officer, as he continued his conversation, studied Clinton from head to foot, but his manner was impersonal. Then he hung up and went on looking at the boy, waiting for him to speak.

"I'm lookin' for Berry-berry Williams," Clinton said. "I'm his brother."

The lieutenant spoke in a loud voice so that the other policemen would hear: "This kid's lookin' for his brother: Berry-berry Williams."

Clinton turned to look at the three men on the benches. None of them spoke; but each of them glanced at him and grinned in a private way.

"You happen to know where he is, sir?" Clinton said.

"When'd you get to town?"

"Just a little while ago."

"How'd you get here?"

"Hitchhiked. A fella picked me up on his motorcycle."

"What fella?"

"I don't know who he was."

"What's your name?"

"Clint Williams."

"Berry-berry's your brother, huh? You carry a knife, too?"

Clinton reached into his pocket. "I got a little one, a fingernail knife."

"Never mind," the officer said. Then, "You sent your brother two hundred dollars. What for?"

"He needed it. He was goin' into the shrimpin' business."

The officer raised his voice again: "Berry-berry was goin' into the shrimpin' business, did you guys know that?"

One of the policemen laughed out loud this time. But the other two only snickered. The behavior of all these men caused Clinton to flush red with embarrassment and annoyance, and he tried to suppress these feelings.

"Your brother hasn't claimed that two hundred. It's still over at the Western Union. Who's Ralph? He another brother?"

"He's my father."

"Your father know where you are?"

"Sure. I told him I was comin' down here. How'd you know his name?"

The officer did not answer this question. "How old are you, Clint?" he asked.

"Sixteen."

"What're you gonna do, stick around, wait for Berry-berry to turn up?"

"I don't know yet. Is he in some kind of trouble?"

"Nope."

"Then he's not here? I mean in jail?"

The officer shook his head. "We don't know where he is."

"Well," Clinton shrugged. "I guess I'll just have to start lookin' for him. Thank you, sir."

When he had reached the door, he heard the officer's voice. "Clint. Come back here."

He went back to the desk. Ramírez asked him to sit

down, and then the two of them had what seemed to be a friendly conversation. The officer asked a number of obtrusive questions, unrelated to Clinton's search; and there were long pauses in which Ramírez looked at Clinton in a quizzical way that caused the boy to squirm in his chair. But Clinton believed that the officer was interested in helping him find Berry-berry.

At length, Ramírez consulted a list of telephone numbers glued to the surface of his desk. Then he picked up the phone and dialed.

"Sellers? Ramírez." He looked at the clock on the wall. "Three-thirty. —'Cause I need to know something, that's why. You sleep too much anyway, fat ass. Listen, where's Berry-berry? —No, nothing like that. The girl hasn't talked yet; she probably won't either. —His kid brother's here lookin' for him, come all the way down from Ohio. —Oh, screw you, you're such a goddam lily. Go back to sleep."

He dropped the receiver into its cradle. "He don't know either. Bail bondsman. Sometimes those guys know everything. But he don't know where Berry-berry is." He put a cigarette in his mouth, but he did not light it. "Your brother used to be in the Festival a lot. That's a strip joint on Gasparilla. But *you* can't get in there, you know."

"Maybe I could just go in there and ask around."

The officer took the cigarette from his mouth and pointed with it. "Listen, you know what I want you to do? At noon tomorrow, there's a bus goes to Naples. You get on that bus and go home, hear?"

"Yes, sir."

The Festival is situated cater-cornered at the end of Gasparilla Street, across the street from the Tin Pot Arms. The pilings that support the building are partly in the

92

water, in the Gulf of Mexico. On its board-and-batten exterior has been painted a myriad of colored bubbles on a field of green, so that the place has the look of an enormous earthbound balloon. Lettering on some of the larger bubbles enumerate its wares: FUN, BEER, DANCING, GIRLS, CONTINUOUS ENTERTAINMENT, FOOD.

Clinton did not hesitate outside the place. He pushed the door forward and walked right in.

The Festival is one huge room. An elongated horseshoe-shaped bar occupies the center of it, and inside this horseshoe is a long spot-lighted ramp. These spotlights seem to be the only source of light in the place, so that its periphery, where the tables are located, appears at first to be in total darkness.

At the bar, a scuffle was taking place that engaged the attention of the bartender and the bouncer. Clinton's entrance was therefore unnoticed by these people. He went directly to one of the tables that lined the walls and sat there in the dark. There were no other customers at the tables, but more than half of the bar stools were occupied. A large cluster of sailors on one side of the horseshoe bar looked across the ramp at a cluster of girls who sat opposite them. Other girls moved about desultorily among solitary male customers. Clinton watched several of these brief dumb shows of conversation but he did not wonder at what was being said because his attention was somewhat divided. A naked woman was making her way down the center of the ramp, unable to keep time with the jukebox music that accompanied her, but shaking various parts of her body in an awkward, lumbering rhythm of its own. Aside from Clinton himself, the only person in the room who paid any attention to the dancing woman was a lone sailor who looked upon her with the cold indifference of a butcher appraising a side of beef. Meanwhile, the bouncer,

93

a wiry cat-like little man, was helping a big drunk with the problem of getting into his shoes.

All this activity in the Festival Night Club took place on a kind of screen projection of Clinton's deepest concern: Berry-berry and his whereabouts. In his mind, when he saw this picture of Berry-berry, he could see only the back of his head, and it kept moving farther and farther away. This caused in him a painful anxiety that was centered in his chest. If a doctor had asked him to describe the feeling, he might have said it was like a wound caused by a poisoned arrowhead under his heart, and it caused his nerves to tingle in a hurtful way.

Suddenly one of the girls was at the table with him. He had not seen her approach. She sat so close to him that her thigh touched his. One of his hands had been in his lap. She placed her own on top of it. "Hello, cuteness," she said. Her tone was impersonal but intimate: "I want a drink, you want company?"

"Okay." His face was hot; it ached from embarrassment. The girl's hand clutched his under the table. Then, moist and cold, it moved about restlessly on his lap until it came to rest lightly on his inner thigh, just below the groin. Her face shone with a kind of waxen deadness, as if the paint had been applied by a mortician, and masses of hair surrounded it like a dull brown shroud. Nothing in this face seemed to have any knowledge of what the hand was doing under the table: it crept about independently, like a wind-up toy forgotten by its owner.

When a waitress appeared at the table, the mechanical girl said: "I'm havin' a champagne cocktail. What about you, hon?" She squeezed his thigh. His blood had risen in him, but this excitement was not pleasurable; it only increased his turmoil.

"I'll have the same," he said.

94

"Really? Well, I don't think you'll like it, honey. Why don't you just get a highball?"

The waitress leaned forward. "Listen, Frances, you lost your goddam mind? Get him out o' here. F'godsake, he's still got his baby teeth; can't you tell by lookin'?"

The girl said, "It idden *my* job to check I.D.'s."

"No, but you could use your *head*."

Suddenly the little cat-like man stood at the table, jumping lightly from foot to foot, glancing from face to face. "What what what, what's goin' on? What is it, what?" He seemed unable to stand still or to focus on one object for more than a split second at a time. But he had already assimilated the situation. Within a few seconds Clinton was on his feet, being guided swiftly toward the door. The waitress and the girl remained at the table, quarreling.

On the sidewalk, Clinton said: "Look, I didn't want a drink anyway. I'm just lookin' for somebody. Ize lookin' for my brother."

"We haven't got any brothers, what brother, who?" the bouncer said, in his rat-a-tat-tat voice.

"Name of Berry-berry Williams."

"He don't come around here n'more, neither d'you, you keep out o' here from now on, completely, crazy kid, lose m'license, what you want? Get away, go." Suddenly the door was swinging and the swift little man was gone.

A low brick wall protected the yard of the house next door. Clinton sat on this wall and lighted a cigarette. He could not imagine what he would do next. It seemed to him that he had run out of alternatives and would remain seated here forever. When he had put out the cigarette, he found that the wall was wide enough to lie down on. He lay flat on his back. Then he put the duffel bag on top of his stomach, folded his hands across it, and closed his eyes.

In order to keep his mind busy, he took a sensory inventory of his belongings: without moving, he could feel the money belt strapped to his stomach, the notebook tucked under his belt, the duffel bag on top of it, his own hands. And above them, the night itself and the sky, the stars. But he felt no sense of ownership about the night: it was part of Berry-berry's leavings. When Berry-berry swept through a place, he seemed always to leave in his wake the garbage of a vampire: everything and everyone empty, meaningless, dead. Clinton saw the entire peninsula of Florida as a giant penis dangling into the sea, worthless, used up, spent; and the town, Key Bonita, nothing but an absurd tattoo on its crown. In his mind, weary, half-dreaming, the town was not a network of streets, but of branches; one did not walk here, one climbed; and the tree itself, in his half-dream, was a poor, withered Christmas tree, decorated by Annabel. She herself, perched in some high branch next to the moon, presided over her collection of shabby ornaments; like a puppet painted to impersonate a crazy woman, half angel, half whore, she gazed down with puzzled, indecisive eyes. "Are you still looking for Berry-berry?" he heard her ask, in a tiny, scarcely audible voice. "You *are* lookin' for your brother, aren't you?" But Clinton could not answer because he himself was part of Berry-berry's garbage, an apparatus of nerves, exhausted, bloodless. He lay on the wall like some pitiful lizard, unable to shed his old skin: duffel bag, notebook, money belt. . . .

"Little boy," said the voice, "I'm talkin' to you. Are you the one is lookin' for Berry-berry Williams? Now, listen, what's wrong with you? I'd like to be your friend, and I just know you can hear me. Are you runnin' a temp'ature?"

The angel-whore lowered her hand, touched his brow. Suddenly, in one motion, Clinton sat bolt upright on the wall. The woman standing on the sidewalk before him was like an enormous nine-year-old. She was no taller than himself, and she was not fat; but her tininess of manner made her body seem outsized, like a child whose glands had gone haywire.

"You sleep with your eyes open, little boy? Say, listen, you're not *turned on*, or anything like that, are you?" she said.

Clinton turned away from the woman. He blinked his eyes several times, then looked at her more closely. Her innocence of face, even under the mask of paint, was flawless: her eyes were moist blue flowers, her skin clear, her lips full and soft, slightly petulant. The toes of her pink high-heeled slippers pointed inward, her stomach thrust forward, her chestnut-colored hair fell in long curls to her shoulders. Even her pocketbook, pink and large, held upside down, took on the aspect of an abused rag doll.

"It was a dream," Clinton said aloud, but to himself.

"Oh! What kind?"

"I don't remember. —Miss, did I hear you say something about my brother?"

"I just ast if you uz lookin' for him is all. My girl friend tole me somebody uz lookin' for him."

"D'you know where he is?"

"No, I don't, but when I seen you were a little boy, I only wanted to be friendly. D'you want to come over to my house?"

Clinton rose to his feet. "You don't even know who I am, hardly."

The girl took his hand and pulled him across the sidewalk toward the street. "C'mon, *please?*"

"Listen, who are you anyway?" Clinton said.

"I'm Shirley. What's your name."

"Clint," he said. Then, "Hey, Shirley, tell me something, *do* you know where my brother is?"

"You already ast me that. And I don't, honest. How come you're lookin' for him? Are you lost?"

"Me? No, I'm not lost. I'm just lookin' for him."

"I hope you're not *like* him. 'Cause he's very, very mean sometimes."

"Do you know him?"

"No, and I've never even talked to him, but my girl friend has."

"Would she know where he is?"

"No, and she says she doesn't care, either. And she won't even talk to you, because you're his brother and meanness runs in families. But I don't believe that myself. *Are* you, though? Mean?"

"What'd my brother do that was mean?"

"I'm not a tattletale. Besides, I wasn't there, and maybe it's a lie. Now do you want to come home with me or not?"

"I can't. I got to find my brother. —Besides, your folks don't know me, or anything. And it's late."

Shirley laughed. "Don't be silly, my folks are *dead!* My whole family is. I live over there." She pointed across the street at the Tin Pot Arms Hotel. "Come on." She guided him into the street.

Clinton saw a police car in front of the hotel. The officer in the front seat was smoking a cigarette. Clinton could not see the man clearly, but he knew that it was Ramírez and that he was being watched by him.

As they passed through the lobby, the old clerk stared at them indifferently. Shirley turned with sudden shrewishness toward the desk and shouted in a lower, almost harsh voice, through clenched teeth: "He's only gonna *visit!* So why don't you mind your own business, you filthy thing!" The clerk looked away as if he had heard nothing, seen nothing. Once out of his line of vision, Shirley giggled, and with a child's sense of conspiracy ran tiptoe up the stairs, with Clinton close beside her. But when she paused to catch her breath at the top, she seemed much older, perhaps thirty or more. She looked at Clinton quickly, almost guiltily, from the corner of her eye: had he sensed this flaw in her game of childhood?

"Come on!" she said, leading the way up the hall. At her door, she stopped once again. "Now you wait here, and keep your eyes closed till I say okay. Okay?" Clinton closed his eyes.

Shirley stepped inside. He could hear the sounds of hurried activity within the room. After a moment, she took his hand and led him to the center of her room.

"Okay," she said. "Now open."

Shirley had lighted three kerosene lamps. The room was large, high-ceilinged, almost barren; but with these soft lights flickering through their glass chimneys, the place was far from dreary; and it was clean, well cared for. Between the front windows was a bed, with an ornamental iron headboard. At the foot of the bed was a wardrobe trunk, covered with a piece of faded purple chenille. One of the lamps had been placed on it and there were ash trays and glasses as well. Completing an intimate circle around this trunk-table were two old straw armchairs, their cushions covered with the same faded chenille.

Shirley searched Clinton's face for a favorable reaction to her home. She was not disappointed, for he said, sincerely, "It's the most beautiful place I've ever been in."

A soft breeze stirred the muslin curtains, and the lamp flames danced gently. There was in the air the good fragrance of a woman, her softness, her lilac and spice; and in the room itself, a cool and easy sense of freedom. It was the sort of a place in which, Clinton felt, a person might do as he pleased.

"Ize told once that lavender was my most becomin' color," Shirley said, "so I spent an entire Sunday dyein' just about ever'thing I own, even my undies and m'panda." She kicked off her slippers and opened a bureau drawer. "He sleeps in here." She held up the panda: "See? Name is Herskelwitz, you want to hold him? I have to take a bath 'fore I do another thing, so you just get comfy."

"Is it okay if I lie down?" Clinton said. "I won't go to sleep or anything."

"You don't have to ast me!"

"Well, it's just, if I'm lyin' down, I can *think* a whole lot better."

Shirley took him by the hand and led him to the bed. They sat on the edge of it, his hand still in hers. "You know what?" she said. "I don't think you ought to think about all the things you got to think about. Nobody should."

"Maybe so, only I've got to."

The girl looked at him for a moment, penetratingly, and then her gaze became diffused, passed through him and beyond him, as she said, "Would it make you feel funny if Ize to call you Willy?"

"Why do you want to call me Willy?"

"You just look like—like you should've been named Willy. I believe it suits you better'n that other name."

"You think so?"

She nodded.

"Okay. Call me Willy."

She started into the bathroom. "Listen, if you're scared to be alone, I can leave the door open."

"You don't have to."

100

"Well, um, wouldn't it make you feel better to know I'm right there where you can holler?"

"I don't care," Clinton said.

"Don't you get scared, alone?"

Clinton saw anxiety in her face.

"Sometimes," he said.

"You *do!*" she said happily. "Well, I believe that's perfickly normal, so I'll leave the door open enough to hear you. In case you holler."

"Thanks."

She hurried gaily into the bathroom. Clinton's head had scarcely touched the pillow when Shirley's face appeared again at the bathroom door. "Listen, if you get so lonesome you can't stand it, we can have a conversation right while I'm havin' m'bath. Just pull that chair over and set with your back to me, is all you have to do."

"Thanks."

"And we can talk about just any old thing till you feel better. Or I *could* give up m'bath altogether. 'Cause I'm clean as a pin. I just need refreshment. And I want to try out m'new cake o' soap. Are you as crazy about soap as I am?"

Clinton could still hear her voice, but it seemed to come from a great distance. He had fallen asleep. Shirley moved quickly to his side and stood there for a long time just looking at his face. And then she touched his forehead lightly with her lips.

Clinton felt the coolness of it; and he heard, as in a dream, the softness of her voice: "You're only asleep. Aren't you, Willy?"

Then Shirley crept silently into the bathroom. The panda named Herskelwitz sat on the toilet while she took her bath.

Later, when Clinton awakened, the character of the room had changed. Shimmering blades of daylight, very thin, but sharp as swords, shone through cracks in the shutters and were softened only slightly by the curtains that now hung motionless in front of them. The lamps had been put out. Clinton knew it was daytime, but it seemed more like night than night itself. Without moving his head, he could see Shirley. But at first he could not believe what he saw:

She was seated on the floor, just inside the closet, smoking a corncob pipe. She wore lavender pajamas and the lavender panda sat on her bare knee. At first, when he looked at her, her body was so utterly without motion, not even breath, that he feared she was in some kind of mysterious trance. But after a long moment, she exhaled, and emitted a puff of smoke. Then she placed the pipe in her mouth again, and with a series of brief and frenzied pulls at its stem, her lungs once again filled with the smoke. She seemed to try to hold this smoke inside of her as long as possible.

The girl, unaware of Clinton, was so intent on her pipe that he felt as if he were an interloper watching through the keyhole as she took part in some curious and private ceremony. Then, to remind her of his presence, he turned over on the bed and stretched his limbs, making as much noise as might seem natural. Without looking at her, he sat forward and put his feet on the floor.

"Hello, Willy," she said.

"I guess I fell asleep. I'm awful sorry."

"You was tired. What's wrong with that?"

"But I shouldn't be takin' up your bed. Where'd you sleep?"

"I didn't. I seldom sleep too much," she said, "except on Sundays."

102

"What time is it?" Clinton said. The words sounded strange to him. There was no time in this room, not now, not any more. Something else had taken its place.

Shirley said: "I watched you quite a bit. Do you mind?"

"Watched me sleep?"

"Uh-huh. I felt like a thief. But it was nice. And nights are long."

She got to her feet and stepped out of the closet.

Clinton said, "Do you sit in the closet quite a bit?"

"Only when I turn on. It's better in a small place. You want some?"

"Some what?"

"Don't you know?" she said, approaching the bed.

"You mean the pipe?"

"You can keep a secret, can't you, Willy?"

"Sure."

She held the pipe under his nose. It smelled like sin itself: exotic, faintly acrid, indescribable.

"What is it?"

Shirley put her mouth next to his ear, and whispered: "It's marijuana." Then she stood straight, thrust her stomach forward in the attitude of a little girl, and gave a false little laugh.

Clinton stared hard at the pipe. "If I tried a little puff, would I become a fiend?" Then, quickly, he added, "I mean, would I get addicted?"

"Huh-uh, not if you got a strong will. Have you got a strong will?"

In his mind Clinton reviewed rapidly certain of his own vices, and the strength of their hold on him. "Not very," he said.

"Then maybe you better not have any," Shirley said.

"Okay."

"What'd you dream about?"

He thought for a while. "My brother, I guess."

"Me, too! That's what *I* dreamt about. My brother."

"I thought you didn't sleep," Clinton said.

"Oh, I dream awake. I do it all the time. You want to hear my dream?"

"Sure."

"You may have to help me some," she said, settling into one of the straw armchairs.

"How can I?" Clinton asked.

"Well, if I start to cry, you have to stop me. Just take hold of my shoulders and say, 'Shirley, you look very pretty in lavender,' and make me listen. Okay? Just in case. But maybe I won't cry atoll. —Anyway, I dreamt about my little brother Willy. It's not my fault or anything, but he's dead. Everybody says it's not my fault because it was accidental. But when I dream about him, we're both settin' in the tree singin' songs. *The Isle of Capri* and *Billy-Boy* and every song you ever heard of. I never think about him bein' dead and all, 'cause I don't really believe in it. We just sing songs and I change the words for him. Like I sing:

> "*'Summertime was nearly over,*
> *Blue* Kentucky *skies above;*
> *I said,* Willy, *I'm a rover,*
> *Can't you spare one sweet word of love?'*

"Which is all purely my own imagination. I mean the part about Kentucky and Willy. But he thought I made up the whole thing for him. And when I sang Billy-Boy, I made it Willy. Don't you think that was cute?"

Clinton said: "I think I heard you singin' while I slept." He rose from the bed and sat in the chair opposite the girl, facing her.

"That's prob'ly why you slept so good," she said. "My

voice is a very soothing quality. —Anyway," she continued her dream story, "we could hear the woman callin' us, but we just stayed put, him on one branch, me on the other."

"What woman?"

"Oh, just some Miss Hoozit we was boardin' with at the time. After m'folks died, me and Willy boarded out all sorts of places. But this Miss Hoozit was the last one, 'cause after that I run off by myself."

"Without your brother?"

"Just me alone. 'Cause Willy'd already had his accident. He fell off the high branch. Y'see, he was tryin' to fly. Cutest thing, believed every word I told him. I used to tell him when his wings got big enough, we'd fly away together, and he believed me. Every day that summer, he'd say, 'Shirley, are they big enough yet?' And I'd say, 'Not quite, Willy, but pretty soon!' And then one day, he di'nt ask me. He just took it on hisself to try."

Neither of them spoke for a moment. Then Clinton said, "Is that what you dream about?"

"Mm-hmm. Except in the dream, him and me both, we just fly all over the country together, we go whippin' right through the air to North Dakota and Delaware and Greece. Even Colorado and Panama City. And we stop on various trees to rest and sing songs."

"Where'd you fly to tonight?"

"No place special. I just sang while you slept."

Clinton said: "You know, I hate to change the subject, but I got two things I want to say. One of them is, I'm gettin' to where I like you a whole lot; and the other one is, I'm gettin' awful hungry."

Shirley jumped to her feet. "You want candy?" She went to the bureau. In the top drawer she found a jar of Hershey's kisses. "I keep 'em in a jar so they won't get ants." She took off the lid and handed it to Clinton. He

105

began to unwrap the little silver pyramids of chocolate and stuff them into his mouth. "If you want to," Shirley said, "you just eat every last one of 'em. You want me to send down for more? 'Cause all I have to do is go to the head of the stairs and holler. . . ."

She started toward the door. Clinton stopped her. "Hey, Shirley, don't do that. I won't eat but one or two of 'em, anyway. But thanks an awful lot. I'm just crazy about these things."

"You really like 'em?"

"I really do. Whenever I see 'em anywhere, I get some. 'Cause they're just fabulous. Want me to unwrap you some?"

"I shoulda thought about you bein' hungry."

"I wasn't, though, till just a minute ago."

They sat facing each other in the big wicker armchairs, Shirley hugging her legs under the big pajama top, Clinton unwrapping the candy. They smoked cigarettes, too, and they were both wide awake.

"Now tell me about *your* dream," she said.

"Okay."

"What'll I do if you cry? Is there somethin' I can say?"

"Oh, I don't think I will. But thanks, anyway."

"Go on then, what you dream about?" she asked.

"My brother."

"Is he dead?"

"No!" Clinton exclaimed. "He's alive! He's Berry-berry Williams!"

"Oh! I forgot." She frowned and looked away for a moment. "Go ahead, what you dream about him?"

"I dreamt I went to see him in jail." He laughed.

"Lord, I hope it was some *nice* jail," Shirley said.

"It *was!* It had these real thick walls and when I got into the cell where he was, they wouldn't let me out."

106

"Were you scared?"

"No. I kind of liked it. It felt good bein' in there with him. It was a nice place, and it had two bunks. So I got in one of 'em, and he got in the other one; and we went to sleep. One of my favorite things is sleepin' in a room where somebody else is."

Shirley leaned forward eagerly, as if a dream held for her more suspense than any tale of an actual event. "Then what?"

"That's all." He felt that his story had disappointed her. "Sometimes I just dream these very crazy things that don't amount to anything."

Suddenly Shirley said, "Do you believe when people die, it's just absolutely ker-*plunk?* Forever?"

"No."

"No what?"

Clinton said: "I don't think they die just absolutely kerplunk forever. I think they sort of float around like when you dream."

Shirley thought that over. "And they still like to have songs sung to them, don't they?" she said.

"I guess they do," Clinton said. "*I* would, anyway."

"Isn't it funny," Shirley said, "how, down on the street, I just knew to trust you?"

The talk went on between these two people, Shirley and Clinton, for a long time. Here in this second-story room at the Tin Pot Arms Hotel on Gasparilla Street, with the shutters drawn against the sun, there was talk of her growing up in various Kentucky towns, and of his childhood in the Old Neighborhood, talk of all the places and towns the girl had worked in during the numberless years that followed her thirteenth birthday; there was talk of Berryberry and Ralph and Annabel, the White Tower and Mevvin from Heaven, and the motorcycle ride through the mangroves; and each one told what he believed in and gave utterance to profound thoughts and deep secrets: life-and-death matters like heaven and hell, love and hate, ghosts and flesh, parents and children, religion and movies and favorite songs, even politics and the brotherhood of man. The discourse was rich and rapid and nobody knew or cared what time it was. Clinton took a bath while Shirley sat outside the door with the lavender panda on her knee, and pretty soon they took to singing songs together: *Red River Valley, For Me and My Gal, The Isle of Capri,* sad songs and fast ones, and *Way Down Upon the Swanee River,* and they dedicated their songs to the ghosts of all the children who had ever died or grown up in the world. And they danced on the wooden floor of this second-story room of the Tin Pot Arms Hotel, humming their own music, Clinton with a towel about his waist, and Shirley in her pajama top. She showed him how to do the cakewalk as they sang:

> " '*I'll be down to get you in a taxi, honey,*
> *You better be ready 'bout a half past eight . . .' "*

And by the time he had learned, they sat on the edge of the bed, breathless, hugging one another, and they vowed to be friends forever. Soon they were lying on the bed in a close embrace, body against body. The boy's mouth was pressed into the hollow of her shoulder and he could feel her hands traveling across his body, on his shoulders and on his back. They exposed to one another secrets of body even more profound than any of the talk had been. For a moment, like children who had not learned shame, they were apart, with only the contact of eyes, and then they were close once again. When Clinton's body had entered hers, there was a moment of perfect stillness in which he prayed for death, an end of time. But this stillness gave place to motion, and the motion repeated itself again and again, and soon they had created a subtle and amazing rhythm of closeness and pleasure, closeness and pleasure, closeness and pleasure, until there was no lavender bedspread, no bed at all, no room, no hotel, no island, no earth. Only this closeness. Followed, too soon, by the sudden terrible knowledge that he had not died. This creation of senses, of nerve and blood and flesh, so exquisitely wrought that the world itself and all time were dissolved by it, had now itself dissolved. The closeness slipped away.

A person is born in the grips of this hunger for closeness; he seldom achieves it and never can keep it for long, but he learns to be grateful for a letup in the hunger itself, even when the letup is brief. Some are always too young to have learned this, and others too old and foolish. Clinton was young. His blood remained high in him. And in a few minutes they began again, he and the woman, his first woman, to build another of these brief universes, perfect and beautiful, and doomed. They built it and for a moment it was there, and then it collapsed. They witnessed the return of the world, the lavender panda, the iron bedstead, their two bodies lying close; and all of it illuminated by the sharper than ever sword thrusts of sunlight through the shutters.

Shirley rose suddenly from the bed. She covered herself with the pajama top and, hiding her face from Clinton, she ran into the bathroom and closed the door. It occurred to him that she might have been crying. He called to her, "Something wrong, Shirley? You okay?" But she did not answer. For a moment he lay on the bed, studying his body like some startling new possession. Then he realized that for perhaps an hour or more he had not given one thought to Berry-berry and his search for him. His notebook lay on the trunk at the foot of the bed, all but forgotten. He moved quickly to it, and made this entry:

[*Clinton's Notebook*]

> Did not think about B-B for more than an hour. Must figure this out. We have been singing songs here, songs for ghosts. There is much to tell about. And trouble. The girl is crying. I don't know what to do. I'm hungry. Must find Berry-berry.

He stopped writing, and listened. Shirley, in the bathroom, was trying to stifle the sounds of her weeping. Clinton stepped quickly into his trousers and stood outside the bathroom door.

"Can I come in, Shirley?"

"No."

"Shirley, I want to tell you something. Can you hear me?"

"Go away!"

She turned on the water faucets. Clinton raised his voice above them: "Shirley, you look very pretty in lavender, do you know that? It's the first thing a person notices about you. I really mean it, too, not just because you're crying either." There was no answer. He could hear nothing but the sound of running water. "Shirley, can you hear me?"

At length, the door opened. Shirley entered the room, drying her face with a towel. She was frowning, and the skin surrounding her eyes was puffed and inflamed.

"You okay?" Clinton said.

She looked at him as if she had never seen him before. "What's your name, anyway?" she said. Her voice was lower, almost husky; and coarse.

Clinton smiled at her. "Don't you know?"

"Yeah, but I don't want to play the Willy game any more. I mean your real name. You don't have to tell me, of course. I don't really care."

"Why shouldn't I? It's Clint. I told you last night."

"Oh. Well, thanks. Thanks for tellin' me about lavender, too. It dudden work in the mornings though. But thanks." She went to the bed and turned back the spread. "I took my pill, so maybe you better go now."

"What pill?"

"Sleeping pill. So now's your chance to scoot. You want to go, don't you?"

"I got to try to find my brother."

"Yeah, I know. Berry-berry." She opened her pocketbook and searched inside of it. "I got something for you." In her search, she came across a mirror, and glanced into it, briefly, displeased with what it presented. "Christ," she said, "I ought to have my butt kicked, foolin' with a kid your age." Then she dug into the purse once again. "Where'd that damn thing get to?"

"What you lookin' for?"

"Newspaper clipping. About your brother. He's prob'ly not even in the State of Florida any more."

"How do you know?"

"'Cause he left town the day after he stabbed my girl friend." She handed him the clipping. "Here, if you don't believe me. *Advertiser* wrote the whole thing up last Thursday. It don't give his name, but take my word."

Clinton sat on the edge of the bed and read the clipping:

GIRL SUFFERS STAB WOUNDS

A girl staggered into the Kit-Kat Bar and Grill, 122 San Lucia St., at 2:30 A.M. yesterday and, according to the police report, fell on the floor bleeding from knife wounds.

The owner of the Kit-Kat, Isobel French, told Lt. Arthur

Ramírez, acting chief of police, that she was sitting at the bar with a friend when Elsie Muller, 34, an employee of the Festival Night Club on Gasparilla St., made her dramatic entrance.

Miss French called police, who rushed the wounded girl to the Bonita County Hospital. She had been knifed on the left cheek and in the breast, it was reported by Lt. Ramírez.

Ramírez said that Miss Muller told him she knew who did it, but that she would not tell, nor would she press charges.

Dr. Charles Ober administered first aid at the hospital. The patient was treated for shock, but no stitches were required. Miss Muller is expected to be released in a few days.

Shirley was now under the covers.

Clinton turned to her. "It doesn't say anything about Berry-berry!"

"No, but it was him that done it."

"Then why didn't this woman give his name?"

"Lots o' reasons. I'm gettin' sleepy."

Clinton went to the side of the bed. Her eyes were closed. He touched her face with his hand: "Please, don't go to sleep now. You got to tell me."

Shirley sat forward, her head propped up on her arm. "Listen, Clint, I don't want to make you miser'ble. But your brother's a mean kind of person. If Ize you, I'd quit lookin' for him."

"Shirley, he's not mean. I'll swear, if you only knew him . . ."

The little girl had become an old woman, her eyes cold and remote, filled with bitter, costly wisdom. "Well, maybe he's not, who knows? Elsie's not really sore at him neither, but she's nuttier than anybody else put together. You know why she didn't *tell?* She didn't want to get your brother sore at her. Idden that a joke? —Besides, she had some pot in her room, and didn't want the cops to find it."

112

"What's that?"

"Pot, you know, like Ize smokin' last night. Marijuana."

"You know something?" Clinton said. "You sure have changed a lot. I mean since before. You act different."

"Look, you're goin' away, aren't you?"

"Yeah. If you want me to."

"If I want you to has got nothin' to do with it. Has it? So why don't you just do it? Go away and leave me sleep. I've already took my pill, you want me to waste it?"

"I'm goin'," he said.

She lay back on the lavender pillow again and closed her eyes. Clinton found the panda on the floor and placed it in her arms. "I'm goin' now, Shirley," he repeated. "But aren't we friends any more?"

The woman's eyelids tightened slightly and there was a crease between her brows. "Little boy," she said, without opening her eyes, "are you tryin' to make me cry?"

There was a sudden loud banging on the door.

Shirley murmured, "Whoever it is, make 'em go away."

Clinton went to the door and opened it. The police lieutenant, Ramírez, entered the room. He reminded Clinton, by the quality of his glance, that he was dressed only in his trousers. Clinton picked up his shirt and put it on. Ramírez did not speak. He walked to Shirley's bedside and looked down at her.

Clinton whispered, "She's asleep."

Then the lieutenant looked at Clinton for a long moment, his eyes curiously aflame; like tongues of vision, they lapped up the room, the boy, the woman. At length, he motioned to Clinton to follow him into the hall.

Ramírez leaned against the railing of the stairwell, and watched Clinton as he buttoned his shirt. "You got a bus to catch," Ramírez said. "Leaves in three minutes."

"I'll never make it, will I?"

113

"You will. The driver's waitin' for you."

"Then I guess I got to get on it, huh?"

"You don't got to," Ramírez said. "But I would. Go get your shoes."

Clinton returned to the room and finished his dressing. Then he checked his belongings: money belt, duffel bag, notebook, a pocketful of assorted articles. When he glanced at the bed, he saw Shirley's eyes, wide open and staring at him. And he heard her little girl's voice once again: "I di'nt roll you!"

He said, "The cop is puttin' me on the bus."

She nodded. He blew a kiss into the air. "Bye."

She smiled at him. "You go straight home now, Willy," she said.

In the police car, as they drove toward the bus station, Ramírez turned to Clinton: "Big night, huh? Did you light up?"

"Light up?" Clinton was puzzled for a moment, and then he understood.

"The pipe," Ramírez said. "Didn't she give you a drag on her pipe?"

"I don't know what you're talkin' about, sir," Clinton lied. "Can I ask you, how'd you know I was up there?"

"How does a plumber fix bathtubs? I got a job to do. —Went di-rect to the Festival last night, didn't you?"

"Yes, sir."

" 'Cause I said not to?"

"No, sir."

"How many times you screw her?"

Clinton looked straight ahead.

"Don't frown at me, kid. I ast you something. How many times, six or seven? I could've busted in there any time I wanted. You know that, don't you? So thank *me*. You got me to thank, hear that?"

114

Ramírez was filled with some puzzling emotion. Clinton could feel this strangeness, even though the officer tried to suppress its signs. But his face was pale and his breathing unnatural. "She was your first. Right?"

Clinton determined not to answer.

"Remember this," Ramírez said. "Whatever you got from that tramp, two or three times, whatever it was, you wouldn't have got it except for me. A gift from Ramírez. Hadn't been I'm big-hearted, you'd of waited for the bus in jail. You know that?"

"Yes, sir."

"All right, now you got a lot to think about, huh? Am I right?"

"Yes, sir."

Ramírez removed one hand from the wheel and raised it toward Clinton. For a moment it hovered in the air, near the boy's neck, caught between an act of strangling and a caress. But without touching Clinton at all, the hand returned to the wheel.

"Goddam you, you got a nerve," Ramírez said, "sittin' there bein' polite to me, callin' me 'sir.' So goddam smart." He stopped the car. "Get out."

They were parked across the street from a variety store that served also as a bus station. The bus was at the opposite curb. The driver, sitting on a bench in front of the store, watched Clinton climb out of the police car. A few passengers, already seated on the bus, watched from the windows as Clinton walked across the street, through the white tropical glare of noon, followed by the police lieutenant.

Ramírez talked with the driver of the bus. Clinton went into the store to buy his ticket. Inside, on the counter, he saw a display of cheese-flavored crackers wrapped in five-cent cellophane packages. He bought seven of them and stuffed them into his pockets and under his shirt. Then he went outside and handed his ticket to the driver and got on the bus.

Ramírez and the driver climbed aboard. The driver got into his seat and accelerated the motor several times, as if testing it. Ramírez conducted Clinton down the aisle, stopping him midway with a hand on the boy's arm. "Not back there. That's for colored," he said.

Clinton sat down. The seat next to him was empty. Ramírez looked at him; and in a voice that was like a politician campaigning for office, he said: "Now, son, you go on back to Ohio with your daddy, and when you're twenty-one, maybe you'll come back and see us. Will you do that? Now, no hard feelings, is there?"

"No, sir."

"Well, I hope not," the officer said. Then he strutted back up the aisle. "Hello, Mary," he said to a lady passenger, seated alone. "Goin' up to see Danny, are you? And do a little shoppin'?"

"That's right, Lieutenant."

"Well. You hurry back."

"I will."

As he stepped off the bus, Ramírez said, over his shoulder, to the driver, "Thanks, Henry."

Then the bus started to move.

part 3

WHEN HER 1929 Dodge touring car went off the road—the road that goes from Cleveland to Toledo—and crashed into the living-room fireplace of a country dentist, Echo O'Brien was instantly killed. This took place in a heavy rainstorm, at 4:45 A.M., on the second Sunday of October. The state police pointed out that the hazardous bend in the road was clearly marked by luminous arrows and large signs that said SLOW—DANGEROUS CURVE. They therefore attributed the accident to weather conditions and a possibly defective windshield wiper. But people who knew her well doubted that the vehicle itself had any defects whatsoever; because Echo O'Brien was a fine mechanic and especially fastidious in the care and upkeep of her 1929 Dodge touring car. Most of them believed that what happened to her was simply a terrible thing for which there was no accounting. The two persons who could not hold entirely to this opinion were Clinton and Berry-berry Williams.

This wreck took place just four months after Clinton's return from Key Bonita. He had come home during the peak of a heat spell so severe that Cleveland newspapers, that same day, carried reports of four different persons who had dropped dead on the sidewalks.

When Clinton walked into the house late that afternoon, himself weak and feverish, he called up the stairs to Annabel: "Hey! I'm home! Annabel!" Then he sat on the floor, his duffel bag in his lap, and leaned against the doorframe.

Annabel rushed down the stairs in her petticoat, pulling a negligee about her shoulders. The first words she spoke to him were, "Clinton! What are you doing on the floor?"

"It's hot," he said.

"Where's Berry-berry?"

"I don't know."

"Didn't you see him?"

"I don't know."

"You don't *know?*" Then she took a good look at the boy and said, "Why, precious baby, you are *peak*ed!" She knelt on the floor and gave him a fever test: by pressing her lips against his forehead, she reckoned his temperature to be high enough for concern. "*Straight* to bed!" she commanded.

As she helped him out of his clothes, Annabel asked what sort of food he'd been eating.

"I ran out of crackers," he said.

"Why crackers? Didn't you have money?"

"*Cheese* crackers."

"What's wrong with you, Clinton?"

"I said I ran out of crackers."

"Look here, Mister traveler, I will not tolerate insolence. Fever or no fever. Now get into this bed and tell me all about your brother."

"He fell out of the tree."

"He *what?*"

"He was eight years old, that's all. Ker-plunk!"

Suddenly his teeth were chattering and he complained of the cold. Annabel soon realized he was delirious. She covered him with blankets and telephoned the doctor.

Dr. Bolz came to the house that afternoon. He was a frail and diminutive man who, in repose, seemed to be a creature of exceptional elegance and grace; but the fact was that he was indescribably clumsy. He seemed always to be tripping over his own feet and dropping things. The Williamses always referred to him privately as Dr. Butterfingers; but in spite of this alarming personal trait, Annabel had perfect faith in his competence as a physician.

He was not a stammerer but he spoke haltingly and in sentences that had no definite endings to them; so that when he gave a diagnosis, one had to guess at its meaning. On this day Dr. Bolz left her with a vague impression that Clinton had contracted some insignificant summer malady called cat fever, which could be cured with plenty of blankets and the administering of his pills every four hours. But on the second day, he assured her that she had misunderstood his diagnosis: the patient had pneumonia. He told her to stop giving the pills altogether; instead, he injected into Clinton's buttock a powerful new drug. On the fifth day of this new treatment, Dr. Bolz pronounced the patient cured. Clinton could get out of bed whenever he felt able; and it was the doctor's professional opinion that Annabel might now safely question the boy about his trip.

Annabel's curiosity had had too much time to grow in her. By now it had become a thing of unrecognizable proportions, a demon over whom her reason had no control whatever. When Clinton told her that Berry-berry had left Key Bonita by the time he himself had arrived, and that he, Clinton, had merely taken the next bus home—Annabel was not only disappointed but dissatisfied as well. She would not leave the subject alone.

"Do you mean to tell me a boy travels thousands of miles to see his brother, and then he gets on the next bus and comes home?"

"I'm *here*, aren't I?"

Annabel could think of no immediate question with which to counter this absurd answer. She sat in the undersized rocking chair next to his bed, silent for a moment, and stared at the portrait of Abraham Lincoln on the opposite wall.

"Well," she said at length, "how d'you feel? Dr. B. says you can get dressed and come downstairs whenever you want to."

"Oh, I don't feel *that* good yet."

"Your temperature's almost normal. Maybe tomorrow you'll feel stronger. Clinton, what did Berry-berry's friends have to say about him?"

"Who?"

"Surely you met some of his friends, people who knew him!"

Clinton remained silent.

"What about the man he was going into business with? Didn't you talk to him? Or if they'd already gone out to catch some fish, there must have been other fishermen who knew *both* of them. I'm not sure you used your head, mister. I'm not at all. Now look: the telegram said they make five-day trips. Anybody in his right mind would wait for his brother to get *back*. Especially after spending all that money on bus fare."

"I didn't see any point in waitin' around. Everybody said he'd left town, so . . ."

"Everybody!" Annabel exclaimed. "Who?"

"I told you, the clerk at the hotel."

"One little clerk is not 'everybody.'"

"All right, I was just now exaggeratin'. It wasn't everybody, it was the clerk. —Besides, talking so much makes me feel dizzy."

Annabel looked steadily into his eyes.

"No kidding," he said. "I feel really lousy."

Similar interrogations were to take place regularly, sometimes two or three of them in the course of a day.

That evening, after dinner, Ralph climbed the stairs and

appeared at the door of Clinton's room. He entered without knocking. Clinton had time to close his notebook, but he did not have time to get it entirely hidden under his blanket.

"Look here, old-kid-old-kid-old-sock," said Ralph, "since when am I the kind of a sonofabitch you got to hide things from?"

"I thought it was Annabel," Clinton said.

"Well, I should've knocked. But d'you think I give a fiddler's fee what you write down in them notebooks? They's nothin' wrong with the English language. As a matter of fact, English is a fine goddam language. When I was on the bum, I read everything anybody handed me. I had to. I was a public speaker and I had to know my onions. You got a dictionary?"

Clinton pointed to the desk. "There's one."

Ralph got the book and handed it to Clinton. "All right, now open it up. Anywhere. I don't care where. And pick a word. Any word they got in there. And I'll tell you what it means."

Clinton said: "Rowan."

"Which?"

"R-o-w-a-n, rowan."

"Is *that* in there?" said Ralph, with disgust. "Here! Give me that book." Clinton handed him the dictionary. Ralph read aloud: "Rowan. A Eurasian tree." He closed the book and examined its cover. Then he made his steam-kettle sound of mirth. "I think it's a crime," he said, good-naturedly, "slippin' all those foreign words into an American dictionary. Webster's *Collegiate*, my ass. Listen, I had a talk with some snotnose college kid in a saloon one night. You know what he said: Glass—now get this—glass is more perfectly elastic than rubber." Ralph threw back his head and emitted a long spurt of invisible steam. "Well, I turned to the poor bastard, and I said, 'Listen, if we leave the world to birds like you, we'll end up looking through rubber windows, and screwing with glass contraceptives."

Ralph and Clinton had a good laugh over this remark, and then the old man said: "Listen, Clint, I think the best step you ever took was drop out o' school. And it wasn't *my* idea, was it?"

"No. It was mine."

"Tell *her* that." He indicated Annabel with a downward motion of his thumb. "She says it was *me* give you that idea. —But whatthehell, if I pressed charges every time that woman slandered me, she'd be locked up for ninety-nine years. —Now answer me, when did I ever butt in on you boys? Or tell you what to do? Ever?"

"Never," Clinton said.

"Oh, well. She can't help it; we shouldn't be too hard on her." He lighted a cigarette. "It was her sent me up here, you know. She wants me to find out what you two bozos did down there in Key Bonita."

"I told her I was only there overnight."

"Didn't see him at all, huh?"

"No, sir."

Ralph nodded. "Listen, whatever you got to say is strictly volunteer. *I'm* not the one with the prosecution complex in this outfit. You know I'm no prosecutor, don't you? You got anything to say, it's up to you—and it don't have to go any farther."

There was a long moment of silence in which Ralph grew uneasy. "I come up here tonight just because—to see how you're gettin' along. The fact is, I miss you down in that cellar."

"I missed you, too, Ralph."

"Well, *shit*, why not!" There was another pause. Then: "Furthermore, I hope you had a helluva good time down there in Florida. I been playin' with the idea o' goin' down there myself before I—before I, uh, decide not to. But then I prob'ly won't go anyway." Ralph studied the top of his shoe for a while. He turned his foot in various ways, considering it from several angles. "I never cared much for the water," he said.

Suddenly he got to his feet. "Well, old-kid-old-kid-old-sock," he said, walking toward the door, "come on down to the cellar one of these days and we'll holler dirty words up the clothes chute to Annabel." He giggled and wheezed and leered at Clinton as he closed the door.

Clinton said, "G'night, Ralph. Thanks for comin' up." But he did not immediately take up his notebook. Instead, he looked for a long time at the closed door, as if it had written on it all the things he had not told his father.

Two weeks passed and Clinton remained in his pajamas.

Annabel continued to carry his meals to him, but now she took fewer pains to make them pleasant for him. At first she had placed early summer flowers on his tray, garnished his plate with parsley leaves and touched it up with colorful extras: spiced apples or red molds of Jell-o to sharpen his appetite. But as the days of his recuperation drew into weeks, and she began to suspect that Clinton might be malingering, the meals grew plainer. Annabel took her time about getting the newspapers to his room, and now and then she arranged to be just out of earshot when he called for ice water. She hoped that with this deterioration of service, the boy might find the sickroom less to his liking and declare himself recovered.

But soon it was July and still Clinton would not leave his bed. He would awaken at dawn and listen to all the morning sounds: the dry swoosh of Mrs. Cardoni's broom on the back porch of the house next door, a variety of bird songs, the stopping and starting of the J. F. Smith milk truck on its rounds. Midmorning, he would close his eyes, trying to pretend to himself that he was asleep. But this kind of fake rest does no one any good, as it is full of wakeful dreams: ugly memories put you in a fog that is hard to throw off later. Annabel brought his first meal at noon, and the hours that followed were endless affairs to deal with. Much of the time he spent just lying there staring at various objects for long periods, or propped up on an extra pillow with the Sears, Roebuck catalogue or the dictionary opened on his lap. Or he would look out the window, not even seeing the roof of the garage or the trees in the yard across the alley. In general, Clinton was not having a good time.

But he could think of no good reason for getting out of bed. He did not want to look for work; he did not want to visit the Old Neighborhood or sit at the Aloha Sweet Shop; and he did not want to sit downstairs under Annabel's eye. He began vaguely to realize that he was in a kind of trap; but there seemed to be no will power in him, and he could not concentrate on figuring a way out of it.

His favorite time of day was five o'clock, the hour of Annabel's long afternoon bath. The minute he heard the first splash of water in the tub, he would bolt out of his bed and run silently, barefoot, all over the house performing small errands for himself. First, he went on a sniping tour of all the ash trays, gathering enough butts to last him through the evening. Then he checked Annabel's writing desk for any fresh mail she might have received that morning. If these letters were insufficiently interesting to warrant copying down in the notebook, which he carried with him for this purpose, he spent the time going through her desk drawers and reading any mail received in June during his absence.

There had been an exchange of correspondence be-

tween Annabel and Bernice O'Brien which was of considerable interest to him. The first letter read as follows:

DEAREST ANNABEL,
Such beautiful weather here. Echo took me for drive in
country Sun. aft., wildflowers everywhere. I thrive in summer,
but Echo very restless. So pathetic, gets dolled up, takes drive,
comes home. No place to go. Stands at front door, looking at
her car in driveway, so proud of it. Odd hobby for girl, but
loves motors, tools. I have full-time nurse now, so Echo free
on weekends. Recent painful experience of very private nature
took her out of swim of things, does not meet new people.
Gets dolled up and rattles her car keys. Hard time sitting still.
So lovable, and not a complainer. But God will find way.
Be glad your boys free to travel. Harder for girl to go place
alone. Clinton can take care of self, and may be good influence
on big brother. Good idea see world while young, don't you be
worry bird.
Your dreams not in least shocking. Shame on you thinking
so. Woman of fifty not eighty after all. I read of French woman
with lover at 72. America backward nation some respects. But
put yourself in God's hands. Who knows what He plans for
you? Excuse awful paper, out of stationery. But write to your
loving friend.

B—

Annabel's answer was of course unavailable to Clinton,
but he could almost read its contents between the lines of
Bernice's second letter:

DEAREST ANNABEL, in haste—
Believe me was not hinting. Rather die. But oh, what miracle. Please do *not* ask Echo if inconvenient, but honestly would
be gesture from God if you sincerely *want* her visit. She's so
considerate, would never come if believed you didn't want
her. Impossible I accompany her, as trips are hard for me.

127

Could you write her note? So it comes from you? Must not suspect *me* involved. Echo dying for trip, studies road maps, could find way to China. Bless you, drst. friend Annabel. Always hold fine thoughts for you. But do not inconvenience self too much!

Your loving friend.
B—

P.S. Was *not* suggesting you take lover! More about this in later letter.

Aside from using Annabel's bath hour to catch up on the daily mail, he often had telephone calls to make. One day he called Western Union and persuaded a clerk to return his unclaimed money order in a plain envelope so that it would arouse no questions from Annabel. He also put in a call to the airport to ask about schedules and ticket prices for flights to Tibet. The woman said they could get him as far as Pakistan or India, but from there on he was on his own. Actually, Clinton was fed up with traveling and had no intention of taking a trip, but occasionally such questions enter a person's head and it is best to get them cleared up.

One afternoon, on a similar impulse, he telephoned Mildred Murphy.

"Hi, Mildred. It's Clinton."

"Clinton? Clinton who?"

"*Williams*, for godsake!"

"Oh! Hello, Clinton."

"How you been?"

"Oh, I'm fine. There hasn't been any letters from Berryberry, though."

"Oh, I wasn't callin' about *that*. I get all my mail at home now."

"You mean you've *heard* from him?"

128

"God, yes; didn't I tell you about my trip? I been to South America and all over. He got in trouble down there on some island. So I helped him out. Then I got malaria and came home."

"Ma*laria*?" Mildred was impressed.

"Pretty near died from it."

"Well, that's just *ter*rible."

"I was delirious and everything. —Say, how many Clintons do you know, just roughly? About five or ten?"

"Oh, just you," she said, "but my mind went blank for some reason."

"So everything's okay over there, eh?" Clinton said.

"Over where?"

"The *Neigh*borhood!"

"Oh. Well, everything's just the same."

"Nobody's house burnt down, huh?"

"Whose?"

"Nobody's. I said, 'Nobody's house burnt down, huh'?"

"Of *course* not! That's a terrible thing to say."

"I just meant, is there any *news*, for godsake." Clinton was beginning to wish he had not telephoned Mildred Murphy at all.

"Oh. No, no news at all. But you'll have to tell me about your trip. Some time."

"Well, there's not really anything I can discuss about it. Actually, everything that happened is pretty much secret. You know how it is."

"I see. —Well, may I ask why you called up?"

"Just to say hello. And to see if there's anything goin' on over there I didn't know about. But I should of known better. Because, let's face it, there's nothing *over* there to begin with but a bunch of *scrags*."

"Oh, really?" Mildred said.

"All right, when did anything ever *happen* over there? Name something, say in the last four hundred years, and not counting Fritz Burns getting shot by a cop in a gas station and losing his left lung. Which is ancient history. Can you?"

"No, I can't," Mildred said after a slight pause. "Nobody has robbed a gas station since Fritz Burns got shot. I'm *aw*fully sorry, Clinton."

"Oh, that's perfectly all right, Mildred. But what do you do when you get so bored you can't *stand* it?"

"Well," Mildred said, "I'll tell you the truth, *I* don't get that bored. But if I did, I think I'd sit down and decide who was the most fascinating person I knew. And then I'd call them up on the telephone."

"Oh, would you?"

"Yes. Isn't that exactly what *you'd* do?"

"No. But it's a swell idea. My trouble is, I don't know a single fascinating person in the whole State of *Ohio.*"

"Isn't that a shame?"

"Yes, it really is. Well, I got to hang up now, Mildred. But I hope nobody over there *drowns* or anything like that."

"Thank you, Clinton. It was just sensational hearing your voice."

"Yeah, I thought it'd be quite a treat for you. G'bye."

There was a click on the other end of the wire.

Clinton heard the sound of Annabel's bath water running down the drain. He hurried up the stairs and had climbed into bed long before Annabel left the bathroom.

When he had entered certain fragments of his telephone conversation, Clinton read all that he had written on the previous day. It began with the rough draft of a suicide note:

130

DEAR RALPH AND ANNABEL,

I suppose this news will come as a shock, but I have just killed myself and am now lying in the upstairs bathtub. Believe me, I am filled with deep regret over whatever mess this causes, but I have taken certain precautions to make it easy on all of us.

I have locked the bathroom door from the inside so that you would not just walk in without any warning and scream because of the horrible sight. I suggest you get a doctor or a policeman to go up there. The key is ten inches inside of the door. Tell the policeman to bring a small magnet and pull it through in this way. Then he can unlock the door and pull out the plug, and all the blood will go down the drain. I have chosen wrist slitting in a warm tub as my method, as it is known to be fairly clean and painless. I am sure the policeman will rinse out the tub if you so request.

You will no doubt be curious why I have taken this measure, but it is my deepest regret that I cannot divulge the most important motives. It is certainly got nothing to do with your not being perfect parents, which you certainly are, and deeply beloved as well, as you well know. And I certainly did not like making a slave of Annabel during my recent sickness and long before.

As to my motives for this measure, they are largely secret. I can say this much, however, as my final thoughts, and I hope it will be a comfort to you.

(A) I have had all the experiences that life can offer, even certain experiences that may come as a surprise to you, which I regret I am unable to divulge.

(B) Ralph has always been of such great stature,

131

never acting like a dominating parent who always butts in. On the contrary, I might say that as an excellent companion and friend, he knows no peer, and with highest principles which he lived unfailingly up to at all times. (Re-work this.)

(C) Annabel has been likewise ideal in different ways, such as big things like seeing to it we are all comfortable and well fed, including small things not usually noticed, such as sewing buttons which is nevertheless tedious and has to be done. Also, Annabel has always tried very hard to do what is right and see to it we all did likewise, which may have resulted in confusion at times, but this is very admirable.

(D) In conclusion, it is certainly not that I did not have a wonderful life with such two parents. I am merely miserable for private reasons and have been meditating in my room on these matters. It is now clear that I must go on to invisible experiences such as one has in deep dreaming, so do not think of me as dead in any way in spite of the mess in the bathroom which may tempt you to believe otherwise. Which incidentally I have also heard of the Fire Department being called in in such cases as this.

Your ever loving son and offspring,
CLINTON WILLIAMS I

I'm really none too proud of this letter. In the first place the style of it sounds smart alecky, and there ought to be some synonym for blood. Now that I see it on paper, the whole idea is just too creepy and would probably bring on heart attacks or worse. You would think science would come up with a pill that would make a person just disappear to death, thereby doing away with embalming and all the expenses of

132

burials. Which could also be fabulous for capital punishments and many other uses.

Besides I am getting curious about this Echo O'Brien who I get the very definite impression is a virgin, even though middle-aged, and is coming to visit from Toledo. She is apparently so car-crazy there is a good chance she will turn out to be a Lesbian or a morphadite, so why shouldn't I wait and get a look at her first, as there is always time for suicide at a later date.

Also Annabel is getting plenty fed up with me being sick and is trying to starve me out of here. Maybe if I sweat it out long enough, she'll be so fed up with me my suicide will be kind of a relief. I think it has already reached such a pass, but a few more weeks will only improve the situation.

Another thing is this, suicide is naturally quite a step to take and I may as well be good and damn sure of myself, even though there is little doubt that fate is ordaining the thing. Of course if I end up in some lousy place like Hell, for instance, it would be a miserable mistake.

The thing I am gambling on is that after death people become automatically ghosts, and possess thereby complete freedom of movement and are invisible. ADVANTAGES: I could follow Berry-berry around from place to place, invisible from cops, modern pirates, and jujitsu experts that throw people out of night clubs. The whole idea has a thousand other advantages too numerous to list as well. But a few of the most colossal are as follows: no need to work at White Tower to save money for bus fare. If I want to ride a bus, okay. When not in the mood to eat, okay. I can then hear any conversation I want to without recourse to laundry chutes, holding a glass to the wall, or taking all kinds of risks of getting caught. Minor advantages include sitting in the Aloha Sweet Shop without being expected to pour Coca-Cola down my gullet by the quart. The only major snag I have not yet worked out is, can a ghost keep a notebook????

(Go easy on the question marks.)

Annabel came up for my tray about ten o'clock tonight. She lets them sit there for two or three hours to punish me for not getting out of bed. If things get much worse around here, I may revise the suicide plan and the leave the bathroom door stark wide open.

Naturally she doesn't ever sit down and visit, not as a rule, except to drop these very subtle hints about what the Army does with goldbrickers, and how miserable it is to get bedsores.

Anyway, tonight we did have a regular conversation, which really threw her for a loop even though she tried to hide it. She had my tray in her hands and was opening the door with her toe when I said the following:

"Annabel, has any of our family ever been psychic?"

"Why of course," she said. "For generations! Why?"

"Oh. Well that explains it."

"What?"

"Why it is I'm in contact with Mrs. O'Brien, that's all."

"What do you mean, in contact?" she said. I knew I had her. She almost dropped the tray.

"Oh, it's nothing important. I mean if it runs in the family, there's nothing *unusual* about it."

"Nonsense. I insist you tell me what you're talking about."

"Look, I didn't mean to start anything, for godsake.

134

But let me ask you, does this daughter of hers work around, uh, garages, or places like that? You know, where they keep cars and tools?"

"No, she works at the automobile club up there." Annabel put down the tray. "But why did you say that about cars?"

"Look. Just skip it, because obviously there's nothing to it. It was probably some kind of a daydream."

"But *what* did you daydream?"

"Well, I know it's crazy, because no woman ever works around cars, but I keep seein' this—Echo?" Annabel nodded her head; she loved every word of it. I went on. "I see her around a big car. She's got tools in her hands and all, and keeps puttering with this car. So I figured she might be some kind of a mechanic! Isn't that nuts?"

Annabel felt for the arms of the rocking chair and lowered herself into it. "Ooooh! Oh, my God!" She was really impressed. "*Wait* till I write Bernice. I may even call her up long distance! —Go on, what else?"

"Why?" I said. "You mean that fits in some way? Her and cars?"

"It certainly *does!*"

"Well, now this is a real shot in the dark, but did you happen to invite her down here for the Fourth of July?"

Annabel took in a deep breath and just held it for about a couple of hours. Then she said in a real faraway voice, "You couldn't have known that any other way."

"What? What did I say? Did I say something?" Maybe it was a pretty dirty trick to pull, but once you get started in a thing like this, you can't just pull out all of a sudden. Anyway, it was clear as hell I'd gone up in Annabel's book about a hundred points.

"What *else?*"

"I always see this very nice lady, kinda fat, sitting in a wheel chair. —Course I knew she was in a wheel chair, so that's nothing. But she sits there watching TV and this Echo is pacing back and forth rattling something in her hand. Car keys, I think. Do you suppose there's anything to all this?"

"Clinton," she said, "first of all, you are not to be frightened. Some people have these powers, and it's not dangerous at all. Not at all. As long as you use them properly. Now, you won't be frightened, will you, if I tell you that you have these powers?"

At this point I felt like a scum. So I said, "No, I won't be frightened." What else could I say?

"Now listen. I *have* invited Echo O'Brien to come here for the Fourth. What do you think of that?"

"I'm very surprised. I can't believe it."

"And she does tinker with cars all the time! She has an enormous old Dodge that works good as new because she's so clever with mechanical things. And she'll arrive at our very door, in that very car, at noon tomorrow. I'd intended to surprise you."

"How do you know she's coming?"

"I heard from her."

(I wondered what she did with the letter, because I certainly never got hold of it.)

"She phoned this morning and said it would be all right. Well, of course, I couldn't have been happier, a daughter of Bernice's, and *devoted.* The poor thing has a silent nature, but she's pretty as can be and waits on her mother hand and foot. But of course, *you* probably know the whole story!"

136

"Oh, no!" I said. "I mean, it doesn't happen too often, just now and then."

I suppose when a person plans to die soon, he gets to where he does all kind of unscrupulous stunts, because nothing matters any more.

The following morning, the third of July, was a perfect summer morning, the kind that reminds a grown-up person of his long-ago summers of childhood, of days in which the blue of sky seemed almost within reach, songs of birds bore secret and promiseful meanings, the sun touched the air with a kind of warm sugariness, and the planet earth was one enormous ripe plum. On such a day everyone will find an excuse to go outdoors: lawn mowers clattered on Seminary Street, children played games on the sidewalks, there was much traipsing from house to house on dreamed-up missions; a sudden happy rash of tree pruning, porch sitting, and automobile washing brought forth people whom one had not seen outdoors since the previous fall.

Even Ralph Williams, an indoors person by nature, wandered outside after breakfast on the pretext of deciding whether or not the house needed a paint job. Annabel found old vases in the cellar and filled them with roses and delphinium; these she distributed throughout the house.

Altogether, on this day of the visitor from Toledo, there was in the world a beauty so keen and simple that it was akin to sadness. But while the beauty was remarked upon by nearly everyone you met, the sadness was a kind of secret that no one mentioned at all.

At noon, Clinton Williams stationed himself, pajama-clad, at the window of Berry-berry's room, which looked out over the front lawn and street. From this vantage point, he awaited the arrival of Echo O'Brien.

At about ten minutes after the hour, in front of the house across the street, Clinton saw the porch swing come to a halt, and the man and woman seated there leaned forward and stared up the street. "Helen Mae!" the woman called over her shoulder. "Come here! Quick!" And immediately another woman came onto the porch and joined in the staring. Two doors up the street a gang of children called a recess in their game and stared at the same phenomenon. Now all of these people looked on with respect and awe as a magnificent old automobile rolled importantly into view and came to a smooth stop in front of the Williamses' house. Polished to a flawless black, this stately car, high and proud and long, with its dignified fenders and long rubber-carpeted running boards, made other cars on the street seem frivolous with their weird balloon shapes and all-day-sucker colors. Eccentric only by reason of age and size, this strange car, with accents of silver glistening in the spokes of its wheels, its bumpers and headlights, gave an impression of overwhelming elegance.

The front door of the car opened and the driver stepped out.

Echo O'Brien was a slender brunette of exceptional height. She was dressed in champagne colors: shoes with spiked heels, a close-fitting silk suit, beautifully tailored, a picture hat with an extravagantly wide brim; and in her hand she carried a huge pocketbook. All of her jewels looked like topaz: enormous ear drops, a choker at the throat, a dinner ring, even the clasp of her pocketbook.

She stood there, one hand holding her hat on at the crown, and looked up. It seemed to Clinton she looked directly into his eyes, but Echo O'Brien gave no sign that

138

she saw him at all. To him, the sight of her standing there in that soft wash of sunlight was so dazzling that only some major disturbance could have drawn his eyes from it.

Now Clinton heard the front screen door open and close; and he saw Annabel rush forward across the path to greet the visitor. His mother had herself been at some pains to make a good appearance, and Clinton was surprised to realize that she did not suffer at all by this contrast with a beautiful, younger woman. With her well-painted face, her chestnut hair, her moss-colored dress and big emerald ear buttons, Annabel looked a handsome, self-assured forty. She talked incessantly, not even pausing when she touched her cheek against Echo O'Brien's. Clinton observed that the visitor did not once get her mouth opened. But she smiled and nodded, and her outsized eyes seemed to scoop up and take in everything that was said.

These eyes were to affect Clinton even more profoundly at close range. They focused on a talker so completely that they seemed to serve the function of ears as well. They opened and closed, changed size and shape, lights danced within them—all in a pure and subtle response to what was being said. You had the impression all your words counted for something and would be remembered forever. You could place your heart itself in these great blue-green depths and it would dwell there safely, sensitively cared for, immortal. The eyes of Echo O'Brien were eyes that cared.

Now Ralph Williams entered Clinton's field of vision. From around the corner of the house, he approached the tall stranger with one arm outstretched, all gallantry and charm. The sight of her seemed to have recharged some inner battery that brought to his welcome a kind of high-voltage sincerity that demanded respect: even Annabel was silent for these extravagant civilities. He bowed, kissed the visitor's hand and held it as he looked up into her eyes and spoke to her. Then Ralph took her luggage from the car (two leather bags, rather large, Clinton thought, considering the brevity of her visit) and, walking with unusual lightness of step, carried it into the house. Arm in arm, Annabel and Echo followed him.

Clinton instantly quitted his station and flew to his bedroom. He put on fresh pajamas, combed his hair, and climbed into bed. There was much talk on the first floor, but he could not make out the words. In his eagerness to hear Echo's voice, Clinton was momentarily tempted to get dressed, go downstairs, and declare himself well. But two thoughts deterred him: Annabel would surely tell Echo that her presence had brought about the cure, and pass remarks about it all through the weekend. And he felt he had to do much more thinking on certain matters before he left the sanctuary of sickness.

All these considerations were soon interrupted by a procession on the stairs. Clinton was able to distinguish one of Annabel's sentences: "You'll sleep in Berry-berry's room, it's much comfier than the guest room and has the best mirror in the house"; and he heard clearly a protest of Ralph's concerning the luggage: "What, heavy? These? Christ, no! What you got in them, cotton candy?" And as the noisy parade drew nearer, Clinton was able to discern a new voice as it spoke a sentence he would remember all of his life:

"Clinton's the one I want to meet. Where's Clint? *He's* my guy."

It is worth dwelling for a moment on the voice of Echo O'Brien. It was akin to her eyes. It might even be said that there was a twinship in the sound and in the look of her: one evoked a sense of the other. Her bigness of eye

140

could be heard in the depth of her voice, a full octave lower than the average range of a woman; and the color was there, too, if you thought about it, a blue-green coolness, slightly rough, and infinitely lonesome.

Now she appeared at the door of Clinton's room, flanked by Ralph and Annabel. Indeed she had won his parents so completely that they now seemed like trophies that decorated her arms. Leaving them behind for a moment, she came toward Clinton and leaned with both hands on the iron railing at the foot of his bed.

"Hi, Clint," she said. "I'm the old maid from Toledo."

And from that moment, Clinton Williams was in love with Echo O'Brien,

[*Clinton's Notebook*]

July 3.

ECHO O'BRIEN FROM UP CLOSE.

Dark circles underneath her eyes make them look bigger. Also a considerable amount of paint. Her mouth is a good size to begin with, but she adds on a little the way women do with lipstick. Usually I'm not too crazy about this stunt, as it's easy as hell to spot, but on Echo it's quite fabulous as a matter of fact. Also her teeth stick out a tiny bit even when her mouth is shut. Actually she's got all kinds of these really sensational flaws that nobody in their right mind would change even a speck. Her hair is short and dark brown, very straight and it glows and comes to a point over each ear, so that you can't see anything of these ears except the very bottom of them. From the side, I'd say roughly her head looks like the top of a question mark, with the earring making

141

the little dot at the bottom. All her eyebrows are plucked away and she's got these long straight lines drawn on instead. Plus she seems to have a damn good figure, the kind you keep on thinking about after she's left the room. Naturally, chances are she's got falsies on, but even so they don't look completely *impossible*.

She came upstairs alone just especially to talk me into eating dinner at the table. No doubt it was a put-up job, but Echo made it like I'd be doing her a big personal favor, so finally I broke down and thought to hell with it, I been sick long enough anyway.

Annabel was way off beam about Echo being a silent person. I guess a lot of people seem that way to Annabel, as she is mostly tuned in on herself. But the fact is, Echo is willing enough to talk; she just refuses to knock people down to make an opening, is all. You ask her something and she'll answer. Like when Annabel was in the kitchen making the gravy, I said:

"How is it you happen to be called Echo?"

She said: "Well, Clinton, I'll tell you. It's because I'm kind of a parrot, you know what I mean? When I was a little girl, the way I'd learn to talk was I'd repeat whatever I heard my mother say, over and over again. See?"

"Doesn't everybody learn to talk that way?"

"Well, now, that's a very interesting thought. I believe you're right. What do you think about that, Ralph?"

Echo turned her enormous eyes on Ralph. He said, "Hmmm," and seemed to weigh the question very carefully. The way Echo looks at a person makes him feel like Oliver Wendell Holmes passing down a decision. Ralph said, "Imitation, yes. I believe that's a very decisive factor in the learning process."

"Wow," Echo said. Then she turned to me. "Clinton, you got a wonderful papa." She tapped her head twice. "What a head on him! We been downstairs workin' a puzzle, and I want to tell you it was a pleasure just to watch." She raised her voice so that Annabel could hear it in the kitchen: "Annabel, you mind me smokin' cigarettes at the table?"

"Not at *all!*" Annabel exclaimed.

"You're a real doll and I mean that," Echo answered. Then she lit a long cigarette with a gold tip, and turned to Ralph. "What was that thing called, Ralph, the one with all the water in the street? The Grankin—Grankin Alla—something or other?"

Ralph passed down another decision: "The Grand Canal of Venice."

Echo said, "That's it! You know, it's hard for a woman to remember a thing like that." She threw back her head and let out a big cloud of smoke that hovered over her head like a halo. Then she turned to me. "Now what was it you ast me, honey?"

I thought for a minute. "Oh, you were tellin' me about Ralph, and the puzzle."

"Oh! Oh, yeah, and how *smart* he is. Which I admire. Well, there we sat, see?" She did a little pantomime of a jigsaw puzzle being put together very fast. "Phht, phht, phht, phht," and then she snapped her fingers and said, "There it was, together! But you better look out, Ralph, because what I'm going to do is practice!" She laughed, and then Annabel came in with the gravy.

The point is that Echo O'Brien is not some kind of

a big fantastic walking brain that stops everybody cold on television quizzes. That is just a completely nother department altogether. In fact with Echo, this Grand Canal kind of thing is fairly common. She makes tons of these really stupid mistakes. But the ridiculous thing is that on her it only adds, because it makes her all the more beautiful. Boy, this is a hell of a hard thing to describe. Now for instance if you committed a murder or fell in love or got in some other kind of trouble, Echo O'Brien would know just what to do. Whereas Einstein would probably be stumped because he'd be too busy worrying about where Venice is, and relativity, etc.

The second thing after her eyes that you notice about Echo O'Brien is this quivering kind of poise she's got. She's graceful as hell and when she moves it's a very definite thing. But what strikes a person as really beautiful is this way she has of quivering underneath. You don't actually *see* her quiver, the way a mere nervous person does. You just feel it. You know that inside she's all alive. And quivering. It's all tied up with the dark circles under her eyes and that deep rippling sound her voice has got in it. It's like her body is just this very delicate shell that she keeps her heart in. I picture it that inside this shell it's almost dark, like a little green shelter in the woods with a brook running through it, and on the edge of the brook, just sitting there lonesome and quivering, is Echo O'Brien's heart. The way it makes me feel is this. I'd like to just come up beside her, walking very softly, and just be there with her.

Tomorrow she's going to teach me how to drive her 1929 Dodge touring car.

July 4.

On a day like this I don't really like to write things down, but when everything's miserable and back to normal again, I'll need all this stuff to help me remember how it all was.

When I got dressed, about nine o'clock, I looked at myself in the mirror and made a solemn vow not to write in this goddam book today. But here I am. When all this excitement dies down I'll have to do something about my will power, some kind of discipline to build it up a little.

Because what happened was, I went bouncing down the stairs with all these good intentions about no eavesdropping or note-taking, etc., when I heard them in the kitchen, Annabel and Echo, and pretty soon there I was stopped dead on the landing with my hands cupped behind my ears, leaning over the railing.

Through the whole conversation, there was a lot of coffee-cup clinking and spoon rattling. I got the impression Annabel must have just finished one of her lectures on life with a liberal. Because here's what Echo was saying:

"Tell the truth, Annabel, and you may hate me for it, but I'm the kind of damn fool would do anything for a man. If I loved him. Wouldn't care if he was a Communist or a what. Is that terrible of me? Maybe so. But I'd go to Lapland and live in a fish barrel, or if he wanted me to I'd stand on Euclid Avenue passin' out leaflets that said Abraham Lincoln was six different kinds of a bastard. Isn't that awful?"

"Of course not, you're as sweet as you can be," Annabel said. "But I just don't believe you mean that.

145

Because if all women felt that way, why! we'd deserve to lose the *vote!*"

"I suppose we would," Echo said. Then she chuckled, and added: "Yeah, I guess you're right about that, Annabel. Aren't I something?" You could just tell Echo wasn't the type to get in a sweat over suffrage.

"Listen, Echo," Annabel said, "why hasn't a girl like you ever gotten married? I just know you've had oodles of chances!"

"Well, I wouldn't say oodles. But I did go with this one fella for about five years. He was a sweet guy, but he got to be a pretty heavy drinker there for a while."

"There!" Annabel said. "And you wouldn't stand for it, right?"

"No, it wasn't like that. 'Cause see, he must've figured he couldn't marry me. He got hurt in the war, and it put him all out of commission, you know what I mean?"

There was a silence. I guess Annabel must have asked the next question in pantomime. Because Echo said, "That's right, just—all out of commission."

"Oh, what rotten luck! Why, that's just a sin!" Annabel said.

"He never said one word about it, was always afraid to tell me I guess. And I wouldn't have cared either. Oh, yes, I'd have *cared*," Echo said, "but it wouldn't've changed how I felt. I'd have married him like a shot. But it wasn't till about a month after he was killed that I got friendly with his sister, and she let fly the whole story. I was so glad I could've hugged her. Matter of fact, I did. I just squeezed her and cried like a real nut. 'Cause if it hadn't been for what she

146

told me, I'd have kept on thinking it was—something about *me*. You see?"

"Of course," Annabel said. "It's so much better to *know*."

"That's it, and you don't feel nearly so miserable. Oh, Annabel, he was a tender thing, I mean it, a devil, but sweet."

"Well, how did he . . . What *happened* to him finally?"

"You sure you want to hear about that?" Echo said. Annabel must have nodded her head, because Echo went on. "Well, don't let it depress you or anything, honey, because it's all water over the dam. I never think about it, never give it a thought, it's all water over the dam, been four years in March, March twelfth. But what he did was asphyxiate himself, isn't that something? Locked the garage door, turned on the motor and just sat there. Think how miserable the poor sweet devil must've— But shoot! I don't believe in just thinking and thinking and thinking about something awful when it's just water over the dam. Do you?"

Annabel said, "Do you know your mother has never mentioned so much as a word?"

"I know, because she's got this theory that telling about a thing creates a—a whatsit? You know, like black thoughts and all. She's dead right, too. I just know she is."

"Bernice O'Brien just *might* be," Annabel said, "the finest woman in the world. Certainly the wisest."

"No question about that," Echo said. "She made me get all new clothes and just did me over in general. That's when I cut off my hair, too. Can you believe it used to be down to *here*?"

"Echo, I *saw* it when it was down to there—when I went up for the class reunion! Now tell me, have you ever regretted it?"

"Nope, because it's easier to take care of. And if I want to I can take a bun and pull it all back like this, see, with lacquer, and wear it in a chignon. But then of course, these ears are a problem. —*You*, by the way, have got adorable ears. And you sure do make the most of 'em."

Annabel said: "That's very sweet of you, Echo, and you're right! But you know they're getting awful *big?* See? When a person gets older, her ears and her nose both has a tendency to . . ."

"Annabel!" Echo interrupted. "Listen to me, honey. I am not going to let you get away with that, nosiree. Old, my foot! Now you quit that or I'm going to get mad at you."

I could hear Annabel's eyebrows go up and her eyes fall shut when she said, "Well, I *am* fifty-*one.*"

"But I just don't see you as the age type. A person look at you, they think, now there's a darn good-lookin' woman, they don't think about age. Y'see what I mean, Annabel? It's like Greer Garson."

"Listen, Echo," Annabel said, getting very confidential. "Less than a year ago, our Dr. Bolz looked me over. Nothing serious, I had some kind of a boomp-boomp-boomp in the heart, *you* know, not a thing but nerves. Anyway, he said that just looking at my body, I could be way way *way* under forty."

"I don't doubt that for a *second.*"

"I am not a vain person, but let me tell you, that did wonders for my morale. Now, this is a terrible thing to call attention to, but you know when a woman gets older, how her nipples turn a kind of brown? —Well, mine are still pink. *Pink!*"

"Personally," Echo said, "I think that's just wonderful. I only hope when I'm fifty-one years old . . ."

"Oh, yours will be, sweetheart," Annabel said. "I just know they will. Say, we're having a real girl-talk, aren't we? Lord, it's fun, I don't know when I've had more fun."

"Me, too," Echo said. "I'm just having a barrel of fun."

"This houseful of *men*, let me tell you it's something."

"You know what I think of that Clint?" Echo said. "I'd just like to eat him up. I mean it, I think he's a real peach."

Which was worth hearing. But then naturally Annabel had to move in and try to cancel the whole thing out. "Oh, but just *wait*," she said, "wait till you meet his big brother."

"Oh! I'm so glad you brought that up," Echo said. "I got a message for you from Mamma. She says you can look for Berry-berry any time now. —Hey, hey, whoops!"

Annabel had spilled her coffee. I heard her chair backing away from the table, and she started bawling herself out. "Now wasn't that *smart* of me? Thank God it was lukewarm, or I'd have scalded myself to death!"

Echo said: "That's a real cute apron, too. But I don't believe it'll stain."

"Imagine!" Annabel said. "Just sat here and poured a half cup of coffee all *over* myself." She started to laugh about it and so did Echo. When I went into the

149

kitchen they were still cleaning up the mess and by that time Annabel was just about hysterical.

Echo looked at me and said, "Morning, Clint, we just had the funniest thing happen."

But I don't think Echo knew what the joke was. Neither did Annabel. Neither do I. I know it's got something to do with how nervous this whole family is every time Berry-berry comes up in a conversation. We all act like he just went down to the drugstore for a pack of cigarettes and will be back in about ten minutes, whereas the truth is we don't even remember what the hell he looks like any more.

Which I actually said once, and Annabel almost flipped her pizza, said I was talking like an insane person. Okay, so he's down at the drugstore and will be back in ten minutes, and Annabel spilled coffee all over herself as a kind of vaudeville act for Echo's benefit. I don't know.

After breakfast Echo and I got right into her car. She said she was flabbergasted how fast I learned. But she made it very easy and did not get flustered when I made mistakes. Anyway, we went rolling all over hell, including the Old Neighborhood. I drove very slow past Mildred Murphy's house. Of couse she wasn't home, the bitch. But I didn't really care. Then on the way home we passed the airport. Echo said she'd never been up in a plane. Me either. They had these signs all over that said,

AIRPLANE RIDES
SEE CLEVELAND FROM THE AIR
$5

All of a sudden I had this very urgent feeling that we ought to take an airplane ride. When I told Echo about it her mouth dropped open and she looked straight ahead and said, "Lord, do you think we should?" We got out of the car and as we walked toward the gate, she said it again, "Lord, Clint, do you think we ought to?" But she was taking big steps and I had a hard time keeping up with her. By the time we got up to the counter, she said, "I don't know why not, do you?" I pulled out ten dollars of my White Tower money, but she grabbed hold of my sleeve and said, "Just a minute, will you, I want to ask you something over here." We walked away from the counter, and she whispered: "Now look here, kiddy-kat, you been sick and I got this real good job, so let me lay out the ten. Okay?" So I said, "I'll tell you, Echo, if it was anything else but an airplane ride, but I got to pay for this, you know what I mean?" Echo said, "Sure, okay. But you see, you and me can have a lot of fun doing all kinds of things. But if I see we're eating up all your dough it'll take the kick out of it for me. You understand? So not *every* time. Right?" That's the kind of a person she is. Anyway, I got the tickets and we went out onto the field. There was this very neat little orange airplane with two open cockpits, one for the pilot and one for us. We climbed into the front seat. Echo said, "I just can't believe I'm in an airplane, can you?" I said, "No, I just can't believe it." The pilot came up and gave us each a pair of goggles. He was just an ordinary guy about forty but he seemed to take everything for granted, the airplane and the goggles, all of it. He showed us how to fasten the seat belts, then he got in and a short man in overalls stood out in front of the plane and pulled on the propeller a couple of times. Then the motor started and Echo turned to me. "Wow!" she said. "Are you

151

scared?" I said, "No," because I wasn't. I asked her if
she was scared. She said, "No, but it sure is a thrill."
Then we couldn't talk any more because the airplane
made so much noise. Pretty soon we started to taxi
out to the end of the runway. I kept looking at Echo
and she kept looking at me, and we were both laughing. Sometimes when she wasn't laughing she'd be
grinning with all her teeth showing, even part of her
gums. Then the motor made more noise than ever
and we were going God knows how many miles an
hour. Echo grabbed my hand and squeezed it. (She's
got nice cool hands.) Then she let go and threw her
hands up in the air and opened her mouth real wide
and screamed because she was having such a good
time. Which kills me when I think about it. Anyway,
all of a sudden we were off the ground, and we could
see Lake Erie and all the big buildings downtown,
busses and cars like little bugs creeping along. You
could tell the layout of everything and how neat it
really is from far away. But they don't give you much
of a ride. Maybe about five minutes, top. Then we
circled the airport and landed, which is the best part
of all because it looks like you won't make it. Now
Echo was in a very grave and solemn mood. She kept
shaking her head and saying "Wow!" over and over
again about seventeen times. The pilot helped her out
of the plane. Then she held out her hand to him and
looked at him with her head kind of lowered and her
eyes open wide. "Sir, I want to shake your hand," she
said, very seriously. The pilot got kind of confused,
but he smiled a little and they shook hands. "That's
all," Echo said, "just shake your hand." Then she
screwed up her mouth real tight, like a person does
who has just learned something very important that

they don't want to forget. "Thank you, sir," she said, "and God bless you. Come on, Clint." She took my arm and we walked across the field toward the gate. People watched us like we were the first humans ever to come back alive from Mars. At the gate, we stopped and looked back at the orange airplane. Echo said, "Now I want to remember every least thing about it." She filled her eyes with it all and clamped them tight shut.

In the car, and all the way back home, she kept saying, "Clinton, what impressed me was the being up there." When we got back to the house, she stopped me on the front steps and said, "Clint, just for your information, that's the best time I ever had in my life." At lunch, she told Ralph and Annabel all about it, too.

Then all four of us went down to the basement because it's cooler there in the afternoon. Besides, it's the only place in the house that's not fixed up all phony, which also helps. We started playing four-handed rummy with deuces wild, the only card game I can stand because when you lose you still get a big score. But all of a sudden I got this very strong urge to do something and get it over with. So I excused myself and came up here for a while and thought it over. I decided finally that whether or not it was a good idea was a small point. So I wrote this note to Echo, very simple, no signature, and put it on the front seat of her car. She'll know who it's from. Nothing but five words with a ball-point pen and no date even.

DEAR ECHO,
    I love you.

Now she's on her way back to Toledo. She's probably read it already. Maybe not though. Maybe she won't see it till tomorrow morning on the way to work. I wonder if it was a stupid thing to do?

Annabel and Ralph asked her to come back next weekend. Echo said she'd love to, but didn't want to "wear out her welcome mat." Then Ralph and Annabel laid on a lot of palaver and she said next weekend for certain.

But maybe I've thrown in the monkey wrench with that note. Maybe she'll never come back because of me being only sixteen and her being thirty-one, etc., which slays me because what's that got to do with it anyway?

Tomorrow I'm going to get a job, maybe at a car-wash place. Otherwise I may go crazy. Besides, what have I got to lose? I was going to kill myself anyway, so from now on it's all gravy.

I wonder why I didn't *sign* the goddam thing? I wish somebody'd kick my ass for me.

The next morning, carrying out his plan, Clinton made the rounds of several big downtown car-washing establishments. He offered a smiling and cheerful countenance to the managers of these places, and before noon one of them had put him to work. The place, called Frankie's Two-Minute Auto Wash, ran a car through its garage on a conveyer belt, where it was worked on simultaneously by a crew of six men. Clinton's job was to jump into a car and wash the insides of its windows while the other men scrubbed its exterior. It was hard work and he liked it.

Annabel made sandwiches for him, and at noon he bought apples and Coca-Cola at a nearby fruitstand. Then

154

he and the other men on the crew, three white men and two Negroes, all older than himself, would sit on stacks of tires behind the garage and eat their lunches together. These lunches were friendly affairs, and sometimes there were conversations that Clinton would write down while he rode home on the bus. The hard work seemed to add certain flavors to the sandwiches. When they had eaten, most of the men used the remaining few minutes of their half-hour for more talk, and smoking. Clinton found that these cigarettes, smoked after a workman's lunch, had an especially good taste to them. And in the evenings when he was tired, he found that he enjoyed the tiredness; he was usually asleep by eleven o'clock.

Now on the Wednesday of this week, Annabel Williams, for no apparent reason, began to suffer from an unusual nervousness. Late in the evening, long after Clinton had gone to bed, and while Ralph napped in his easy chair in the basement, Annabel sat in the living room, alone as usual, watching a television comedian. It was during this time, on the Wednesday, that these demons of uneasiness crept into the room and stole into her mind. Their approach had been soft and stealthy and had taken place while her mind was partly occupied with the entertainment.

While the commercial was being shown, Annabel suddenly became aware of her condition. It was as if she had undergone a real fright. But it was nameless and invisible to her. She walked across the room, slowly, her flesh chilled, and turned off the machine. This sudden silence made her more acutely aware of her solitude. She began to gasp for breath. The open windows terrified her and she wanted to draw the blinds; but for the moment her consternation was so great she was unable to move. When this first shock passed, she felt gradually easier.

Without thinking, she started toward the basement. From the landing, she looked down and saw Ralph at the foot of the stairs. He was standing there, the Lord alone knew why, in an attitude of puzzlement, suspension, just looking at her.

"Annabel?" he said.

She stopped on the landing. "Yes?"

"You all right?" he said.

There seemed to be a kind of nightmare silence between each word that was spoken. But neither of them made any mention of it.

"Why do you ask me that?" Annabel said.

"No reason."

Annabel and Ralph Williams had lost, a long time ago, the habit of reporting to each other these secret fears. Therefore Ralph went back to his card table. Annabel sat by his side until bedtime. Even though neither of them would speak his thoughts, both the husband and the wife were comforted by the presence of the other.

On this night, Annabel's sleep was fitful, disturbed by dreams of a vague and disquieting sort; during the long moments of wakefulness, she was unable to focus on their content.

The following morning, a florist's truck delivered a splendid bouquet of long-stemmed American Beauty roses. Echo O'Brien had telegraphed them from Toledo with this message:

"God bless all the Williamses see you
Saturday noon with love from Echo."

These flowers were a welcome distraction, but now Annabel carried with her a constant sense of foreboding so

156

strong that it was like an actual knowledge of impending trouble. No matter what else commanded her attention, she was aware of this knowledge that hovered just outside her field of understanding, tormented her like some real and palpable thing, too capricious to show its face. In some curious way, Annabel felt there was something shameful in her anxiety, and she mentioned it to no one at all.

She had also a second secret: her belief that Berry-berry would come back soon, just as Bernice O'Brien had predicted. Perhaps it was natural that she would not fit these two secrets together, and make a piece of them in her mind. Because a mother is not commonly expected to admit, even to herself, that she fears the return of a long-awaited child.

Nevertheless, on that Wednesday evening, while Annabel experienced her fright in the living room, this is what had taken place outside the window:

A blue Ford pickup truck, with its headlights off, had driven up Seminary Street and parked at the curb across the street from the Williams house. On the side of this truck, in gray letters, a sign had been painted:

APPLE MOUNTAIN PLUMBING COMPANY
APPLE MOUNTAIN, O.

In the front seat sat Berry-berry Williams. He sat there for a long time, just looking at the house. For the first ten minutes—while he smoked two cigarettes and took several quick pulls from a half-pint bottle of cognac from the glove compartment—the young man still believed that he would actually go up and knock on the door or just walk in. He thought he was just taking his time about it.

But as the minutes passed, he found that he could not do it. However, he did walk barefooted up onto the porch

157

and stand there for a long time looking at Annabel through the window. When she rose to turn off the television, Berry-berry knew that she felt herself being watched. So he crept silently off the porch and, passing between the house and a big white-flowering bush, he stole into the driveway and crouched next to a lighted window in the basement.

From here, he took a good long look at Ralph, who was asleep in his easy chair next to the table. Then the old man woke up with a sudden start: he gripped the arms of his chair and sat forward. Berry-berry felt he could almost see Ralph's ears cocked for sounds like a smart old hunting dog. He wanted to knock gently on the window and lock eyes with the old man, just to reassure him. But this impulse was no more than a slight tension in his hands. Instead of following it through, he backed away from the window altogether.

Then the young man, running softly, returned to his little Ford pickup truck and drove away.

On Friday evening, he came back. The Williamses had just sat down to dinner. They heard the opening and the closing of the front screen door; and Berry-berry's voice: "Where *is* everybody?"

Annabel clenched her fists and looked at Ralph. Ralph stood up. Clinton, from where he sat, looked into the living room.

Before any of them could speak, Berry-berry had entered the room and was standing just inside the archway.

Clinton stared at him incredulously, as if his brother had been long dead, and now, suddenly, magically, his image had been evoked by the mummery of some wizard.

Perhaps the most startling aspect of Berry-berry's sudden appearance—indeed more difficult for Clinton to believe than any act of magic might have been—was the simple flesh-and-blood reality of his being there.

Though he knew him instantly, he found that he had forgotten many details of Berry-berry's appearance. For instance, he had always thought of him as handsome in an oddly individual way, but now Clinton was aware of an actual impression of beauty. This impression was not even marred by the fact that Berry-berry's eyes were slightly bloodshot and that his skin had taken on an unhealthy, almost greenish pallor; these were defects that seemed only to enhance.

He wore khaki trousers and a long-sleeved sweat shirt. His feet were bare. His hair needed cutting; it was of a dark chestnut color with streaks of red in it, a mass of large unruly waves that contributed to an over-all look of wildness about him. He was a six-footer, slender, with broad shoulders and slim hips. If he did not give an appearance of height, it was because of his posture: his weight usually rested on one leg, and he held his head down and to the side. He had a fine face with prominent cheekbones, a strong jaw, a deeply cleft chin, and eyes that were rather small, but of a vivid blue color.

There was in his appearance an over-all strangeness that would be remembered longer than anything else about him. More vivid and more disturbing than any of these features that can be clearly named and described was an unlikely combination of invisible elements, qualities usually thought of as opposed: weakness and strength, kindness and cruelty, ease and tension, humor and sadness. And the balance would shift from one pole to another with all the quickness of a blinking eye, a gesture of the body, a tilt of the head—or the sudden death of a smile.

159

Now as he stood in the archway, it was apparent to everyone that Berry-berry had had a good deal of liquor to drink; but no one made any mention of it. More cautious and deliberate in his movements than a sober man would be, he made every attempt to appear comfortable and easy. He walked over to Ralph, the member of the family closest at hand, and embraced him briefly. "Hi, Ralph." His tone seemed to suggest that he had been gone only a week; but there was about him a sense of emotion deeply felt that clearly belied all of this elaborate casualness. As Berry-berry moved around the table toward Clinton, the younger boy rose quickly to his feet, and thrust his hand forward. Berry-berry pressed him close to his chest for a moment, and it was good to have that contact; but of Clinton's five senses his eyes were the most eager for a feast. He watched Berry-berry move behind his own chair and approach Annabel.

Now the simple act that was about to take place would remain for all of his life in the eye of Clinton's mind: an act that seemed utterly simple and at the same time infinitely mysterious.

Berry-berry and Annabel looked at each other for a long moment, a glistening look of suspension in the eyes of each of them; and then the son moved briskly forward and placed his arms about his mother. His face was buried for a moment in her hair, and then, suddenly, with an abruptness that was awkward, almost harsh, like the result of some crazy impulse, he kissed her full on the mouth. And for a moment so brief that it hardly existed at all, Clinton forgot who the man was. And he forgot who the woman was.

Then Berry-berry moved swiftly into the kitchen.

Annabel's hands had been clenched for so long that they were now a pair of red fists, white at the knuckles. Her

face, contorted with emotion, told that she was under an
agony of strain. But this condition was inexplicably becoming to her. Clinton thought she often looked silly, almost ugly, when she had spent too long at her toilet,
preparing too carefully her face and her attitude; but it
was at moments such as these, in which she was totally
unaware of herself, that Clinton was reminded of Annabel's beauty.

Now he heard Berry-berry's footsteps on the basement
stairs. Clinton started into the kitchen to follow him, but
Annabel stopped him with her hand.

Ralph said, "Just give him a minute down there, Clint."

The three Williamses sat down again but there had been
a general loss of appetite. Annabel started to pick up a
water glass, but withdrew her hand. Then suddenly she
burst into tears and ran upstairs.

In a moment, Clinton and Ralph heard her bedroom
door slam shut.

Ralph looked at Clinton and made the steam-kettle
sound that was his laughter; but it did not have much force
behind it. "Nerves, you know," he said, of Annabel. "A
terrible thing for a woman; can't help themselves."

Clinton was thinking about Berry-berry. "You think
he's still down there?"

Ralph said: "You never know about that Galbralian,
where he is."

In a moment they heard Berry-berry climbing the stairs,
and then he came into the dining room. His eyes took in
the emptiness of Annabel's chair. He leaned on the back
of it with his arms folded, and he was grinning again.
"Listen, Ralph, I think I'll drive around the block a couple
of times. You know, for about five minutes. I want to get
used to this place—gradually. Know what I mean?"

"Go on ahead," Ralph said.

161

"You're lookin' good, Ralph."

"Are you kiddin'?" Ralph tilted his head forward and pointed at the middle of his baldness. "Look at this, not a *blade*."

"But you're not the kind of a guy *needs* a lot of hair. You look good."

Ralph was eager to be taken in. "Yeah? Well, maybe so. What the hell, I look all right."

"Yes, you do, you look really *good*," Berry-berry said. Then, indicating Clinton, he added, "By the way, who's your friend here?"

Clinton was glad to have this attention. It caused him to smile in a way that he could not control, and he felt like a foolish gargoyle. But he was glad to feel that way.

"Oh, *that* little sonofabitch," Ralph said. "You got to keep your eye on him, he's gettin' to be the worst one in the whole tribe. Stand up, Clint."

Clinton said, "What for?" And then he stood up.

Ralph said, "Look at the arms on him, and that chest. It's enough to scare a sensible person."

Clinton stole a glance at Berry-berry. Berry-berry was looking him over, and he seemed to approve of Clinton.

"You want to come with me, Clint?" he said.

"Sure; where?"

"Oh, just around the block. Is that okay, Ralph? For about five minutes?"

Ralph answered in a slightly belligerent tone: "What the hell you telling *me* how long for? Do I ask you how long? Go on, get your asses out o' here, for Chrisake."

Berry-berry started out of the room. "Come on, Clint."

Clinton followed. At the front door, he shouted to the house at large: "I'll be gone for about fi'minutes! I'm takin' a ride with Berry-berry!"

These words repeated themselves silently inside him.

"I'm takin' a ride with Berry-berry, a ride with Berry-berry, with Berry-berry." And they kept echoing back and forth in all the chambers inside him until they were all but meaningless. Clinton knew that *the visitor* was *Berry-berry*, but he could not fit the two together. "*Realize it*," he begged himself, as he climbed into the truck. "You got to realize it."

Ralph went to the window in the living room and watched the young men climb into the truck. He read the sign on the side panel, and said, aloud to himself, "He's no *plumber*, for godsake."

He went to the hallway and looked up the stairs, but he could not hear any sounds up there. He heard noises outside: distant motors, the faraway chattering of children, a woman giggling on the porch across the street. But his own house was silent now. He went back to the window and looked out into the street. The truck was gone. The Williams boys had driven off somewhere. The two of them together.

This is how Berry-berry Williams handled an automobile, or in this case, a truck: he took all the quick speed he could get out of the first gear; then he shoved in the clutch and threw it into second, gunning the motor hard for all the power that was in it. In the city itself, he seldom had any use for the third position. The corners came too fast. He would slam on the brakes and start out again.

He drove this way for a few minutes and soon they were on a four-lane highway, headed south, downstate. He shifted into high gear and steered the little truck with just one hand on the wheel. Then he leaned to the right and opened the glove compartment and removed a small bottle of brandy. He whistled loud between his teeth and said, very clearly, separating the words:

"It is good to get out of that hell hole. Take that cap off for me, will you?"

Clinton took the bottle, removed the cap, and handed it back. Berry-berry took two short drinks from the bottle. With each swallow, he tightened the muscles of his throat as if the brandy had caused him pain. Then he handed it back to Clinton with a smile: "I needed that. Help yourself. You drink, don't you?"

Clinton said, "Now and then. You know, I can . . ."

"Take it or leave it alone? Me too. That's the way I am. I like the stuff, but I don't *have* to have it. —She looks pretty good, a little older maybe. I was surprised."

"Who?" Clinton said.

"Annabel. How old is she anyway? About fifty?"

"I guess."

"Well, I have had it. That dose will last me for about another two years. Just curiosity, you know. That's all I went back for. You're the only one I wanted to see, and that's the God's truth. People say to me all the time, Don't you miss your family? And I say, Not a bit, only my kid brother."

"I missed you, too."

"You know what I expected? I expected you to be gone. I thought you'd take off by now. I did."

"I did for a while," Clinton said, "but I had to come back 'cause I got sick."

"Yeah? —Where'd you go?"

"I'll give you about a thousand guesses."

"Go on, where?"

"Key Bonita," Clinton said.

"Key *what?* No shit!"

"Yeah. I thought you might be around. And I was going

to take off anyway, so I went down to Key Bonita. I didn't care where I went."

"When? When did you go down there?"

"Oh, it was about the time Ralph got that wire, I think. Yeah, it must've been along about then, I guess."

"Why didn't you *say* you were comin' down? I'd've waited!"

"I just figured, if you were there, okay, and otherwise, what the hell." Clinton drew in a breath and held it for a moment. "Then I—uh—shacked up with this broad for a while and . . ."

Berry-berry said, "You *did!*" And then he started to laugh. He put both hands on the wheel, looked straight ahead, and laughed for a long time. Clinton looked at him carefully, trying to judge the meaning of this behavior. Then his brother reached over to him, as if to encourage him, and squeezed his shoulder. "Go on, tell me what else, you little bastard. Oh, you kill me, goddam you, you little cocksman you, you really do! You know you're the only one I missed in this entire miserable hell hole of a town? That's the truth! You know what you are? You're just like me. We're neither one of us any different." Then he laughed some more.

Clinton was deeply pleased with this impression he was making. Through some divine inspiration he had struck just the right attitude with which to win Berry-berry's interest and respect. He was not yet at his ease in this wild world of a speeding truck headed for no place special, but the brandy helped him some. He wanted to get the feeling that this ride was really taking place, but there was something disturbingly false in the core of it. It was as if he had forced it to happen by the strength of imagination and desire; it was an event of the will, without his flesh being involved in it, without truth.

165

"You know what I get the feeling of sometimes?" he said aloud. "It's like we're not really here."

"That's where you're wrong, Clint. We are. And that's *all* we are. We're just *here*." Then he laughed again.

Clinton said: "I guess you're right about that. We're just here." But he no longer knew what they were talking about. Clinton wanted to be agreeable. Anyway, maybe it was not important.

Then Berry-berry said, "I suppose you know I hate her guts."

"*Who's* guts?"

"*Annabel's*."

Clinton had not known this. He listened in amazement, as Berry-berry went on:

"It's true, and I can't help it. She makes my flesh creep. That's mainly why I don't like to come around. I'm always afraid I'll do something rotten. But I don't want to, so I keep the hell away."

"What d'you mean, something rotten?"

"I don't know even. I'm half nuts, you know. I am, I'm a mess. What about you? Are you a mess?"

"Yeah," Clinton said, "but not like that. Course me and Annabel don't have much in *common*. But I don't feel like *that* about her."

"But you're a mess; aren't you?"

"Oh, sure I am. God, I do really crazy things. For a while, she almost sent me to this psychiatrist even. But I didn't go."

"We're *both* nuttier'n hell," Berry-berry said. "And I don't even care. Do you?"

"Naw, hell," Clinton said. "I don't care."

"We're Ralph Williams' two prize Galbralians, that's what we are," Berry-berry said. "I feel sorry for the old man. I *do*. I can't hardly *look* at him even. You know what he'd be doing if it wasn't for her? He'd be sittin' around in a whorehouse drinking beer. He would, I swear."

"Yeah, I guess maybe you're right about that."

"You know, Clint, she bamboozled the poor old bastard. She's got him bamboozled. God, I'm glad I got out of that hell hole."

The talk between the two young men went round and round in this way. Clinton was soon hungry and dizzy. They stopped at a roadhouse. Clinton ate a sandwich and Berry-berry drank brandy. They sat in this place for a long time, sat in a back booth that had linoleum on the counter, and for perhaps three hours or more, Clinton listened while Berry-berry told these several stories of his escapades in the last two years:

Most of his experiences had been based on two discoveries he had made during the first summer away from home. First of all, he found that work was disagreeable to him. His first job had been as a cherry-picker up north in Michigan. The bosses paid so much a basket, so that your earnings were in direct ratio to the effort you put out. Berry-berry found that when he whistled and daydreamed and took his time, he earned only enough for food and lodging. But when he worked fast, he was too tired at the end of the day to enjoy spending whatever extra money he'd made. No matter how he went at it, this job required no mental activity of any kind; and all day long his mind was busy with thinking up schemes by which he might get a living without any work at all. Ralph had always preached that if a man earned only enough at his work to pay for his daily bread, then that man was in fact selling his life to his employer in exchange for the mere privilege of remaining alive. Berry-berry began therefore by telling

167

himself that he wanted to avoid becoming a victim to such an absurd injustice. Ralph had also said that in a capitalistic system, a man's only chance of winning out over this evil was to become an employer himself. But Berry-berry quickly observed that most of the employers he had known seemed to put out a good deal more effort than the men who worked for them. If they made a lot of money, chances were they had big families to squander it on. But Berry-berry was alone, and money was a secondary matter; what he wanted was ease and pleasure and freedom. —The second discovery had to do with his power over certain women. He had known even in childhood that they found some quality in him irresistible, especially women who were somewhat older. They doted on him. They liked to muss up his hair and invented opportunities to touch him and squeeze him and kiss him. Now during this first summer away from home, he found that there were a number of these women who also wanted to get into his bed with him. At the cherry orchards, he fell in with a crowd of other single men who spent their weekends at nearby lake resorts. The managements of these places, for the most part, closed their eyes to the intrusion of these male non-guests who came in on weekends and made free use of the swimming pools and tennis courts and other facilities; in fact, since there were not enough men to go around anyway, these intruders were welcome and became a valuable, though unadvertised, feature of the establishment. Toward the end of the summer, Berry-berry took up with an unmarried woman of thirty-four, a schoolteacher from Cincinnati who was spending a week of her summer vacation in a scantily veiled search for a husband. At the end of her week, she offered to pay Berry-berry for his time if he would drive her car back to Cincinnati, as she claimed she was afraid to travel alone. He had planned anyway to make his way south for the fall, and so he set out with this woman to drive her to Cincinnati. After a night in a tourist court outside Dayton, the woman maintained that she was in love with him and could not live without him. Within a few days, Berry-berry was living in a rented room in Covington, Kentucky, just across the river from Cincinnati, and the schoolteacher was paying his bills and supplying him with pocket money. She contrived to spend as many as possible of her non-working hours with him, many nights and all weekends, without the matter coming to the attention of her superiors on the school board, or of the fellow teacher with whom she shared a small residence in Cincinnati. As for Berry-berry, he spent more and more of his days with other loungers in the less reputable quarters of these two cities, and after a while had given up any thought of finding work. By the time winter came, he was engaged in intimate affairs with two other women, one of whom was the wife of a naval officer stationed in a foreign port; and each of the women, three of them altogether, were contributing money for his support. Meanwhile, the secret life of the poor schoolteacher, through some incautious confidence with another teacher, became known to the school board, and she was summarily dismissed as a person unfit for daily contact with young and unformed minds. She began to demand more of Berry-berry's attention, which he was unwilling to give. In fact he tried to break off with her altogether. Then she began to pursue him like a crazy person, seeking him out in public places and upbraiding him in the presence of others. All of this behavior led to the incident of his knocking her down in a tavern on that Christmas eve of the telephone call. He never saw her again. The judge told him to leave town altogether, and he was glad to go. The naval officer's wife left her family and went with him.

She and Berry-berry drove to Norfolk, Virginia, the base to which the officer himself was expected to return in a few months' time. They took up residence together, living off the income of the cuckolded party. When the man came in from his sea duty, late that spring, the woman was pregnant with Berry-berry's child. Berry-berry had been instantly repulsed by the news of her pregnancy. He had found that whenever the thought of motherhood entered his association with any woman, he became impotent with her and could no longer bear to touch her. Now the officer's wife was angry and offended by his response to her condition. Therefore, when her husband returned, the bold creature not only confronted him with all the facts of her infidelity but, in retaliation for Berry-berry's coldness toward her, told the officer just where the culprit could be found. This led to an automobile chase down the highways of Virginia, Berry-berry in the officer's car, being pursued by the officer, who in turn had borrowed a Navy station wagon. When Berry-berry sought to elude the man by turning sharply and at great speed into a country road, his wheels skidded in the dirt and the car was overturned. But he himself was not hurt. When the officer arrived on the scene, he did not even get out of the station wagon. Now that he had caught up with this devil who had been sleeping with his wife, he did not have the least notion of what to do with him. So the poor man merely sat in the station wagon, and wept. After a while, Berry-berry got in and they rode back to town together. Notwithstanding his grudge, the officer behaved toward him in an exceedingly friendly way, and even ended up by forgiving Berry-berry for fornicating with his wife. Therefore, Berry-berry was taken completely by surprise when the police came for him the next day and locked him up in jail. He was charged with stealing and demolishing the officer's car. Ralph wired the money for his bail, and the case awaited trial. But as the date of this trial drew nearer, Berry-berry's lawyer became less certain of victory for his client, and secretly urged him to forfeit his bail money and run off to California. He said it was unlikely his opponent would want to bother with the expense and red tape of extradition. Besides, they'd have to locate him. Berry-berry flew to Los Angeles. During the first few days he expected to be tapped on the shoulder by every policeman he saw; but gradually this fear left him and he drifted over to San Pedro, a nearby port town, where he fell in with the same kind of seaport riffraff he had known in Norfolk. One of their number, with whom he became particularly friendly, was a big, ugly American Indian by the improbable name of Silas Rents His Ox. Silas was a panderer who dealt in marijuana and prostitutes. He maintained a kind of floating office that shifted from one to another of various waterfront cafés. Intimate comradeship often grows swiftly among lawbreakers, and so it was with Berry-berry Williams and Silas Rents His Ox. The older man even took a kind of fatherly pride in the quick aptitude Berry-berry demonstrated in learning the secrets of his trade. The Indian showed him how to keep track of his women, and taught him certain methods of tripping them up when they tried to withhold income from their manager. He also taught Berry-berry to smoke marijuana in cigarettes and in pipes; but because of the serious legal consequences of being apprehended as a peddler of the stuff, Silas, out of a real fondness for his apprentice, would not allow him actively to participate in this branch of his illicit enterprises. For his own pleasure, Berry-berry had his pick of any new girl that might turn up in the quarter looking for a manager under whom to ply her trade. He would keep her to himself until she ceased to interest him as a bed partner, and then put her to work. Certain of these women developed crazy attachments for him, and even liked to be beaten by him. The act of love, as a rule, had lost its meaning for such a creature. But if she could provoke her man to violence against her, she might imagine she held some real power over him. Berry-berry learned to take part in these twisted games, and even discovered in them a source of actual pleasure to himself. He liked the company of these barren women for whom any thought of marriage or childbearing was as remote as an imagined sun in some distant heaven; these were matters that never came up at all. Life had become a dizzying round of pleasure and violence, benzedrine tablets and women, alcohol and leisure. Berry-berry had found a life in which he could do as he pleased. But he made one serious blunder: he had begun to withhold considerable quantities of money from Silas Rents His Ox. One day in the winter of the year he was summoned by this person to talk the matter over in the back booth of a saloon called the White Horse. The Indian did not seem to be angry. He merely gave Berry-berry a drink of liquor and started to lecture to him in a fatherly fashion on the ethics of his behavior. But while the man talked, Berry-berry sank quickly into a heavy stupor and lost consciousness altogether. That was the last time he laid eyes on Silas Rents His Ox. He woke up on a Greyhound bus that had just pulled into its station in Albuquerque, New Mexico. The driver was telling him that passengers bound for Biloxi, Mississippi, had to change coaches at this stop. Berry-berry had never heard of Biloxi. But the bus ticket he found in his pocket was clearly marked for that destination. He was still in a fog from the drug Silas had administered to him, and it was to this condition that he attributed his inability to remember the purpose for his trip. It was not until he reached Biloxi that his situation became clear to him: he had been gotten rid of. On the December day of his arrival in this Mississippi town, a cold wave had blown in from the Gulf of Mexico, and Berry-berry wandered through the streets shivering with a chill, and in a general state of misery and bereavement. The small quantity of money in his pocket forced him to choose between food and liquor. His choice was a poor one: the liquor caused in him an almost overwhelming dizziness. Perhaps it set off some residual powers of the drug that was still in his system. At any rate he found himself, long past midnight, on the main shopping street of Biloxi, staring contemptuously at a Bethlehem manger scene in the window of a department store. As he tried to move away from this display that was so galling to his sensibilities, he fell to the sidewalk. In order to get to his feet, he had to cling to a movable traffic sign that happened to be close at hand. As he leaned on this sign for support, his eyes were once again assailed by the Christmas display. The attitudes of the little sculptures depicting the Holy Family so filled him with resentment against their heavy sentimentality that he was suddenly enraged. The longer he looked at it, the more he blamed his own desperate fix on this wicked myth of the Madonna, with all her smug purity, kneeling there, fondling the Infant. At length he began to imagine that this bit of papier-mâché window dressing held some actual hypnotic power over him. And in a moment, without realizing quite that it was he himself who had caused it, a burglar alarm was ringing, the shattered store window lay in smithereens at his feet, and the Bethlehem scene lay in ruins under the burden of the traffic sign. The display no longer depicted the joy of a birth celebration; it had become an image of devastation, an innocent peasant dwelling crushed under the wrath of some mighty and wicked monster. Once again, Berry-berry Williams was locked in jail. This time he telegraphed not only to Ralph for assistance, but also—on a kind of hunch based more on cunning than on guesswork—to Mr. Silas Rents His Ox in San Pedro. When the Indian came through with money, Berry-berry was none too surprised. He then made his way slowly along the Gulf Coast and into Florida, following always the line of the sea, stopping briefly in several towns along the way, and ending up, more by chance than by design, in Key Bonita, where his next unholy adventure awaited him. This strange island-town, though generally wide open to vice of all kinds, was also the scene of an erratic tug of war between the police department and the sheriff's office. Each of these public servants vied constantly with the other for the position most favorable to the collection of graft from the many whorehouses and saloon operators. The flak from this battle had the panderers and barkeepers of Key Bonita on tenterhooks; they could never be quite easy in their relations with the law. Berry-berry thrived on these tensions. He was forced to use his wits and he enjoyed it. On a few occasions he ran afoul of these authorities, but they were fond of him and the matters were seldom of a serious nature. From Silas Rents His Ox he had learned to keep his pockets empty: money was often used as evidence. And he had learned that an office should be a floating proposition, shifting from bar to bar, with all records filed, so to speak, in the head. He checked in at the Tin Pot Arms Hotel, and in no time at all Berry-berry had a brace of exotic women—a Panamanian mulatto and a German refugee—earning good money for him. In a weak moment he might even have married the mulatto, "just for the hell of it." This black-haired harlot intrigued him with the almost ludicrous dignity she brought to her profession; she walked the streets like a queen, commanding more respect than any official had enjoyed in this town in years. Far from toiling under the yoke of guilt that twisted the sensibilities of most of his women, it seemed to Berry-berry that she instinctively accepted her way of life as unimpeachable, perhaps even sanctified. For on the wall above her bed was a cardboard painting of an enormous eye, the eye of Santa Lucia. This eye disturbed the puritanical consciences of more than one of her patron-lovers, who were driven to perform their sins under its gaze. But the mulatto herself felt protected by it; she was certain that Santa Lucia drove away all evil influences. Berry-berry was half in love with her utter lack of any sense of wrong whatever; he found himself bringing gifts to her like a real suitor, and even suffered slight pangs of jealousy when he imagined her activities with other men. This peculiar affair might have continued to bring him all of its idyllic rewards for a long time to come, had it not been for the German woman, a perfect antithesis to the mulatto who was her rival. This blonde hellion thrived on suffering. Berry-berry grew bored with the repeated beatings she provoked from him. She would hold out money from him and then, by the purposely faulty concealment of her misdemeanor, challenge him to punish her. Perhaps the richest possible fulfillment of this strange lady's life would one day be brought about by some man who loathed her sufficiently to cause her death. Berry-berry's disdain for her was of no such exalted order. However, one night in her room, driven nearly to murder itself, he did accommodate her to the extent of delivering, with her own knife, which she handed him for this purpose, a minor surface wound of the face; and he slashed her right breast for her. The depth of this second wound was substantial and brought forth a good flow of blood. She

175

begged him to complete the task, but Berry-berry, sobered by the sight of her blood, refused. He leaped from the second-story window of her hotel room, and hid himself at the bosom of his mulatto. The German woman was left to run screaming down the stairs of the Tin Pot Arms, smearing herself and the banisters and the floors of the place with all the blood she could squeeze from her wounds. Then she ran into the street to display her terrible aspect to all the passersby, and ended by fainting in the barroom next door. It was from this establishment that the police were called to her aid. The next edition of the Key Bonita *News-Advertiser* carried an account of the incident, and because of all this public attention the sheriff's office had to make some show of effort at rounding up the person who had wielded the knife. Besides, the sheriff was interested in demonstrating to the public the incompetence of the city's police. Berry-berry's culpability was known to every underworld character on Gasparilla Street, but since he had no enemies among them, no one gave his name to the investigators. And of all the persons who knew of his guilt, the wounded party herself was the least inclined to divulge his name or bring any charges against him. But the sheriff would not leave the matter alone. Therefore, Lieutenant Ramírez (the same mustachioed personage who was to usher Clinton out of town a few days hence) appeared that night in Berry-berry's room. In return for certain lewd favors Berry-berry had in the past arranged in his behalf—the man, incapable of any direct participation in the sexual act, derived some modicum of satisfaction from witnessing the pleasures of others—he apprised Berry-berry of the dangers of his position: he reminded him that a convict in the South usually ends up on a chain gang. And he caused Berry-berry to realize that the power to deliver him into this fate lay entirely in the hands of a

176

sheriff with an ax to grind and a half-crazy German prostitute. Summer was coming on anyway. Berry-berry decided to head north. He went immediately to a hangout known as the Seven-Eleven Club in search of his mulatto. But when he tried to induce her to travel with him, she betrayed no interest in such an adventure. She had always claimed that a good deal of her spare time was spent in attendance to the needs of her great-aunt, an old, crippled woman who lived in the Negro quarter; and this was the reason she now put forward for her inability to leave town. Some instinct in Berry-berry told him that she lied, and he determined, for his own satisfaction, to learn the truth. Late that night, unaware that she was being followed, the mulatto led him to an old vine-covered Bahama shack, which she entered with the familiarity of one who made her home in it. Berry-berry hung around outside for a few minutes and then crept around to the back of the place and peered into a lighted bedroom. Here he found his shadow-laved queen of Gasparilla Street in the arms of an enormous black lover. After a few minutes, he slipped away. The town had, after all, pretty much fallen apart for him anyway. He gathered his few belongings, including several caches of money he had stashed in various places. By the time the sun had risen, he had driven in a hired car all the way to Naples on the mainland. And during this drive he had conceived of Apple Mountain, Ohio, as his destination. This town had always held many attractions for him, and now, not the least of these was its proximity to Cleveland: he wanted to look in on the family. In his boyhood, the mere mention of Apple Mountain had been a wicked stimulant to his imagination. The place had been known to him, as to most of the males of Cleveland and all the other surrounding towns, as a wide-open center of sin. But its appearance was deceptive. Scarcely even touched by the plastic and neon under which the Victorian charms of most of her sister cities now lay smothered or hidden, Apple Mountain seemed to have been preserved by some historical society in the interests of showing a real Ohio town as it used to be. The face it presented to the casual visitor was that of a modest resort town with a few of its great old houses transformed into sedate hotels that featured mineral baths for the aged and the infirm, and fine churches representing eleven different Christian denominations. And so, to the routine pleasures of Berry-berry's profession was now added this mild but titillating sense of the profane. Within two weeks of his arrival, he had three girls, the cooperation of many of the town's taxi drivers, a silent partner, and a base of operations. The latter was a small farmhouse on the edge of town. Its owner, a drunken widower by the name of Vinnie Agricola, had never actually farmed the place. Before his wife had died, it had been their home and an office for his plumbing business as well. But in his grief he had turned heavily to drink; and now, of the business itself, nothing remained but his tools and the little Ford pickup truck. The place had become, by a series of simple maneuvers on the part of Berry-berry, a whorehouse: in exchange for the use of his home, Berry-berry kept this lonesome plumber in liquor and gave him the use of his women. Operating in a definite location was a concession to Berry-berry's usual business principles, but in the present circumstances the risk to himself seemed minimal: in the event of trouble, Agricola, as legal owner of the place, would be left holding the bag.

"We're only a few miles from there," Berry-berry said. "You want to go out and look the place over?"

178

Clinton's stomach was full of roast beef and ginger ale, and his head was whirling with all these tales of Berry-berry's adventures. Now, many things puzzled him, but of one fact he was certain: his great dream, which had always seemed so improbable that he had all but abandoned it, had practically come true. Berry-berry was, in a way, asking him to go traveling with him.

"You mean it?" he said.

"Why not?"

"Okay, only let's give Annabel a ring, 'cause we said five minutes, and it's been . . ."

"Agh, why bother?" Berry-berry said.

"Well, it's just, you know, bein' gone for two years and then all of a sudden . . ." But then Clinton stopped talking. The bewilderment on Berry-berry's face made him feel he had committed some blunder. "Okay, to hell with it," he said, "let's go."

They drove through the long main street of Apple Mountain and over a small wooden bridge which marked the end of town. A hundred yards beyond the bridge was a narrow dirt road. Berry-berry followed this road to the first driveway and turned into it. Clinton saw the lights of a small house shining from the middle of an orchard that surrounded it. Berry-berry stopped the truck and flashed his headlights twice. In a moment he received an answering signal from the porch lamp of the house. Then they proceeded up the driveway and stopped again at the house.

There were no stars in the sky. A light rain had begun to fall and the air was cool. Berry-berry reached into an apple tree and plucked a piece of the fruit. He handed it to Clinton. "They're sweet as hell," he said, "but watch out for worms. This place should've been sprayed, see, but . . ." Then, with a gesture that took in the entire or-

chard, he said: "Look! More goddam apples than a . . . !
We got thousands of 'em! And they just fall to the ground
like . . . !" This abundance seemed to disturb him, but he
could not express himself. He shook his head; and then
he pulled his sweat shirt up around his neck to protect
himself from the rain. He looked all about him, into the
heavy branches of the trees and beyond them into the
black sky.

"You know something?" he said. "I hate life."

"You do?" Clinton said.

"Yeah. I do."

"Me, too. I hate life something awful."

"We're getting all wet," Berry-berry said.

"Berry-berry?"

"Hm?"

"How come you hate life?"

"How come *you* do?"

"I don't know," Clinton said. "I just said that." He
wished there were some way he could persuade Berry-
berry to take a good run through the orchard with him.
The rain made it seem like a crazy idea, which was partly
what he liked about it. But he was afraid of making another blunder.

"Wouldn't Annabel do a double take," Berry-berry said,
"if she knew I was running a whorehouse?"

"Yeah, she sure would. Boy, she really would all right.
How have you got it? Divided up in little cubicles?"

"You'll see."

But neither of the brothers made any move toward the
house. They just stood there, under the light rainfall, separated by a dozen paces of rich black earth. Each of them
seemed to be engaged in a desultory study of his surround-
ings. Occasionally their eyes met.

"Berry-berry?" Clinton said.

"What?"

"Why are there people? Anyway."

"You mean in the world?" Berry-berry said.

"Yeah."

Berry-berry thought for a long time. He stretched his arms and took a deep breath of air. Then he held one hand out in front of him, and looked at it, its fingers extended. He let the rain fall on it and watched it get wet. As he did this, there was a startled and innocent look on his face; to Clinton, the entire scene was like an illustration from a children's book: Berry-berry, a man-child, lost in a forest, examining some precious treasure, his own hand. "I don't know," Berry-berry said at last. "I guess for screwing." And then he smiled and made a series of big sounds that were almost like laughter. "Come on," he said; and he led the way into the little farmhouse.

Clinton felt, at the first moment, like an intruder in the domestic peace of some poor and respectable family. Paper drapes from the ten-cent store hung at all the windows and wrinkled lace doilies sagged on the back and arms of a badly worn davenport. There were a rocking chair, a big old-fashioned radio, a false fireplace with a gas heater dusty and cold on its hearth; there were pictures on the walls, including a calendar that still showed April, with an illustration of two angels at the tomb of Christ, depicting Easter Sunday.

Agricola, a fat and swarthy black-haired man of forty-five, had been asleep in an easy chair when the brothers entered the house. But he came instantly awake and studied their faces with his black, dying-tiger eyes. Then his mouth opened and his tongue, like some eyeless red creature in search of its own lips, popped out and began to dance about over the surface of his mouth.

"Jeez! I could've *swore* that was real."

"You shouldn't sleep down here, Vinnie. You ought to go upstairs to sleep," Berry-berry said.

"D'you ever have a dream where it's so goddam real you say to yourself, 'Christ, this is just like a dream, only it ain't?' And then you wake up and it *is?*"

Berry-berry said, "Anything going on?"

But Vinnie was still absorbed in his dream. "I even half woke up like; and I heard some noise in the kitchen. It must've been *her* out there." A nod of his head indicated a lighted area beyond the small dining room. A woman sat on the kitchen table, eating a piece of salami and reading a magazine; her bare legs swung back and forth nervously.

"But I thought it was *Gloria*," Vinnie continued, "like she was *alive*. I could've swore it. So I dozed off again and I thought, Well, Gloria's out there cleanin' up the place, and she's not dead or nothing any more. See what I mean, how it all fit in?"

There was an open bottle at his side. He took a drink from it. Before he had swallowed all of it, he started to laugh. This caused him to choke and he spat liquor on his shirt and trousers. Berry-berry slapped him hard on the back. When this seizure was over, Agricola went on laughing. He grabbed hold of Berry-berry's hand and looked up into his face: "But when I woke up and seen *you*, buddy-boy, I knew where I was. I knew I was right back in the front room of a lousy whorehouse."

This joke was followed by another drink, and a renewal of his convulsions. He got to his feet and went to the kitchen, where he began to repeat the story to the woman on the table. But she made no show of listening. Without even a glance in Agricola's direction, the woman walked out of the kitchen and into the living room. She was a dark-eyed French-Canadian, plump and untidy, but not unattractive. Her toenails were painted red.

182

She approached Clinton, and tousled his hair, giving him a big-eyed look of approval. Then she took his hand and guided his arm around her waist.

"For this I get paid?" she said.

"Where's your shoes?" Berry-berry said.

She held her foot straight forward and displayed freshly pedicured toes. "They're still wet, doll. Listen, I asked you something. Is he mine?"

Berry-berry looked at Clinton. "You want her?"

"Not just now," Clinton said, politely. He turned to the girl: "But thanks, anyway."

"Well now," she said, "don't you lose that raincheck!"

"Okay," Clinton said.

"Listen, mess," Berry-berry said. "Do something about yourself, will you?"

"My *name*," she said to Clinton, "is Dorothy."

"You hear me?" Berry-berry said, eyeing her in an expressionless way that seemed to change her mood.

"I'm sorry," she said. "I'll go get all pretty, okay?" She blew a kiss in Clinton's direction and hurried into the bathroom.

Agricola came stumbling in from the kitchen, his big frame falling against the woodwork as he entered the room, a newly opened can of beer foaming over his hands. He was still laughing in his fierce and morbid way. "So I woke up—plunko—in the middle of a crummy whorehouse!"

"Why don't you shut up, Vinnie?" Berry-berry said. And then, to Clinton, "Come on upstairs."

He led the way through the kitchen, with its squalid array of empty beer cans and unwashed coffee cups, and up the back stairway. They had to walk single file up the stairs because half of each step was used as a shelf for empty soda bottles. At the top of the stairs was a tiny hallway, with one attic room on the right and another on the left. Berry-berry entered the room at the left, feeling his way into the darkness.

"Wait'll I get the light," he said. "I can never find the damn string. —Come on, you bastard, where are you? There!" Now the room was illuminated by a bulb in the ceiling, covered by a ten-cent store shade; a long piece of butcher's string had been tied to the chain. There were a double bed, a chest of drawers with a mirror over it, and an easy chair. One corner of the room, fitted out with a broomstick-clothes pole and a curtain on a wire, was used as a makeshift closet. Clinton imagined that in the days of Gloria, the room had been cheerful and modestly attractive.

But nothing he had yet seen corresponded with Clinton's imagined picture of what a real whorehouse should be. Nor was he disappointed: oh, perhaps if he ran the place himself he might put one of the prostitutes to work cleaning up the place now and then, and put a few colored light bulbs around; but he guessed Berry-berry simply hadn't got around to these finer points as yet.

"Is this room all yours?" he asked.

"What, this?" Berry-berry said, with a deprecating gesture that took in the room.

"I mean, if you get like a—a *rush* hour—will we have to get out and let . . ."

"Are you kidding?" Berry-berry said, with a touch of annoyance. "You think I have those tramps up here? Listen, they wouldn't dare cross that threshold. Look, Clint, I'll tell you something right now. This is a strictly temporary operation. I don't like it at all; it's not what I'm used to. In fact, it's the first time I've ever had anything to do with a house. I'm only doing it *now* for the *exper*ience! Christ, *look* at that mess down there; you think I can live

184

like that? Never. This is strictly for the jolts, and to tell you the truth, I've had 'em, all the jolts I want. It's nothin' but a headache. See, the kind of a pig that likes to work a house is just too damn lazy for the better stuff. No initiative, no class. You can't even get 'em to shave their goddam legs unless you keep after 'em like a house mother. To hell with it. Look, I wanted to try a house, just once; okay, now I've done it. I'm ready to move on. —Why? Do you think I'm *trapped* here?"

Clinton said, "Huh?"

"'Cause I'm not. Look here, I want to show you something."

He opened the bottom drawer of the bureau. It was empty, except for a copy of the Cleveland telephone directory. "See that?" he said.

"What, the telephone book?" Clinton said.

"Is that all it is? A phone book?"

"Well, I guess so."

"Look." Berry-berry turned back the cover. The centers of all the pages had been cut out, and the big directory was used as a hiding place for certain small treasures: several articles of jewelry, a bundle of twenty-dollar bills, and a revolver. "See? This is my freedom. I keep my freedom in here. And any time I want to, I put this stuff in my pocket, and take off like a big-assed bird. Go ahead, look it over, if you want to. I got a real sapphire in there, worth seven hundred and fifty."

He removed a bottle of brandy from under the bed, and took a swallow from it. "Here, you want a drink."

Clinton hesitated for a moment. "Yes, please." He reached for the bottle. Berry-berry held it away from him.

"Look, if you don't *want* a drink, you don't have to take it just because . . ."

"But I *do*."

185

"Okay." He handed Clinton the bottle. Clinton took a drink from it.

"You know where I got that ring?" Berry-berry said. "A woman from Palm Beach gave it to me. She and her husband had this yacht—an eighty-footer worth I don't know *how* much—they had it tied up in Key Bonita. *She* gave me that ring; no kidding. I may never sell it, either, I may just keep it." He breathed on the ring and rubbed it against his sweat shirt. "See those cuff links? Those I bought. And that night, I wore them with a two-hundred-dollar black suit. Everybody else was in white and cream and beige. Not me. Black. Listen, I could've had any woman there. I mean *any*. You think that's bragging?"

"No," Clinton said, "but where?"

"At this party on the yacht. And you know why I got invited? Not because I own half the town or because I'm the mayor or some other hot-shot. Because I'm not. I'm nothing. But, Clint, I'll tell you, I don't understand it myself, but there's something about me that a woman—well, they take risks, they lie, they'll do anything—just to latch on to some of it, whatever it is, this thing I got. And it's not that I'm hung like a horse or anything either. 'Cause in that respect I'm just a normal healthy guy. —Anyway, here's what happened. You won't even believe it. I was standing in a bookshop. A *book*shop, for godsake, just hanging around, and—you remember Madeline Carroll? Well, just like that, only black-haired, and she came walking into the place. Really bored, you know. So *bored*, oh, boy. And pretty soon we were having this conversation. Nothing; just, I need a book for a sick friend, and all that; just a conversation. And so she bought a book and started to walk out of the place. Then she stopped, you know, like she'd forgotten her change or something, and said: 'By the way, have you got a white suit and a black tie?' I looked her up and down and I said, 'Why, have you got one you've outgrown?' And then she told me to come to this party on the yacht. I said, 'How do you know I'm not some dangerous maniac that goes around murdering beautiful women?' And then she said, 'Well, in that case I won't need a sleeping pill tonight, will I?' And she walked out and got in her car. So I walked out there, real slow, you know, not anxious or anything, and I said, 'Look, are you serious? Because I may just show up on that yacht.' She said, 'You'd better!' So I said, 'I thought you had a *hus*band.' And you know what she said then?"

"No, what?"

"She said, 'Yes, I do, but I don't think he'll appeal to you.' And drove off. Just like that. And Clint, I swear, things like that happen to me all the time. *Wild* things; I don't even understand it my*self*. So who knows, maybe next winter I might even try some of these resorts. Palm Beach, Nassau. And *I* mean, breathe some *air*. D'you know a reason why I shouldn't?"

"No, why?" Clinton said.

"No. I mean, can you *name* one. A reason why I shouldn't?"

"Oh." Clinton thought for a while. Then, "No, I can't *think* of any right off."

"I don't know what I'll do next," Berry-berry said. "I never know myself. I just follow the breeze."

"Or else you get kicked out of town, huh?" Clinton said.

Berry-berry searched his face quickly, and finding no malice in it, he smiled and said, "Yeah, I've had my share of that, too. You can say that again."

"What the hell, though," Clinton said, "that's part of the game, huh?"

"Sure."

187

"How old," Clinton said thoughtfully, "does a guy have to be?"

"For what?" Berry-berry snapped.

"Oh, I just mean, to travel around, without having a cop put you on the bus and send you home."

"Clint?"

"What?"

Berry-berry had his mouth open, but he said nothing. His eyes seemed not to focus on anything in the room, but on something inside his head.

Clinton said, "What're you thinkin' about?"

"Peanut butter."

"*Pea*nut butter?"

"Yeah. You still eat it?"

Clinton nodded. "Uh-huh. Why?"

"Nothin'. I just got to thinking about peanut butter is all. The time Annabel couldn't find it in the kitchen, and you had it in bed with you."

"I did?"

"You used to eat it with your fingers. You don't remember, hunh?"

"Huh-uh."

Berry-berry, lost in his own thoughts, looked at Clinton for a long time. Clinton knew that he himself was somehow the subject of these secret thoughts, and so he studied Berry-berry's face, hoping to get some clue to whatever it was that was unspoken. The two brothers went on looking at each other in this way, without speaking, until at last, in combination with the brandy he had drunk, this staring created in Clinton a sense of dreaming. All feeling of flesh-and-blood reality eluded him: Berry-berry was not there any more. He was an image he had dreamed up, a private fiction of his own making. Then Berry-berry, no longer real to him, lay back on the bed and closed his eyes.

188

Clinton sat in the easy chair and went on looking at this projected image of his brother.

Suddenly he felt that he had to move, do something, speak, or he would himself cease to exist. He stood up and looked at the opened bureau drawer. He glanced at the contents of the treasure box, his brother's freedom: the gun, the money, the jewelry. Then he closed the cover of the directory, closed the bureau drawer, and walked over to the other side of the bed. Berry-berry was asleep. Clinton quietly lowered himself onto the bed and lay there next to him, his head propped up on his arm, and scrutinized every detail of Berry-berry's sleeping face. He thought of the many times, before the move, that he had been in this position as a child, studying his brother.

Now Berry-berry had revealed to him many secret matters. But still, almost as if he, Clinton, were thirteen again, he had to reach over with his fingertips and touch his brother's nose—to make sure he was really there.

He wondered, if the choice were put to him, whether he would go traveling with Berry-berry or stay around Cleveland to be where Echo was. His last thoughts before falling asleep were of this sudden confusion of riches in his life.

But when Berry-berry awakened him at dawn, Clinton's mouth was bitter from cigarettes and brandy, and his thoughts were black.

The morning itself was decent enough: the sky was blue, birds were singing, the country air had in it the scent of apples and earth. Berry-berry had bathed and shaved himself. He had put on fresh khaki trousers and a clean white shirt, open at the throat, the sleeves rolled up; and out of this linen whiteness, the flesh of his arms and hands,

189

of his neck and face, retained that faint patina of green-blue that Clinton had seen there yesterday, the puzzling color of some remote, unheard-of race, sad and beautiful, and so subtle that only the eye of love, or hatred, could ever perceive its presence.

But the fine morning, and Berry-berry himself, had no power to bring him pleasure. Because some dream that he could not even remember lingered heavily in him. He felt that while he slept, and as the earth had completed another turn, some mysterious event of the night had blighted his good fortune. His whole body ached with the disquiet these thoughts brought with them and, at length, he determined to stop their progress, if he could, by an act of will.

Berry-berry said: "Come on, wake up, Clint. I got to drive you home, for godsake." He led the way downstairs to the bathroom, where Clinton splashed cold water over his face and rinsed his mouth. Then they went out the kitchen door, and into the rich morning of the orchard. They gathered up many of the good apples that had fallen from the trees and filled a bushel basket with them.

"You might as well take these with you," Berry-berry said. They placed the basket in the back of the truck.

Berry-berry drove fast, but not with the reckless speed of the night before. He frowned slightly, looked straight ahead, and kept both hands on the wheel. He did not speak.

Clinton also stared straight ahead, seeing nothing. He lighted a cigarette but it tasted as if someone had stuffed it with poison; so he stepped on it with his heel and threw it out the window onto the highway. He could feel, without even looking at it, the nearness of Cleveland. In a way it seemed that they were standing still and Cleveland was coming at *them* at sixty miles an hour.

190

And he knew something else: that even though Berry-berry was at the wheel of this truck, his brother was, in real fact, headed in some other direction, to a region more distant even than Key Bonita or Brazil. Berry-berry would drop him off at the house on Seminary Street, maybe even help him unload the bushel of apples, and then move on and away, body and soul, all by himself, to that faraway place. Clinton wondered if he might have preferred that Berry-berry had stayed away altogether. Because he was like some drug to which the family, he and Ralph and Annabel, were all addicted; and after this small taste, wasn't there a danger they might go crazy with yearning for him? No, Clinton answered himself, they wouldn't go crazy, but they might continue to languish for another couple of years, or forty, Ralph in the basement, Annabel on the first floor, himself on the second, in the kind of haunted silence, broken only by occasional lies and hollow half-talk, that had filled so much of the past. But Berry-berry had given him a lot to write down, to think about, and for this Clinton was grateful. Then he realized, too, that there was an off chance Berry-berry might continue for a while at Apple Mountain; and that Echo O'Brien would be around after that, to save them from themselves, and from one another.

The truck stopped in front of the Williams house.

"Clint?"

"Yeah?"

"I'll be back," Berry-berry said. "Soon, too. Maybe even tomorrow."

Clinton remembered the promise they had given Ralph the night before: to return in five minutes.

"Yeah," he said. And then: "Listen, Berry-berry, I had a really swell time. It was the greatest night I ever spent, honest to God."

"Me too, I had a wonderful time," Berry-berry said. "Just *talk*ing, too. Which is wild because—anyway, we got a lot in common, haven't we?"

"Oh, Christ, we really have, it's amazing. About ten million things in common. Um . . . !" Clinton hesitated for a moment; then he said: "Listen, Berry-berry, will you do something?"

"Sure. What?"

"Will you come in the house. For a minute. And have a cup of coffee and a piece of toast. With them." He nodded in the direction of the house.

"How come you want me to, buddy?" Berry-berry said.

"*I* don't know. *You* know." Clinton looked at the house. Suddenly it was like a skull, empty, no eyes, no teeth. . . . Then, he mumbled, half to himself: "It'll give 'em something to talk about. For another couple of years."

[*Clinton's Notebook*]

It's absolutely unbelievable how everything can just change, like snapping a switch. I woke up today feeling like the devil, and it turned out to be the most perfect day of my life. In spite of a couple of puky details which I may not even honor them by writing down.

But the main point is, Berry-berry is in his room, in this house, at this exact second. Is putting on his PJ's. Is going to go to sleep there in his bed. Berry-berry Williams is here in this house, is the point.

Not that he'll stay or anything.

And my other main point is, Echo O'Brien is in the guest room, also about to go to sleep. Ralph and Annabel and Berry-berry and Echo O'Brien and me,

Clinton Williams I. The place is loaded. We couldn't sleep another person here tonight if we had to, unless we made beds on the floor or doubled up somehow. Ralph is peeing in the downstairs bathroom. Annabel's in the upstairs one giving herself a cold-cream job. The rest of us are in our PJ's. I may go around visiting various rooms before anybody turns out their lights. Christ, you'd think this was some kind of a regular goddam hotel. We're jammed to the gills. Ralph flushed the toilet just now, and Annabel flew through the hall, so nobody'd get a squint at her without the paint. Which I don't blame her. Because it helps. The point is, there is way too much going on around here for anybody to get it all down in a note-book or anything.

How it all happened was this, Berry-berry just plain followed me the hell in here this morning and—(What I *should* be doing right this minute is write down every word we talked about last night, because it could easily just slip away and I'd be caught short, not able to remember it later. Well, I'll just have to trust my memory to get it all down. For what? I still don't know for what. But I've got to.) —Anyway, he just plain walked in with me. Said he'd give me a hand with the apples. So I just said, Okay, if you want to. As if I didn't give a fiddler's fee one way or the other. So we put them in the kitchen, on the floor. And then Berry-berry went to the sink and started filling up the steam kettle.

· I heard Ralph and Annabel moving around upstairs so I just glided up the stairs about a hundred miles an hour and told them for Christ sake to just come on down and have some coffee with us, but not make some big-ass fuss over Berry-berry, because everybody would only get nervous and pretty soon . . .

Clint, stop. Slow down for Christ sake. You want this to be a notebook full of crap? Okay, that's better. Discipline, goddamit.

At any rate, having controlled their emotions to the degree that I deemed proper in middle-aged personages, especially Annabel, whom, as it has been averred, is given to flights of fancy not un-akin to insanity, we descended the main stairway of the abode and strode casually into the kitchen, whereupon Annabel, behaving like a real dream, which shocked the shit out of me, gave Berry-berry a perfectly natural peck on the cheek and started to make toast, at which point Ralph, with likewise naturalness, reached into his bag of dirty jokes, withdrew the oldest and moldiest one he could find and, turning to Berry-berry, who had seated himself under the ivy pots on the windowsill, inquired, "Have you seen anything of Herby lately?" At which, Berry-berry, playing along dutifully and with considerable pleasure to himself, inquired, "Herby who?" Ralph answered, "Herby Hind." This was followed by general laughter, and a reprimanding ogle from Annabel who, notwithstanding her self-appointment as guardian of the world's moral fibers, was thrilled pink by the familial felicity of the gathering at large, and whipped out a jar of marmalade. In view of the great age of this delicacy, which she has been hoarding since B.C., I was pleasantly stunned to perceive that it had not turned moldy on the shelf, and helped myself to abundant portions, having developed an eager palate during my night of revelry in Berry-berry's brothel.

(Not that I think this is great or anything, but I know my style improves when I slow down. Also ex-

194

perience helps, plus misery, etc. But, to get back to the point . . .)

Anyway, pretty soon it got around to just general talking. Ralph spiked his and Berry-berry's coffee with Old Grandad. Me, of course, being only four and a half years old, I got passed up completely. Small point, to hell with it, I don't even particularly like the stuff. But I might just add that I wouldn't mind once in a while getting a chance to say no thanks. Small point, though.

Then it got to be quite a bull session with Ralph and Berry-berry comparing notes on travel experiences, and both of them lying like hell, Berry-berry for obvious reasons and Ralph because he can't help it any more. Annabel started peeling potatoes and acted like she was really interested in every word, but the wheels in her head were grinding about a mile a minute, because she knew she wasn't getting the whole scoop from Berry-berry. But she controlled herself and did hardly any real prosecuting to speak of, except for a couple of minor nudges. Like when Berry-berry made some passing remark about Biloxi, she asked if he was employed as a window dresser by the department store where he smashed hell out of the Christmas display. I think she knew damn well he hadn't been. Anyway, Berry-berry said, real cool, without even hardly looking at her, "No, as a matter of fact, I was drunk," and then he went right on talking about something else. But anyway, the truth seemed to quiet her down. I didn't even listen to everything they said. Oh, I listened, but now and then I sort of checked out and thought about Echo, and what I'd do when she pulled up in her Dodge at noon.

I'd like to see her really open it up on the highway.

She's got superchargers on it that make it go as fast as a brand-new car, and she drives better than any man. Going sixty-five miles an hour on the open road, she told me she could give herself a complete change of make-up, including mascara, without even slowing down. Which is true, naturally. Whereas an ordinary man driver has trouble even lighting a cigarette at that speed, which proves that sex differences are just like age differences. Some people at sixteen are no more grown-up than a baby, for instance, and others have been all over hell and had millions of experiences, and they don't even think anything of it. So what if I've been down to Key Bonita and went through a whole damn love affair, etc., plus been in and out of whorehouses, and passed up all kinds of opportunities to smoke marijuana. An ordinary person my age probably would have grabbed at the chance and got *hooked,* for godsake. But I just happen to have this maturity, that's all there is to it. Even so, I'm going to take it very slow, I mean with Echo and all. Because there's a matter of finances, and being under age. *Technically,* that is. And a person has to make certain concessions once in a while to the stupidity of people like Annabel who think they're so goddam old. Which brings me to a very important point.

I really like Annabel, I really honest to God like her. I tried to feel creepy about her this morning when we were having coffee, but I don't. And it's not like some Oedipus business either, I just happen to *like* the woman. I think Berry-berry does too, way down deep, only he gets nervous around her for some reason which I haven't figured out yet. For instance, at dinner—

Slow the hell down, will you? Back to the breakfast table.

During this pleasant music of family chatter and tinkling coffee cups, I distinctly discerned the sound of a new but not entirely foreign instrument in the symphony that assailed my eardrums. Could it have been the approach of Miss O'Brien's big, black and august chariot? Calling no attention at all to my nonchalant movements, I rose quietly and skillfully from my position at the family board, and with serpentine speed and feline quietude, slipped out the side door.

The way I figured it, if we had just one little moment alone, Echo would have a chance to slip me a note or speak her piece about any *private matter* that might happen to be on her mind!

Nothing.

Not a word.

I'm such a fabulous genius about conducting love affairs that the note I wrote her either got stolen right out of her car by one of the million heartless criminals that live on this street, either that, or the damn thing blew away. Anyway, I figure the whole matter set me back about a week. Which may be the hand of God, because on such short notice the note might have knocked her right off her pins and sent her into shock. I am determined to take this thing slow. A person that looks as young as I happen to look, which is lousy luck considering the fact that Abe Griswold shaved and had hair all over his goddam body when he was *fourteen* and had to go to school on Saturdays for remedial reading classes—hair and all!! Anyway, my point is, I could easily make a big fat ass of myself by getting carried away.

Echo had on orange slacks (tight) and a white kind

of a knitted top made out of jersey or some insane material. I have had some second thoughts about whether or not they're false. Not that I've absolutely made up my mind either. But the matter is now in abeyance. Besides, I don't think it's healthy to dwell on it too much.

The important thing is the way her eyes lit up when she saw me. They sparkled like wine. (Better re-do this later.)

She said, "There's my guy!" and started to give me a little bitty kiss on the cheek, but I grabbed her and hugged hell out of her. She kept talking all the time so I didn't kiss her right on the mouth, but I have no regrets. Except that she brought me a present, this very fountain pen, and I was too stupid to think of getting a present for her. Which is one of the puky details of this perfect day. Because now if I get her something—well, I'll figure that out later. Anyway, I started to give her a thank-you kiss, when Annabel came running out at just the right psychological moment to make me wish I was an orphan, and then we all went in the house, the *three* of us, which was not the way I had the thing planned at all.

What I'd planned was to walk in with Echo, arm in arm, so that Berry-berry would get the picture without having to be shown a sixteen-millimeter movie of the situation. As it turned out, everything's okay in that department, because later, when he went to the bathroom, I took the opportunity to follow him in there and acquaint him with the fact that I had certain designs, etc. And he was wonderful about it, and did not even look funny about her being somewhat older than me. I'll bet it did not even cross his *mind*. Which convinces me that Berry-berry is probably the finest person I have ever met, except Echo.

I honestly do not understand just why it was he obliged all those whores by beating the hell out of them. You'd almost think he'd rather get some other job than pimping. I mean, when it gets to the point where you have to stab the pigs to keep them happy, it might be better to tell them to go to hell instead. Of course, I don't yet know *everything* about the prostitution game. Meanwhile, I have to leave open at least the bare possibility that Berry-berry has got this terrific mean streak in him.

Which is ridiculous because all day long today he treated Annabel and Echo like they were empresses, and if he was some kind of a son of a bitch, even way down deep, it would have showed through. I'm not *that* dumb.

What I've got to learn is to write things down in order of occurrence. Back to the breakfast table.

Echo took a paring knife and helped Annabel with the apple peeling. There were already two great big bowls full of apples all cut up, but they went right on peeling. When things are going her way, Annabel has this tendency to overdo in the kitchen.

So there were five of us in there now, the biggest mob of people I've been around for some time. I sat between Echo and Berry-berry, which was okay, except that Ralph had the really best seat, because he could look at both of them all he wanted, without craning his neck back and forth. It was like having the place crowded with movie stars, only far more superior, because Echo and Berry-berry are far more fantastic and I know them personally. For instance, Berry-berry had his arm around my shoulder half the time, and Echo kept sticking pieces of apple in my mouth. So I definitely was not just somebody hanging around where he wasn't wanted. Far from it. They're both crazy about me. I may give Mildred Murphy a blast on Monday, just to ruffle her feathers. No I won't. To hell with her. Who needs it?

Finally Annabel said, "Good lord! What'll I do with all these apples?" And Echo said, "Applesauce!" So they got out the pots and the sugar, and while the stuff was simmering on the stove, we all went outside and stood around Echo's car. She got out her camera and took pictures of us for her mother, and then we all went for a ride. I drove, which scared the hell out of Annabel. Puky detail number two. She kept spotting police cars, half of which turned out to be taxis, and said I'd have us all in prison for driving without a license. I figured, what the hell, let it pass, let it pass, but she kept hammering away at the fact that I'm a minor. So finally, I pulled over to the curb and said maybe Berry-berry would like to have a crack at the wheel.

Which he did.

Well, no use going into all the hair-raising details, but suffice it to say that maybe next time Annabel will let well enough alone. We all got hauled in. Speeding. No Ohio driver's license. Running three red lights in a row. Berry-berry's theory seems to be that traffic lights are only there to give these drab intersections a little splash of color. So we all went filing into the police station. Ralph was getting a big kick out of the whole thing, he kept making jokes and giggling and poking everybody in the ribs. I thought we looked like a pretty shady bunch. Except for Annabel. She walked in with her head up, looking real noble and resigned like Katherine Hepburn about to get her head chopped off.

When we got up to the desk, Ralph sort of took over. He put his hand on Berry-berry's shoulder and give this fantastic oration about how "this fine and gallant young son of his had just returned from a long, long tour of this great country," and how he was just "carried away with emotion at seeing once again the landmarks of his boyhood in this fine metropolis." I don't think he actually came right out and *said* it, but you got the impression that Berry-berry was some kind of an unsung hero, and if it hadn't been for him and that long long tour of his, the whole United States would have got flushed right down the toilet.

So we came out of it scot-free, and Echo drove us back to the house. Ralph was the hero all the way home. We kept talking about what a wonderful public speaker he was. Berry-berry said if Ralph had gone into politics, he'd probably be President—which is not as farfetched as it sounds. Echo clinched it. She said Ralph had his heart right on his tongue, and that's what kept us all out of the clink. Ralph loved this topic. He didn't say much, but he ate it up. Now and then, when it looked like we might accidentally get off the subject, Ralph would slip in a comment to keep us on the right track. "You think I did all right, do you?" Then we all started in again and kept snowing him under with compliments. Except Annabel. She seemed to be just very very slightly miffed. I think she had her heart set on that guillotine.

Go easy on the veries.

Now I'm getting to a part I really like to put down. Back at the house, the women went into the kitchen to look at the applesauce, and Ralph followed them in.

(He's got a slight crush on Echo. Nothing *dangerous.* But he can't stand to have her out of his sight.) Berry-berry and I just kind of hung back, and sat in Echo's car for a while, smoking. (I got to cut down.)

For a while, not a word. And then he said, "You know, Clint, that's not really a hell hole in there."

I said, "No. It's not really a hell hole."

"I mean I'm *enjoy*ing myself," he said.

I had about forty things to say, like, "Why don't you move *in* then?" Because, to tell the truth, if it was always like today around here, I'd rather stay home than go traveling to other places. But I kept my mouth shut. If you want something with all your heart, sometimes it's a good policy to shut up about it.

All I said was, "Me, too. I'm really having a good time."

Also, I wanted to ask him if he felt any different about Annabel. But I thought I better play that cool, too. Which was a good idea, because tonight at the dinner table a certain inconsequential incident took place of a very minor order, and I don't know what to make of it. Maybe nothing.

Ralph said something to Echo about how Berry-berry had his own plumbing business out in Apple Mountain. Naturally this is a subject that isn't exactly expected to make Berry-berry feel perfectly *relaxed!* Ye gods, I'd have probably started shaking, if it had been *me.*

Annabel said, "Well, I'm so glad Berry-berry doesn't have those awful stumpy-looking hands that plumbers always seem to have." She took hold of his hand and said, "Look at this, perfectly beautiful, an octave-and-four at least. Wouldn't any piano player give his right *hand*—I mean . . ."

Ralph said, "Well, maybe he wouldn't go *that* far."
Then he and Echo laughed like Faust.

But I was watching Berry-berry all the while. At
first when Annabel took his hand, he got all tense.
You could see it in his face. And then it was like he
was telling himself not to spoil everything. "Come on,
Berry-berry, don't be such a selfish slob all your life."
I could almost hear him talking to himself. "To hell
with how *you* feel for a change, make these people
happy." Then he kind of relaxed.

It was plain that Annabel had something like that
going on inside of her, too. But I don't know what
exactly. I can't even guess. Women are cagey.

The applesauce made a big hit with everybody. So
Berry-berry got to talking about his orchard, and how
he could get all the apples he wanted, just like these.
He talked like he was not a plumber but a farmer,
and proud of his crop. He talked so much about his
apples that I almost left the table. I wanted to go hide
out in the garage and cry for a while. Not that I was
sad or anything. But I just stayed there at the table
and thought about what big liars we all are, and in a
way I hoped that none of us would ever tell each
other the truth. It's a lot better sometimes to just sit
around the table till ten o'clock at night, with everybody lying his ass off. What the hell difference does a
few little secrets make? I mean will the earth cave in
or something?

Because take right now for instance. I'm sitting up
here in bed and if I want to I can write all night.
Which I may do. I've got to get Berry-berry's travels
in here. But what I mean is, here I am in bed, and all
these scads of other people are right here in the same
house, all of them in their beds. And we're all really

crazy about each other. So just say that something terrible happened to me in the middle of the night. A nightmare or something. I don't know what exactly. But terrible things do happen to people in the middle of the night. Then all I'd have to do is holler, and all these people would get into their bathrobes and come flying in here to help me out. And if it was them that hollered, I'd do the same. But I wonder what the hell I'd do if any of them *died?????*

They won't.

And don't get hysterical in the question-mark department.

Now on to Berry-berry's fantastic two years . . .

Now it's Sunday morning and I just woke up with this tremendous hangover from smoking. I counted twenty-two butts and it took me nineteen pages to get Berry-berry up-to-date, so I'm averaging a butt a page. Writing all that stuff down got me nervous, and I couldn't sleep for a long time. I got to thinking about how all that time I was at the White Tower frying hamburgers to save up money to go traveling with Berry-berry, he was running all over hell beating up these women so they wouldn't get any fancy ideas about having babies, etc. Which is not the way he explained it at all, but that's the screwy way my mind was working in the middle of the night. I just don't happen to have a lot of experience with prostitutes. Like I always thought they had false eyelashes and purple silk stockings, and squandered all their money putting their little brothers through school and paying hospital bills for old ladies that eat in cafeterias and all that. Which shows how naïve I used to be, because the fact is most of them are half nutty and too lazy to put on their shoes, and go around pestering some poor bastard like Berry-berry to gig them with knives and stuff. But that doesn't sound exactly right either. Actually, I'm still a little hazy on this whole subject.

So I went to sleep and had this crummy dream about Shirley and her little brother, Willy. They were both little children in the dream, and they were sitting in a candied-apple tree, way up on a high branch, singing songs and fooling around and having a high old time in general, like kids do—when all of a sudden a certain person came along and he started to climb up the tree. This is a really crummy dream. I don't even know why I bother to write it down. Anyway, this stranger had a real wild look in his eye and you could tell he was the kind of a creep that absolutely despises all little kids. So Shirley got scared, and Willy started to cry. But this person climbed right on up anyway and started to shake this high branch for all he was worth. On purpose, too. I mean it wasn't any accident. And then Willy fell out of the tree and got killed. The point is that this sinister person in the dream was quite a bit like—in some ways, only not really too much—I'd say he just *reminded* me of some people I've known casually in the past, but nobody in particular.

It really makes me feel like a turd to put all these crummy things down. But lately I get this crazy feeling when I look at an empty page. It's like the face of a blind man who doesn't even have any eyes. And if I don't fill it up with this stuff, the poor bastard will never be able to see at all, as long as he lives.

Which doesn't exactly lighten my worries. Because I wonder if people that have such thoughts don't eventually just flip altogether?

Berry-berry doesn't seem to ever get bothered with these thoughts. When we were sitting in that beer garden out near Apple Mountain, and he told me all the things that happened to him, once in a while I butted in and asked him why he did this or that, or why somebody else did. And all he'd say about it was, "Oh, it just happened, that's all." Or else he'd say, "I don't know, but isn't it wild?"

He just doesn't happen to have this analytical mind the way I have. Because the way I analyze the whole thing is that he'd be better off if he got a real job and had a wife. It seems to me even washing cars is a lot less wear and tear on your nerves, etc., not to speak of the dangers of ending up on a chain gang or with some kind of a disease. And then he wouldn't always be behind the eight ball, borrowing money from Ralph and all.

But what I've got to remember is that everybody in the world is a separate person, with different ways of being nutty. For instance, maybe Berry-berry has got whores in his blood just like the way I always put everything down in this notebook.

I hear people stirring around in the kitchen. I better get the hell down there and see what's going on.

The Williamses and Echo O'Brien went for a long drive in the country. They took iced tea with them and hard-boiled eggs, and Ralph had some liquor in his pocket. They drove past places where horses and cows grazed, and past big fields where corn and oats and alfalfa grew. They looked at silos and barns and farmhouses, at country churches and hillside graveyards. They took off their shoes and stopped at a creek to go in wading. They shopped at an open roadside place that sold tomatoes so cheap they wondered how the farmers made any profit. After dark, Echo O'Brien started to sing *The Daring Young Man on the Flying Trapeze,* and then the Williamses got into it, and they sang all the way home. Before long the Williamses were home in bed with a fine Sunday behind them. And Echo was on her way back to Toledo.

On Monday, there was trouble waiting for Berry-berry at the farmhouse in Apple Mountain. Two of his women complained that the business, which had hardly even got started in the first place, had gone to pot altogether. They were not making any kind of money at all. Berry-berry offered a few feeble promises, but he had no real heart for the enterprise. By the end of the week, these two women left the place altogether, and there remained only the French-Canadian named Dorothy. Dorothy was in no way an ambitious girl. She was content to stay on in the place, sharing Agricola's bed with him in return for her board and the use of his television set. Berry-berry maintained his quarters in the attic room, making use of them during the weekday nights.

Agricola seemed relieved that these whores had left the place. By the following Monday, he had sobered up and had put Dorothy to work cleaning up the house. Berry-berry had a telephone installed and set out to get some plumbing work for Agricola and himself. He had no experience whatsoever in this trade, but Agricola promised to teach him everything he would need to know. He placed a large advertisment in the Apple Mountain *Record:*

BACK IN BUSINESS

APPLE MOUNTAIN PLUMBING CO.

- no job too big
- no job too small
- guaranteed satisfaction
- free estimates

BERRY-BERRY WILLIAMS
VINCENT AGRICOLA   DIAL 4140

The next day there were two responses, and the Apple
Mountain Plumbing Company repaired a toilet tank in
a boardinghouse and installed a sprinkling system in the
grounds of a private residence.

On Friday a letter was delivered to the farmhouse, inviting them to submit a bid to a contractor who was
building a small housing development for a nearby town-
ship, Ashton Wells. Berry-berry learned from Agricola
that this contractor was related by marriage to the town-
ship's official inspector and that all the subcontracts
would be assigned on the basis of graft payments to the
inspector. Agricola had no real talent for skulduggery; he
was inclined to ignore the invitation altogether. But
Berry-berry, for his part, felt that his underworld experience might stand him in good stead, and these shady
details even added a certain spice to his first legitimate
venture.

On Saturday at noon, when he arrived on Seminary
Street wearing a necktie and a new summer suit, and at
the midday meal displayed to the Williamses and Echo
O'Brien the advertisement he had clipped from the
Record, and read aloud to them his company's invitation
to bid on the Ashton Wells project, Clinton excused him-

self and went upstairs to make this brief entry in his notebook: "Berry-berry's whorehouse has folded up!!!!"

But when he went to bed that night, Clinton felt somewhat less inclined to indulge in exclamation points.

[*Clinton's Notebook*]

Saturday Night.

Well, every day can't be perfect. And I'm not complaining either. Nor am I going to sit here and write a lot of vomit. I'll just tell everything the way it happened.

We roasted weenies in the back yard, the whole five of us, and we played cards and worked jigsaw puzzles on the front porch. We all move around in this wonderful kind of a cluster, like one big person with ten legs and five sets of teeth. All the neighbors were sitting on their porches. They kept glancing over here, and they all looked kind of glum to me. I think they wanted to get in on all this activity we had going on. That big old German woman who's always sucking her teeth and lives in that weird-looking purple job, the second door from the corner, she walked past here about forty-five times, and each time she slowed down, trying to get an earful. The way I figure her, she's some kind of a scout they send out in this neighborhood to get information about us. Which I don't blame anybody. Because if *they* had these strings of fantastic cars lined up in front of their places, I'd probably go nuts wondering what was going on. So this one time when she went creeping by, I gave her a big smile and said, "How do you do, ma'am?" She glanced at me like somebody caught at the keyhole, and went scooting up the street like a rocket. I actually like the old broad, though. And I wouldn't mind getting her to fill out a few question-naires about some of the other odd-balls I've seen on this street.

Well, tut-tut.

Tonight I got a sniff of some real trouble ahead. Oh, I'll get through it. Ye gods, what am I? And I'm not going to go racing into the bathtub with any goddam razor blades either. Nor am I sore at any-body. Because nothing even happened. But I've defi-nitely got grounds for being depressed. Berry-berry and Echo are driving each other crazy. They're in love.

Of course he hardly ever looks at her. And vice versa. They don't even talk much, except in cases of politeness, like lighting cigarettes for her, etc.

I wouldn't even have noticed that all this was go-ing on between them—if it hadn't been for what did not take place at the drive-in movie tonight, which as far as I'm concerned, completely puts the frosting on *my* little cake. The whole thing is tragic. I hope the full realization of it never really hits me. Thank God I've got a sense of humor.

But at the time, which lasted about three years (they make these endless movies nowadays), I was praying science would come up with some new shriveling-up powder that would make a person about the size of a snail. Because personally, my presence was about as useless as a brass monkey's—well, I'll be damned if I'm going to be shoved into that kind of cheap metaphor just because for the mere reason that it's appropriate. However, tut-tut, there I was, sitting square in the middle, with Berry-berry on one side and Echo in the driver's seat, and Vera Ralston and

George Brent and Constance Bennett running in and out of jungles and hotel lobbies, like a bunch of neurotics, right in the middle of the Amazon.

Meanwhile there's this big loud nothing going on back and forth between Berry-berry and Echo. Not a word. It was like a fuse burning and we all three sat there pretending we'd never even heard of dynamite, and stared at the screen. In the first place, the picture was about as entertaining as having a boil in your armpit. Because I, for one, have never heard about them having all these big flashy hotels in the middle of the Amazon before, and I get fed up with movies where people like Vera Ralston are always getting the short end of the stick. Which I think she got, but I'm not sure. And now I must admit they did have an airplane trip somewhere in the middle of this picture, so it's just possible the goddam hotel was supposed to be in Paris or Baghdad or some other lousy place. Besides, I wasn't paying any attention to the damn picture. How could I with Berry-berry's arm in front of my face, reaching over to light about three cartons of cigarettes for Echo, who has never struck me as the helpless type, with her pocketbook full of wrenches. And you could hardly class Berry-berry as a real out-and-out cigarette-lighting type either. As a matter of fact, I get the impression that hordes of women have burnt their little pinkies lighting *his* for him. Well, to hell with it. I'm not sore about all this. I just don't happen to get a thrill out of sitting there right under my very own nose being a fifth wheel, that's all.

Big pause here.

Because Berry-berry just this minute left my room. We had a conversation that lasted about sixty seconds, but in that little bit of time, the whole world changed.

He walked in and leaned on the doorframe.

"Clint. I got to talk to you."

"Come on in and shut the door."

He sat in the little rocking chair with his arms and legs sprawling all over the room. Then he looked right at me, and for some crazy reason, I got nervous as hell.

"Clint. I want her. And she wants me."

"Yeah, I know it."

"Well, what do you think?" he said.

"What do *I* think?"

"You saw her first."

"I'm sixteen," I said. "She's thirty-one."

"Clint, I won't even look at her, unless you say the word."

Then I had two thoughts: I thought about Echo's eyes, how immense they are, and lonesome, and how, that day at the airport, she kept filling her eyes up with everything she saw, so when it was over she'd have something left. And the second thought I had was about this tremendous power I had in my hands.

"Berry-berry," I said. "You love her, don't you?"

Love is an embarrassing kind of a word, but sometimes you have to just say it. Anyway, he looked at the picture of Abraham Lincoln. Maybe I'll take that picture down someday, just to see what the hell people would do with their eyes when they don't want to look at me.

"Yeah," he said, "I guess I do."

Then he got up and started fooling with the junk on top of my bureau, and all of a sudden I got scared. I thought if I said, "No, leave her alone," then Berry-

berry would think I didn't trust him. And then I'd
lose both of them. Echo, because I'm too goddam
young, let's face it, and him, because of not trusting
him enough. Besides, they wanted each other. And
he was decent enough to ask me first, which is a big
improvement over just snatching her right out from
under me, which he could have done without any
trouble.

So I just said, "Treat her nice, will you?"

"What the hell you *think* I'm gonna do?"

"You sore?"

"Sore at you? Why should I be sore at you?" he
said.

" 'Cause I didn't mean anything."

"What're we talking about?" he said. "I don't even
know what we're talking about any more. Do you?"

"Huh-uh."

"I better get to bed," he said. "Thanks, Clint. You
hear me?"

"Thank *you.*"

"For what?" he said.

"For talkin' to me about it."

"G'night." And then he went to his room. Now
they're all in bed. I really feel pretty good about
everything actually.

A few weeks ago I was practically a mental case,
couldn't even get out of bed like a normal person.
And now my ship has come in and all my old wishes
have come true. Plus I've even got a job, and have
greatly curbed my appetite for reading Annabel's
mail, etc. (I still *read* it, but I don't always copy it
down any more.) So what kind of a person would I
have to be to get sore just because Echo O'Brien, aged
thirty-one, doesn't happen to be passionately in love

with me, aged sixteen? A nut? I'd have to be some kind of a neurotic for godsake! Besides, how many people have these fantastic sister-in-laws sleeping in all the spare bedrooms? And brothers that are so wild they're practically crooks, and then all of a sudden turn into tame ordinary people with neckties and big plumbing corporations?

Well I, for one, happen to feel just sensational about this whole thing, practically.

Tomorrow I'm going on a health binge, get some filter cigarettes and start doing push-ups every night. Maybe I'll do some right now, to make myself sleepy. Because I've got about forty-seven big knots in my chest, and they hurt.

Au revoir, notebook, old pal, old thing. You've had it. This is my last entry. If Berry-berry can go straight, so can I.

FINIS

In the summertime a family of Clevelanders will experience some distressing hot spells, but on the whole it is not a miserable season. Any extreme in the weather is apt to provoke trouble among persons who are sad to begin with. But as far as contented people are concerned, the mercury may do as it pleases without placing much real strain on the spirits.

And so it was for the Williamses of Seminary Street and their frequent visitor from Toledo. During this long and happy summer Echo O'Brien spent most of her weekends in Cleveland, and the three full weeks of her August vacation as well.

For her and for Berry-berry it became the summer of their romance. The love affair between these two was known to each member of the family; and its continuance was so fervent a wish in each of them that no one ever risked any direct mention of the possibility to either of the lovers: perhaps, as a thing of beauty, it seemed too fragile to meddle with at all.

Ralph Williams, on the weekdays, saw to the upkeep of his rental properties. And he sold a small apartment house that had been on his meager list for more than fourteen months. His own commission from the transaction was negligible, but his chief profit was in his own view of himself: it made of him once again a man of affairs. He took pleasure in the most tedious details of the deal, and when it was concluded he even took the seller and the purchaser downtown and bought them lunch in a hotel. At this lunch, Ralph himself swallowed nothing more substantial than a shrimp cocktail. He drank a good deal of liquor, however, and when the party broke up, his spirits were such that he was unable to locate his automobile. After searching the streets for more than an hour, he finally arrived home in a taxi and headed straight for the telephone. Annabel was unable to dissuade him. Nor was Ralph to be contented with a mere report of the situation to the Police Department. Among the calls he put in that afternoon were three to various officials at the City Hall, including the City Attorney himself, and one to the City Desk of the *Plain Dealer*. To each of these gentlemen in turn, he enumerated the ghastly dangers implicit in their flagrant indifference to the crime wave that was sweeping Cleveland. The next day the police located the car for him, on the street where he had parked it and the whole affair caused no one any serious trouble. But Ralph was back in business; and the following week he started to clean out his old file cabinets.

Annabel attended with renewed pleasure to her household duties. It was in her nature to be a good housekeeper. She liked making lists and paying bills, and the sound of a vacuum cleaner was no mere nuisance to her ear: it gave her comfort. On long afternoons alone, rather than let time go stale on her hands, she wrote lengthy letters to Bernice O'Brien or attended matinees at the Cleveland Playhouse; and sometimes she made popsicles out of Kool-Aid and passed them out among certain pint-sized friends she had newly cultivated in the neighborhood.

Clinton continued with his job at Frankie's Two-Minute Auto Wash. All in all, he was having a good summer, but his problems were these: how to persevere in his resolution to keep away from his notebook; and how to refrain from insinuating himself into the love affair between Berry-berry and Echo. He found that he was not actually jealous of Berry-berry, but of the secrets the two of them shared. He was forever creeping about the house, barefooted, spying on them and listening to their private conversations. If they were on the front porch, Clinton was at the side of the house, sitting in the bushes. If they were in the basement, he was crouching in the driveway outside the window, or sitting on the edge of the bathtub with his head inside the laundry chute. When he got hold of something worth listening to, he then had to summon all the powers of his will to restrain himself from writing it down. Often, when the lovers planned to drive off somewhere to be alone for an evening, they would find Clinton hanging about the car; and without ever asking to be included in the outing, he sometimes presented to them a demeanor so forlorn that Echo and Berry-berry, after a brief and whispered exchange among themselves, would insist that he come along. These occasions were usually painful from beginning to end; he knew they wanted to be alone, just

216

the two of them, but he seldom found the strength to refuse.

In this way, Clinton's problems fed one another and grew larger and larger until, at last, it occurred to him that if he returned to his notebook he might have greater success in keeping out of the way of the lovers.

[*Clinton's Notebook*]

I hereby choose, of my own free will, to write things down again, whenever I goddam well feel like it. Why shouldn't I? I went practically the whole entire summer without it, which proves I'm not some kind of a madman on the subject. Also, I certainly don't want to turn out to be the kind of a person that makes a resolution, and then he'd rather kill himself than break it, which would be really nutty. Then it would be like the resolution was some terrible kind of a habit that you couldn't get away from. In fact, the way I see it, resolutions can be very harmful to a person.

For instance, I missed a hell of a lot of good stuff this summer. Frankly, though, I don't mind at all. Because I've definitely noticed that when people are sore at somebody else, or they're miserable, or they've got some kind of a gripe, then they have this tendency to say more interesting stuff. Take this summer for instance, Annabel's been going around making potato salad and singing songs in the kitchen and making excuses for people. This stuff is not any too interesting to put down. I'm crazy about it and all, but it sort of goes in and out of my ears without making much of a dent. She says all these nice things about everybody, and about the weather and the flowers. And not phony either, because she means it, and is not half as nervous any more either. I think it's because Reason A, she's gotten over the change of life, and Reason B, Berry-berry's around all the time. Plus Echo. Also, she's been doing quite a bit of praying. Every now and then I catch her at it. I see her at the side of her bed, kneeling down and all, and my own personal hunch is that she's praying about Berry-berry and Echo. I get the feeling that Annabel thinks if she holds her breath long enough and keeps praying a lot, the two of them will get married and have about twenty kids. Which I personally wouldn't mind at all either, because it's quite nerve-racking to just wonder about it all the time, I mean about whether or not you're going to have all these nephews and nieces and sister-in-laws living about a block away. Personally, I wouldn't mind it at all, a whole neighborhood full of little kids I'd be the uncle of, and pretty soon I'd have about forty of them around my neck, wanting to horn in on everything and be taken places and bought things for. They'd probably drive me out of my head and keep me broke half the time, but frankly, I wouldn't mind it too much. It's just that at the moment there's quite a bit of suspense about the whole thing. The way they're going at it, I mean Berry-berry and Echo, the way they're doing is like there's no tomorrow. They're always getting in and out of cars, or flying hell-bent up the street, or running into the house to change clothes and eat and fly back out again. It's nerve-racking as hell. What I'd like is to be sliced right down the middle and have half of me sewed on to Echo and the other half sewed on to Berry-berry, and then when they were flying in and

218

out of the place, and up the street a hundred miles an hour going Christ knows where, then I'd not only *know* where they were going and what they were doing, I'd be there, and doing it with them, and it still wouldn't be like three's a crowd, or anything.

These are the kind of nerve-racking things I've been thinking about quite a bit this summer, because of all this suspense around here.

The world needs to have its Indian summer. The sun has retreated, deep into the skies, a kind of death has taken place. Indian summer shows the world in its most brilliant colors, and most sad, too, lying, as it were, in state. As a rule, in this gentle season, the people pass by, paying their respects, and in this way accustom themselves to the approach of winter.

But the autumn of this year was a freakish season. The warm time had no real September in which slowly to wane and die; the last weeks of this ninth month were as cold as any ordinary November should be. The leaves had hardly turned color before strong winds and icy rains had beaten most of them from their branches and made a pulpy slush on the sidewalks and streets. Even on fair days the sunlight was muted by a vast and heavy veil of clouds, and there was not much color to be seen in the city—only on the traffic lights and certain bold umbrellas. The early days of October did bring sudden and sunny splotches of warmth, intermingled with more rains, so that on certain afternoons children could walk home from school with their sweaters under their arms or tied about their necks, and there were brief and frantic rashes of roller-skating in the streets; but even on the finest mornings, most people, already made cautious by so many bleak surprises, left their houses wearing raincoats and rubbers.

It was as if the sun, by some awful accident, had suddenly been snatched from the world, and in the place of Indian summer was this terrible art of the skies, a phantasm of gloom and judgment and anger, with only the briefest glimpses of blue and gold.

And so it was, right into the second week of October, when Ralph Williams contracted a cold. Annabel had heard of recent instances of older persons who had gone from colds into pneumonia and died from it. Ralph hated the idea of death, and he offered only slight resistance when Annabel, after a telephone diagnosis from Dr. Bolz, argued that he should be put to bed.

Therefore when Saturday came around it looked as if Ralph's room would be the family's weekend headquarters. When Echo O'Brien arrived from Toledo at noon, she rushed straight up the stairs and found him and Clinton engaged in a game of checkers. The old man received her with a bleary-eyed grin. He was propped up on pillows and wearing brand-new green pajamas with a mandarin collar that made him look like a jolly and wicked old Buddha. Echo paused just inside the door, pocketbook in one hand, car keys in the other, her eyes big with concern.

"Ralph, I swear, if I'd known you was sick, I'd have brung my thermometer and nurse's cap and two barrels of beer. Good lord, now listen, tell me how you feel?"

"Terrible. I got enough germs to wipe out this entire town."

Echo started toward him, but he withdrew like a leper. "No, no, no! Unclean, unclean! Oh, Christ, woman, don't come near me!" But she went over and kissed the top of his bald head.

"That's better," he said.

220

She gave Clinton a kiss on the cheek. "How's m'guy?" she said. Then she started to pace the floor, rattling her car keys.

"I'm okay," Clinton said. "Only I was afraid you weren't comin'. What happened?"

"Well, baby, two weeks is about all I can go without a look at you. I mean it, too, that's the awful truth."

Clinton watched her as she wandered aimlessly about the room. He liked to watch her move. Her clothes were always cut in a way that made them move with her body, in the same rhythm.

"Besides," she said, "Mamma wanted me to come. Makes her feel bad if I stay home just for her account. Where's Berry-berry?"

"He didn't get here yet," Clinton said.

Echo leaned on the windowsill and looked at the sky. "It started out like a real pretty day. Didn't it? I can't tell what it's gonna do next, though. Oh, but I had such a *scrumptious* drive comin' down. Made it in just under two hours. I mean, sweetheart, I *moved!* I'm not claimin' I set a record, but who'd believe that old girl had so much speed left in her." She walked over to the bedroom door. "I got something to tell Annabel." She called down the stairs. "Annabel! I know you're in that kitchen. And I know what you're doin' in there, too!"

Annabel's voice came from the downstairs hallway.

"Well, aren't you just *starved?*"

"Now, see? That's what I mean. And if you fix me anything, I'm goin' to slap your fingers. I got something to tell you."

"But I *know* you're starved!" Annabel said.

"I'm not really, darlin'. I'm truly not. Can I help with Ralph's tray?"

"*Ab*solutely not. Just keep him busy up there." Annabel's voice receded as she returned to the kitchen.

In the bedroom, Ralph studied the checkerboard. "I don't know how I got into this hole," he said. "I think my mind is deteriorated. I think I'm senile is my trouble."

Clinton watched Echo in her aimless progress about the room. She sat at Annabel's dressing table, her keys silent for a moment, and she said: "Now, let's see. I had three things to tell, for cryin' out loud, and I can't remember a one of them."

Now, unaware that Clinton was watching her every move, Echo suddenly focused on her own image in the mirror. Some aspect of what she found there caused her to tremble; for a brief instant her eyes closed and her body seemed to buckle from within. Clinton felt that what she had experienced in that moment was not physical pain—but a flash of terror. It had been so brief he could not even be certain that it had taken place at all. But he had lost all interest in the game, and watched her more closely than ever.

Echo began immediately to chatter once again, as if nothing had happened. "Oh, I know *one*, anyway. This one's for Annabel when she comes up. The Buckeye China Company's havin' this gigantic sale, seen about a dozen big signs on the highway." She had turned from the mirror and fixed her gaze on something outside the window. Clinton thought her face looked slightly puffed. In spite of a heavy application of powder, there was a darkness showing through under the skin surrounding her eyes; and in the eyes themselves, usually alive with such profound inner brightness, there was an almost beladonna-like glaze that suggested some mild hysteria. She had painted herself with exceptional care, but perhaps somewhat too heavily.

She turned suddenly to Clinton and gave him a big smile, and winked at him. He knew he had been caught staring, and looked quickly at the checkerboard.

"Where'd you move to ?" he said to Ralph.

"Where the hell *would* I move to?" Ralph said. "I'm in a goddam corner, for Chrisake."

"And the second thing is," Echo said, "I had an offer from a Dodge dealer who'll give me seven hundred and fifty on a trade-in for my limousine."

"I hope you spit in his eye," Ralph said.

"Well, I said, 'Mister, you're going to have to do better'n that. This car's a lady and don't like insults!' —Course, I wouldn't sell her, Ralph, you know that. So what if she drinks oil like an elephant? I told him, too, I said, 'Listen, she drinks oil like an elephant.' But he don't care. He just wants to have her settin' out front, to show off how a Dodge gets to be a million years old without even a whimper. Which is *smart* on his part. Don't you think he's smart?" She walked over to the window and looked down at the street where the old Dodge was parked. Clinton went to the window and stood at her side. She linked her arm in his, and said, "Look at that sweet thing. Now I'm going to say something goofy, but you know, that gorgeous old flivver puts me in mind of the Queen of England. I don't mean the real *queen*-queen, but the mamma queen. You know which one? —Listen, if I had to put *caviar* in her crankcase every ten minutes, I wouldn't sell her for a million bucks. Now that's a lie, baby, I *would*. But you see what I mean?" She turned away from the window. "Now I'm going to play the winner. Who's the winner, gentlemen? Look out, 'cause Echo Malvina O'Brien is rollin' up her sleeves!"

"*You* play, Ralph," Clinton said.

"But you *won*."

"I want to watch."

"Well," Ralph said, resetting the board, "I don't mind playin' another game."

"I just thought of number three," Echo said. "Now listen, Ralph, this is for you. Mamma's takin' up phrenology, and she says you got more on the dime than Albert Schweitzer. You know, *Schweit*zer! That went to Africa with the mustache? Who Mamma has read every single word of, that's he's written."

Ralph looked at Echo. "Where'd Bernice O'Brien ever get hold of a sample of my handwriting?"

"No, Ralph," she said, "phrenology is bones. Skulls and noses and all. Remember them snapshots I took a while back? Well, she took one look at you and said, 'Ralph Williams is a genius!' "

Ralph's hand went instinctively to his head. "Is that what she said? I wonder if there's anything to it?" He felt his skull with his fingertips.

"Oh, a hundred per cent," Echo said. "Listen, I showed her a picture of Felix Frankfurter, who she'd never laid eyes on before, and what do you suppose she said right off the bat? 'Why,' she said, 'I don't know what that man *does,* but what he *ought* to do is be a judge!' —I'm tellin' you, she absolutely floors everybody in Toledo. But the point is that you are a humanitarian of the first water. —Now am I red or black?"

Clinton said, "Did you show her a picture of me?"

"I sure did!" Echo said.

"What she say?"

"Well, she said if you had a haircut, she'd know more. But she swears you got a dandy imagination."

"What about Berry-berry?" he said.

"What about him?"

"I mean," Clinton explained, "did she say what kind of bones he's got?"

"Who, Berry-berry?" Echo said.

"Yeah."

"Oh. Uh-huh. Well, it was all kind of complicated. Sometimes Mamma gets astrology mixed into it. —Now I've got to concentrate. I'm black, right?" She moved one of the checkers. "I had a system for this game once, but it's gone completely out of my head. Clint, will you reach into my pocketbook and help yourself to a cigarette and light one for me? Lately, if I'm not smokin', my mind turns to oatmeal."

"You want a little drink?" Ralph said.

"No thank you, Ralph, it'd put me right to sleep."

Clinton went to the dressing table and opened Echo's pocketbook. He had been through it before on a number of occasions, both at Echo's request and on his own initiative. A person's intimate belongings had always held for him as much fascination as any private conversation or even a personal letter. Echo's pocketbook contained the usual female paraphernalia of cosmetics, Kleenex, address book, identification cards, money, a pocket flashlight; and along with these a pair of pliers, a set of small wrenches, a screw driver, an assortment of nuts and bolts and headlight fuses that were as essential to Echo O'Brien as her mascara and lipstick. —Now a new item had been added: a small medicine bottle containing a clear red liquid. Clinton read these typewritten words on its label:

> For nerves.
> 1 tsp. every 4 hrs.
> Do not exceed.

Clinton removed one of her gold-tipped cigarettes and

225

lighted it for her. As he handed it to her, he heard a car stopping in front of the house.

"There's the truck," he said.

Echo started to rise. "Huh?"

"The truck. I just heard it."

Echo sat down again. "Oh." She looked at the lighted cigarette in her hand, and waved it toward Clinton. "Thanks, lover." Then she took a couple of deep puffs, and as the downstairs door banged shut, she started to sing:

> " 'Hail, hail, the gang's all here,
> What the heck do we care.' "

Berry-berry's footsteps were heard on the stairs.

> " 'What the heck do we care,
> What the heck do we care no-ow?' "

Then she wrinkled her forehead and poured all of her attention onto the checkerboard.

Berry-berry stood at the door of the bedroom. "Hi, everybody."

During the moment in which greetings were exchanged in the room, Clinton continued to study Echo's face. She looked up from the checkerboard and said, "Hi, handsome. Your daddy's skinnin' me alive." Then she gave Berry-berry a smile so filled with love that Clinton felt a pang of deep sadness. It was like a blow to the chest and it had caught him off guard. He wondered why this smile should have so great a power over him: simply because he coveted it for himself? Then why not other smiles on other days?

There was a graver reason that he could not name, even in his own mind, but it was within him and he felt it: that in Echo's gift of love was some unearthly purity that Berry-berry could never return. Then suddenly the sadness grew and extended itself beyond any connection with the persons in the room; and for a moment Clinton knew that in this difference, the difference in the love offerings people make to one another, lay the reason for all the pain of the world. And immediately this knowledge was gone from him. It had been like the visit of some ghostly bird, a truant from heaven: at the instant he had tried to catch hold of it, the creature was gone. Of its message, nothing remained but a vague sense of doom.

Clinton imagined that in some way Echo O'Brien knew these thoughts that were going on in him, and perhaps even shared them.

Now Berry-berry stood between Echo and Ralph, studying the checkerboard. He touched Ralph's shoulder and indicated a possible move.

Ralph said: "That's what I was gonna do anyway. Listen, you think I need help? You're crazier'n I give you credit."

Clinton thought of the bottle in Echo's pocketbook. He wished there was something he could do for her that would give her such perfect calm and peace that she would have no need for the nerve medicine. But he could think of nothing at all.

"He sure *don't* need any help," Echo said. "I bet you didn't know this; I bet you didn't know my worthy opponent has got a bigger brain than Albert Schweitzer! Mamma said it's a fact. She studied his bones in a snapshot."

"Echo," said Clinton.

"What you want, baby?"

"I feel like washing your car. You want me to wash your car?"

"Oh, kiddy, that's a mean job. I wouldn't let you."

"I want to. I feel like it."

"Listen, how *could* you feel like it, washin' all them cars five days a week? Nosiree-bob, honey, nothin' doin'."

"Please?"

"You mean you want to? On a Saturday? —Well, lord knows it needs a good washin'."

"Will you let me move it myself? Into the driveway?"

"Into the *drive*way! I'd trust *you* to move it anywhere you want to. But I feel like a heel."

"Give me the keys."

She took them from her lap and handed them to him. And as she did so, her smile was like a beautiful instrument of torture. But the pain it brought him was in her behalf. He wanted to take Echo away and lock her up in some soft and luxurious place, a place protected by thick stone walls, and he would stand next to her, forever, like a sentry, guarding her.

As he started down the stairs, Clinton heard her voice: "Clinton's a peach, do anything for a person. —Hey, what the hell happened to my kings? Ralph, you are a rat, r-a-t. Lord, where was Echo when they passed out the skulls?"

Clinton put the Dodge in the driveway. He used a whisk broom on its upholstery, swept out the inside of it, wiped the dashboard and steering wheel, and washed the windows. Then he got out the garden hose and several soft rags, and set to work on the body of the car. During much of this time, the sun was shining, and the harder he worked, the better he felt about Echo O'Brien. He had begun to learn that it was possible to shed some of his worries by the simple process of turning his attention elsewhere, especially to some labor that would use up his energies. After a while, a small group of neighbor children had formed in the driveway and soon his imagination was engaged in answering their questions about this strange car. He explained to them that this valuable relic had enough mileage on it to have traveled around the world twenty times over; that jealous manufacturers of competitive cars had offered thousands of dollars just to keep it off the streets, and the lady who owned it was always being hounded by these big executives from Detroit, but she herself was so rich she would not even bother to talk with them. When he had covered the car with a milky liquid wax, he distributed soft rags among these youngsters and allowed them to help with the polishing. Annabel came out later and passed out cookies and prunes and peanuts; and she said, Wasn't it a shame that Berry-berry's pretty blue truck had all that mud on it? Clinton drove the truck into the driveway, and while he and his young crew were busy washing it, Berry-berry and Echo came out to watch. When the job was done, the children climbed into the back of the truck and Berry-berry took them for a ride around the block. Then Echo took them for a ride in her Dodge. When they got back to the house, she gave them all the loose change she had in her pocketbook. The young mob went home happy, and Echo told Clinton her Dodge had never looked better.

Ralph came down to the dining room for the evening meal, and sat at the head of the table in his bathrobe. It seemed to Clinton that everyone was in good spirits. He thought that Echo, to whom he gave most of his attention, was in better form than ever before: perhaps the nerve medicine in her pocketbook had caused him to imagine, earlier in the day, that some deep problem existed, when in reality she might simply have suffered from the effects of a bad night, troublesome dreams of no significance whatever. Because now Echo was herself again, alert, interested, gay, causing the conversation to flourish by touching off in each person, as if by some magical intuition, his secret sources of gold; and drinking in with her eyes all the faces and voices, her responses reflecting with quicksilver sensitivity the mood and quality of each moment. Clinton saw that Berry-berry, too, was attentive, considerate, absorbed by all the talk and activity at the table.

By the time dinner had ended, Clinton had all but forgotten his earlier fears. He accompanied Ralph to his bedroom, and when Annabel had finished with the supper dishes, the three of them sat for an hour reading the Sunday papers. There was not much talk, but they were together in a warm and easy companionship that had been restored to them with the advent of Echo O'Brien in their lives, and with Berry-berry's return. Annabel and Ralph had learned not only to tolerate each other, but to overlook or forgive in each other many of the qualities that had for so many years driven them to separate corners of the house. Ralph had lost much of his former eagerness to offend Annabel's sensibilities; and she, in turn, was less inclined to take issue with him when she found his behavior objectionable. Clinton knew that it was Echo who had, by her own example, brought them to this truce, and led them even beyond it to the pleasures and comforts of mutual sympathy: it seemed to him very much like love; and life itself had gradually been restored to them.

As they sat reading in this fine silence that had been given to them, there was a knock on the bedroom door, and the beautiful people, the lovers, came into the room, dressed for an evening in the night clubs: Echo O'Brien, her slim body sheathed in black and teetering elegantly on the spiked heels of her black slippers, drops of topaz depending from her ears and throat; and at her side, Berry-berry Williams, eyes alight with pride in his companion and the deep pleasure he took in his own animal beauty; his necktie, like his smile, ever so slightly askew,

230

a subtle and good-natured mockery of the manners and customs of the tame and the ordinary. Together they had come into the room to give, from their bounty, this staggering glimpse of themselves, a marvel of luminosity like the glow of angels.

When they had said goodbye and started down the stairs, Annabel and Ralph and Clinton looked at one another and shared, at that moment, the same mindless, wordless sense of wonder. But no one of these three persons knew how often, in the future, this moment would be dredged up in memory, to be looked at and savored, and endlessly pondered.

Ralph soon fell asleep, and Annabel declared herself ready to retire as well. She gave Clinton a good-night kiss and went into the bathroom for her nightly preparations of cold cream and hairpins.

Clinton went to his own room. He thumbed through his notebook and picked up his fountain pen. But he found that he had no desire to record all of the small happenings of the day: Echo's arrival, and the evidence, so trifling as to be almost imaginary, that he had found to support his own fears in her behalf. When a day had been as nearly perfect as this one, it seemed to him that any impulse to dwell on its defects should be thwarted as unwholesome, even wicked. Perhaps, in a few minutes, when Annabel was in bed, he would take his notebook downstairs to her desk, and catch up on the week's mail. But as he lay back on his pillow, to wait for her to finish in the bathroom, his eyes closed, and soon he was fast asleep.

Some sound in the night brought him suddenly to full wakefulness. He wondered how long he had slept. His light had been turned off and there was a bathrobe covering his legs; Annabel must have placed it there. In a moment he heard footsteps on the stairs and the whispering of Echo and Berry-berry. He turned his lamp on, in hopes that one of them, or both, would see the light under his door and come in to visit with him. Then he heard the gentle opening and closing of doors, and the tiptoeing sounds of journeys to the bathroom. In a few minutes there was silence; and then he heard a gentle rapping on the door of his own room.

"Come on in," he whispered.

The door opened. Berry-berry, still dressed, put his head in and looked around. "Where is she?"

"Who?"

"Echo. I saw your light and thought maybe she came in to say good night."

"Huh-uh. But come on in."

"She's not in *her* room either," Berry-berry said.

"Maybe she's getting something to eat. Where'd you go, to Wood's Inn?"

"Yeah, and the Shamrock. You know; all over."

"What time is it?"

"About two. I'm not drunk either."

"Is she a good dancer?"

"Oh, yeah, she's a *good* dancer." Berry-berry seemed unable to stand still. He walked from one end of the room to the other. Then he sat on the bed, and instantly arose. "I wonder where she is though."

"Eating something?"

"No. 'Cause we had a hamburger. I think I'll go see."

"You had a good time though, huh?"

"Oh, God yes."

"Did everybody stare at her?"

"Sure. They always do."

"I don't blame them," Clinton said.

232

"Neither do I."

"If I was them, I sure would."

"Me too." Berry-berry had started toward the door, but abruptly returned. "Have you got some butts? 'Cause I'm out."

"Here." Clinton tossed his packet to Berry-berry.

"Thanks. Only what if you want some yourself?"

"Take 'em. I got more."

"You sure?"

"Sure."

"Okay then, thanks. She's probably downstairs."

Clinton stopped him. "Hey. Did you get any photographs taken?"

"*Photographs?*"

"In the night club. You and Echo at the table. *You* know."

"Oh. —No, they didn't have any of that."

"Oh."

Berry-berry went out and closed the door. Clinton got up and went to the bathroom. On the way back to his room, he paused at the stairway and listened for their voices. Then, barefooted, he went down to the landing and inclined his head toward the kitchen. There were no sounds at all. He went down to the front door. Echo's car was parked in front of the house, and Berry-berry's truck right in front of it. Then Clinton noticed a small patch of light on the driveway, reflected from the basement window. As he stepped out onto the porch, closing the door softly behind him, he could hear their voices from the open window. He stepped into the driveway and stood there, pressed against the wall of the house, listening. The first words he could make out were spoken by Berry-berry.

"I can *tell*," he said.

"No, you can't, baby," said Echo. "You're just bein'

sweet and considerate. I should've known better'n drink that coffee is all."

"Maybe Annabel's got a sleeping pill."

"What, and wake her up? Huh-*uh.*"

"She won't mind."

"No, what I'll do is throw this puzzle together and carry it up to Ralph tomorrow. You go ahead on up to bed, hear me?"

"You want me to close the windows?"

"No, thanks, I like the air. Now, listen, I mean it, I want you to go on on up. I'll be sleepy in no time."

Clinton was afraid Berry-berry might go back upstairs and notice his absence. He hurried back into the house and up the stairs to his room, and waited for several minutes, expecting to hear Berry-berry's footsteps. He knew that if Berry-berry remained in the basement, he himself would be unable to resist eavesdropping on their conversation. He tried to will himself to sleep, but as the moments passed he knew that sleep was impossible for him. Berry-berry had been questioning Echo, apparently about her insomnia. She had blamed it on a cup of coffee. If Berry-berry had believed her, wouldn't he simply come to bed and let her amuse herself with the puzzle until she felt inclined to sleep? In Clinton's heart, he knew that sooner or later he would be crouched outside the basement window, listening. Certainly it was within his power to resist the temptation altogether, but somehow he had convinced himself that there was a *reason* for his witnessing their conversation: it had to do with Berry-berry's restless demeanor of a few moments ago, and his own deep concern for Echo.

Clinton turned out his light, closed his door, and went downstairs. He went this time to the opposite side of the house. He knew that from the vantage point of the win-

234

dow nearest the furnace, he could see without being seen, hear without being heard. The ground was damp, but he knelt down, and waited.

Echo was seated at Ralph's card table, sorting out the pieces of the puzzle. Berry-berry was standing on the other side of the table, looking at her. An unnatural silence was taking place, and Clinton felt it sharply. Echo continued with the puzzle: by family procedure, one began by placing all pieces of like value in separate groups around the edges of the table, and all border pieces in the center. Echo, her cigarette hanging from her lips, moved through this early process with considerable speed, her full attention apparently on the table.

"Why is it," Berry-berry said, "you have to pretend you're so goddam interested in that puzzle?"

Echo took her cigarette from her mouth and looked at him with genuine concern. "Berry-berry," she said, "I'll stop. This minute, if you want me to. Do you?"

"Don't you have something to say to me?"

"No, baby, I don't," she said gently.

"I think I better have a drink."

"Will you pour me a thimble, too?" she said.

Berry-berry moved out of Clinton's line of vision. Apparently he had gone to the kitchen for Ralph's liquor. Echo watched him leave. Then she straightened her body and took a deep breath of air. Looking up, her eyes somewhere in the rafters of the basement, she made the Sign of the Cross, as Catholics do; her lips moved in some brief and silent prayer. Then, quickly, she returned the cigarette to her mouth, and went to work on the puzzle. Berry-berry came back carrying one glass and a bottle nearly half full of bourbon. He poured some of it into the glass, and set the glass on the table. Echo took a sip from it.

"Whee!" she said. "Straight!"

235

"You want water?"

"This is fine, thanks. Now listen, if you want to talk, and this puzzle makes you nervous—just say so."

"Go ahead if you want to, I don't care. I'm not that touchy. God, I hope I'm not that touchy."

"I want to thank you for tonight, lover. Best time I ever had."

"You shouldn't call me lover, not around here."

"I'm sorry. —Boy, I'd like to've danced my heels off. Usually a man wants to quit after two or three."

"Has that been your experience?"

"Mm-hmm. But I could go on all night."

"Could you?"

"Yes. I could. —Now, Berry-berry, the reason I came down here was so you all could sleep. And I think you *need* it. So go on on up, for heaven sake."

Berry-berry was silent. Still standing, he leaned with both elbows on the table. After a long moment, he said, "Echo. Why did you tell me you were a virgin?"

"Because you *asked* me, honey. And I was. It just happened to be the truth. And as far as my *new* status goes, I wouldn't change it for all the tea in China. So quit worryin' about it, why don't you?"

"Because your boy friend was impotent? Is that why?"

"Yeah. That's why."

Berry-berry stood straight and took a long drink of whisky. Then he sat down in the big chair and threw his leg over the arm of it.

"Did you ever try to—*help* him?"

Clinton watched Echo's face. The meaning of Berry-berry's question reached her slowly. Then she looked at him and said: "There wasn't anything there to help. You understand what I mean?"

"Yeah."

236

Echo took another sip from her glass, and lighted a fresh cigarette. Berry-berry reached for it. She gave it to him, and lighted another one for herself.

"Why is it," Berry-berry said, "you never married anybody else?"

"I guess I'm just backward."

"Or even went to bed with anybody else?"

Clinton felt there was a definite edge on Berry-berry's voice; he seemed to be trying to provoke an argument, and Echo knew it.

"You know, Berry-berry," she said, "something tells me not to answer that question."

"Why?"

"I think it might make you sore. Am I right?"

"Maybe. Would that be so terrible?"

"Maybe not. But let's just skip it anyway."

"No, I want to know. Why?"

"You *know* why."

"Because you didn't love anybody else?"

Echo made no attempt to answer this question.

Suddenly Berry-Berry said:

"You're pregnant, aren't you." He made it sound more like a statement than a question. When Echo offered no comment, he repeated, with unmistakable annoyance in his voice: "*Aren't you.*"

In the moment that these words hovered in the air, in the moment before they set out on their path toward the future, Clinton saw, as in a dream of war—thunderous bright red explosions and the aftermath, blood and pain and death—saw and heard all the colors and sounds these words would evoke: saw the officer's wife in Norfolk, the Christmas madonna in Biloxi, numbers of wounded and bleeding women, saw these words as palpable things like buttons that had been pushed, releasing some terrible

237

energy that no one could ever stop; it would go crashing blindly into the next moments, bruising, cutting, crushing whatever lay in its path, and then go on, careening into the hours that followed, the weeks and months, and perhaps into the years as well. —But he knew with even greater certainty that there was nothing he could do about it; only listen. And watch.

Echo continued to work on the puzzle. "Whether or not I'm pregnant," she said, slowly and with a careful effort at making herself understood, "is none of your business."

"Because you aren't ready to spring it. Is that it? Want to choose your own moment?"

Echo turned to face him for a moment. Perhaps she wanted to believe, as Clinton wanted to, that the cruelty in his eyes and in the twist of his mouth was not actual but illusory, a trick of light and shadow, an accident of her own vision. She looked away from him, and then spoke:

"Why don't you give a little thought to what you're saying?"

"All right. I'm sorry."

"No need to apologize."

"Are you pregnant?" he said quietly.

"Yes, I am." Echo took another drink, and turned her chair toward Berry-berry. "I've got a few things to say to you, handsome."

Berry-berry sat motionless in his chair, his face immobile now, betraying an absence of emotion more terrifying than fury.

Echo leaned forward in her chair and spoke so softly that the words were scarcely audible to Clinton.

"You've given me all I want from you. Do you hear?"

There was no sign from Berry-berry that he had heard her at all. But she continued to speak, quietly, and with

238

strength: "I'm gonna try to say something clear, real clear. Now just give me a minute."

She settled back in her chair and closed her eyes for a moment, as if the words she would speak were written in her own private darkness. "When you and me, when we first got together, the two of us, and I knew how I felt about you—I decided I'd take a gamble. And I did. I took a gamble that someday you'd get to where you loved me. I don't mean marry me. I mean love me."

She stopped talking. Her eyelashes were wet. Clinton felt that in this brief silence Echo prayed for strength with which to restrain these tears; and he tried to pray with her, in his own way, by willing that some miracle would bring Berry-berry to her side.

Echo leaned forward again, and opened her eyes. "Listen, Berry-berry, I guess I must've lost. But *you* didn't. You're free as the day God made you. You hear me, baby?" She laid her fingertips on his hand, and Berry-berry, withdrawing instinctively from her touch, rose to his feet with a movement so violent that it caused her to gasp. He backed away from her and stood looking at her for a moment, as if all his will were required to keep him from retreating altogether.

"Oh, God," Echo said, "I wish I hadn't done that! I'm sorry! I shouldn't ever've touched you like that! Believe me, I . . ."

Berry-berry turned suddenly and was gone. Echo's impulse was to follow him, but she stopped after taking two or three steps. "Berry-berry. Berry-berry." She spoke his name so softly that it seemed not to be intended for his ears at all; it was a sound of mourning.

Clinton heard the side door of the house as it slammed shut. Echo removed her high heels and murmured aloud to herself. "Oh, God, make me behave, don't let me be a

239

fool!" Then she hurried to the stairs and followed Berry-berry.

Clinton stood up. He no longer cared whether or not his presence was known to them. He walked around to the front of the house and stood in the middle of the lawn. Berry-berry had jumped into his truck and started the motor. Clinton watched its rapid progress up the street. Then he saw Echo hurrying down the driveway in her stockinged feet, carrying her shoes. She ran down past the sidewalk and into the street.

The truck turned the corner and was out of sight. Echo remained standing in the street for a few seconds, apparently too confounded to move. Then, suddenly aware of herself, she looked at the high heels she carried and studied them as if she had forgotten what they were or how she came to have them in her hands. She looked up the street again, in the direction in which the truck had gone, and then she looked at the house; and then she saw her car. The big old Dodge seemed to be the only object that was familiar to her. She walked over to it, and reached out to touch its fender.

Clinton wanted to call out to her, go to her side. But he felt that in her bewilderment his sudden and unexpected presence would frighten her. As he tried to think of some way to avoid this danger, Echo started up the path to the house, and went inside. Clinton moved closer to the front steps so that he could watch her movements inside. She stood in the front hall for a moment, and then went into the living room, turned on the light, and sat at Annabel's desk. Annabel's stationery was in a box on the shelf. Echo took a sheet of paper and began to write. Then she stopped, put the paper in the wastebasket, and started over again. After a moment, she paused, read what she had written, and placed this second attempt in the wastebasket with the first. Then she turned out the lamp and hurried up the stairs to her room.

Clinton went inside and withdrew the crumpled papers from the basket. In the light of the hallway, he read them. The handwriting was so large and sprawling that the words "Dear Annabel" alone took up an entire line:

DEAR ANNABEL,
Mamma's nurse just called me up and

The second note began:

DEAR ANNABEL,
I could not sleep and all of a sudden for no reason at all I got worried about Mamma and thought

Clinton folded the two sheets of paper and put them in his hip pocket. He knew she was upstairs packing her suitcase, and he wanted to go up and stop her. But their voices might awaken Annabel. He decided to wait for her on the front porch. He turned on the light over the door. She would first see the light, and then him, and his presence would not startle her. He sat on the front steps, clearly visible from the door, and waited.

In a moment, Clinton heard her footsteps on the stairway, and then she was at the door.

"Echo?"

"Yes, honey. It's me. Did I wake you up?"

"No. I was awake anyway."

He got up and opened the door. He held out his hand, and she let him carry the suitcase.

"I guess you wonder what I'm doin'," she said, "sneakin' out like this." Echo's voice and manner were subdued without being solemn or sad. There was no sign that she had been weeping. It seemed to Clinton that her calm had been achieved by an act of will that commanded respect.

All of the things he had wanted to say to her froze inside him.

"Do you have to go?" he said.

"I have to, Clint. I have to go."

He had meant to embrace her, to express his love for her, to offer his help. He had imagined that he would take her in his arms, hold her close to him; and she would weep on his shoulder and empty her heart to him. But now he could not even look at her. Her self-possession so dumfounded him that he could only walk down the path at her side, carrying her suitcase. Echo had become a royal figure, exalted by her own anguish. Clinton's love for her made him proud to be her fool, and with the fool's wisdom he was silent.

"Will you tell Annabel not to worry?" Echo said. "I'll call her up tomorrow."

He put the suitcase in the back seat of the car.

"I'll tell her," he said.

He opened the door for her, at the driver's side, and Echo climbed in. Clinton stood next to the car as she started the motor.

"Maybe you better roll up the windows," he said. "There's no stars out or anything."

"I love to drive in the rain," Echo said. "I just love it. —Have you got a light, handsome?"

He took a book of matches from his pocket and struck one of them, holding it in a special way that guarded the flame from the wind. She inhaled deeply and looked at him, and as the smoke rose from her face she said:

"You want to kiss me g'bye, lover?"

"You're comin' back, aren't you?"

"You bet your boots I'm comin' back." She offered her cheek and he kissed it. Then Clinton offered his own cheek and she kissed him back. Clinton stepped away from the car. Echo placed the gear into position and raced the motor with her foot. Then she hesitated for a moment.

"You wrote me a note once, didn't you?" she said.

He nodded.

"Well, that note, I just wanted you to know—it goes double."

As she started to smile, her face seemed to crumble from within; and her tears had begun to flow. Then the car was in motion. And Echo O'Brien was gone.

part 4

WORD OF Echo O'Brien's death reached Seminary Street on Sunday, a few minutes before noon.

Her mother's nurse and companion, a Mrs. Foss, delivered to Annabel on the telephone only the bare fact itself—that there had been a crash in which Echo was killed. An hour later, when the first terrible waves of anguish and consternation had subsided in the Williams household, Annabel and Clinton stood by as Ralph put in a call to Toledo.

He learned from Mrs. Foss, in this second conversation, that Echo's automobile had left the highway, just forty-some miles south of Toledo, that it had crashed into the brick chimney of a private residence, that death had come during the first instant after the impact. The accident had taken place during a heavy storm, but its exact cause was not known.

Ralph suggested that Annabel's presence in Toledo might be helpful to the girl's mother. Mrs. Foss agreed. She said that the doctor had given Bernice O'Brien an injection to induce sleep; but that, in her opinion, the comfort to the poor woman, if Annabel could be at her side when she awakened, might be invaluable.

Ralph offered to drive her to Toledo in the family car, but Annabel held that it was the duty of Berry-berry to accompany her. Besides, she insisted, Ralph should remain in bed.

Annabel refused to believe that Berry-berry would stay away for long. Though Clinton had offered no information at all concerning the events of the night, Annabel had deduced, from the absence of both of the lovers, that some quarrel had taken place between them. But now, because the girl had died as an indirect result of it, Annabel could not permit herself to imagine that this quarrel had been of any real importance to either of them.

Therefore, while she prepared for her trip, Ralph, at her insistence, made several attempts to reach Berry-berry by telephone at his establishment in Apple Mountain. But as these attempts failed, it was decided that Clinton would drive his mother to Toledo; and in the evening he would return, alone, to Seminary Street. Then, in two or three days, he and his father—and Berry-berry, if they could find him—would drive up together for the funeral.

By midafternoon Clinton and Annabel had set out on their trip. The sun was shining. The sky was blue. There were the sounds of Lake Erie's strong winds, which made the earth seem flagrantly alive. But the journey was otherwise a quiet one. Annabel occasionally gave voice to her inability to believe that this dreadful thing had actually taken place, but from time to time, when the fact itself momentarily overwhelmed her disbelief, she wept silently into her handkerchief.

There were, however, in Clinton, no such fluctuations: no disbelief and no sorrow. He was waiting. His mind and his heart and his spirit were waiting. He knew, though he could not have put the knowledge into words, that there was still some event that had yet to take place. And when it had—whatever it was—his feelings would then take some outward form. Meanwhile, it did not even occur to him to question his lack of emotion. Instead, he drove through the afternoon and across northern Ohio, experiencing only a kind of elation that was almost pleasurable. And he waited.

They arrived in Toledo during the first moments of twilight. The O'Brien cottage looked familiar to Clinton, even though he had never seen it before. As he drove the car into the driveway, he saw the garage at the end of the yard, its doors flung wide, yawning with emptiness. The sight of it caused him to shudder.

"I guess I better not come in," Clinton said.

"Well precious," Annabel said, "to tell you the truth, I don't know what shape she'll be in. —Will you do something about food?"

"Yes."

"And before you start that long drive back. Promise?"

"I promise."

They kissed each other. "Bless you," Annabel said, "for being so sweet."

" 'Bye," he said.

Clinton backed out of the driveway and started at once on the trip back to Cleveland. He had no intention of eating. The possibility, even when Annabel had mentioned it, did not actually touch him at all. He filled the gas tank at a station near the edge of town, and even before the twilight had ended, he was on the highway again.

He could not remember a time in which his senses had been so keen. His eyes beheld colors and forms with a new clarity that gave to the pavement and the countryside and the sky a fresh kinship with one another, and with himself. The steering wheel did not seem to him any different from his own hands, but an extension of them, of himself; and it possessed no lesser degree of life and reality than his own flesh.

Not only in his senses, but in his mind, too, he experienced this peculiar clarity. He felt that he knew everything, understood everything. He had only to turn his mind to the basement on Seminary Street and, with no further effort at memory, it presented to him a word-for-word re-enactment of the conversation he had overheard there between Berry-berry and Echo. During the drive back to Cleveland, he tested this power over and over again, and not once did it fail him. He could see these people with photographic accuracy, hear their voices, witness over and over again the cruelty, the pain. And with this same facility, his mind could evoke for him the sight of Annabel's hands, clutching the receiver at noon: Annabel's hands, assuming the ghastly shapes of disaster, had told the tale more eloquently than either her face or her voice could have done: "Echo," they said, spread-fingered. "Crash," they said, twisting into themselves, against the instrument. "Dead," they said, suddenly still. "I don't believe it," they said, massaging the receiver as if to revive it.

And Ralph Williams, bare-legged, clad only in his bathrobe, frowning with anguish, his mouth open: "Ooh. Oh. Oh," he repeated over and over again. He went out to the front porch and looked up and down the street, searching for the car in which Echo had been killed. Then he had come back into the house and held Annabel in his arms, uttering over and over again the pained monosyllable that expressed his profound reluctance to accept the truth; and he shook his head back and forth more than a hundred times, trying to wish it away from them all.

Clinton had at his disposal all of these images and sounds, and he could review them at will. This gave him a sense of power that was akin to actual physical joy. At one moment, it even occurred to him that if he wanted to he could re-enact in his mind the moments of love-making with Shirley in Key Bonita, and with such reality that they would result in an actual orgasm. This thought alone caused his blood to rise, and for a moment he was frightened by it, intimidated by his own powers.

He knew there was another thought, an idea, growing in him, waiting to take hold of him, and that when it came, the moment of this thought, his body would again act in obedience to it; and the result would be violent, ugly. This was the thought his mind was trying to evade and postpone, as he forced it to concentrate on the highway, the sky, the waters of Lake Erie, the overwhelming present.

Now, it has been said that this state was almost pleasurable. But there was something lacking in it. The lack was profound. It was like a poison that brought fear and anxiety in equal portions with the pleasure. The fact was that Clinton was in a condition similar to that of a man to whom some evil drug has been administered. He experienced a similar, uncanny sense of power; and a similar poison as well: the total lack of any love whatsoever. And in this void was anger, anger so profound he could not even dare admit to himself its presence.

The trip from Toledo to Cleveland takes, under normal conditions, and in a decent car, about two hours and a half. Clinton made repeated efforts to maintain the legal speed limits, but as his mind was absorbed mostly by other matters, the car seemed to charge forward on its own at the rate of some eighty miles an hour. In no time at all, it seemed, Clinton was guiding the car into the driveway at Seminary Street.

There was one light burning behind the upstairs window shade of Ralph's bedroom, but the rest of the place was dark. It had the look of disaster about it. Clinton felt that any passer-by could take one look at the house and see clearly reflected in it the anguish of the people who lived inside. In his shocked condition, with his new, keener perception of the world, he assigned qualities of sense and spirit to everything he encountered; and the house was sad; contemptuous, too, of all the wickedness that had taken place in its shelter; as he passed under the porch roof, he touched its supporting pillar and found that it had gone cold. He opened the door and went inside.

249

"*Ralph!*" he called. "*I'm back!*" He went up to Ralph's room. The old man was propped up in bed. There were newspapers on the floor and in his lap, but he did not seem to have been reading them. The crease between his eyebrows was deeper, his nasal folds were wrinkled, the edges of his mouth turned down. Like an unhappy old monkey, dyspeptic, bewildered, he turned his wide-open eyes to Clinton.

"How'd you do? The car handle all right?"

"Yeah, it handled good. You want some food?"

"Naw, I had baloney, beer. —You left her there okay, huh?"

"Yeah."

"Her bein' there is the right thing."

"Sure it is."

The old man looked at the foot of the bed.

"He was here."

"Berry-berry? He was here?"

"Yeah," Ralph said. "He left, maybe an hour ago." The old man studied his wrist, and then he began to rub it with his thumb, trying to form a noodle.

Clinton said, "What'd he have to say?"

"Oh, he—uh—needs some money."

"I mean, what'd he say about—what happened?"

The old man seemed ashamed. He mumbled evasively: "He didn't have much to say. He—uh, said it was a terrible thing, just terrible."

Neither Ralph nor Clinton could look at each other. Ralph made a thorough study of his entire left arm. Clinton looked at the bedside stand, the telephone, the medicine bottles, Annabel's ship's-wheel lamp, the ash tray.

"Where is he?" Clinton said.

"I don't know."

"I guess he'll go out and maybe get drunk, huh?"

Ralph shrugged. "I suppose. I suppose that's what *any-body'd* do. Thing like this, you know, it's a shock, it's a terrible thing. If Echo O'Brien was an ordinary girl, it'd been bad enough. But she was a queen, for godsake."

Clinton nodded. "Does he figure to go up with us? Tuesday?"

"I don't know about that. Doesn't look like he'll be able to make it. He wants some money."

"From you?"

"Yeah, that's right."

"To go away?"

Ralph made no direct answer to this question. He looked straight ahead for a moment. His face bore the blank and senseless expression of a person who imagines himself alone. When finally he spoke, there seemed to be no wind supporting his voice: "He wasn't sure he'd be able to make the funeral."

Now it happened that at this moment Clinton's eye went to the bottom shelf of the bedside stand and came to rest on a copy of the Cleveland Telephone Directory. This thick book held his full attention for a long time; even as he spoke brief, mechanical phrases to Ralph, his mind was caught and held by it.

Ralph said, "He was talking something about he wanted money. I told him we'd look into that—at another time. But I let him have twenty. You think I did right?"

"I guess." Clinton studied the image of Mercury on the cover of the directory, the glistening body, the winged helmet, the feathered feet, the hand held high, pointing, beckoning. "Ralph, I want to ask you a favor. Can I borrow the car? For another while?"

"I wonder," Ralph said. Then he lay back on his pillow, folded his hands across his stomach, and looked at the ceiling: "You know, I've made it a point never to—never to clamp down on you bozos."

"Can I use it?" Clinton said.

Ralph nodded; but he had not even heard Clinton's request. Clinton started out of the room. Ralph said, "Where you going?"

"Just out for a while. You want anything?"

"No, I don't need anything."

"G'bye."

Clinton hurried down the stairs, pausing on the landing just long enough to light a cigarette; and then he proceeded out the front door and into the car. As he put the key in the dashboard, something cautioned him against driving at any reckless speed: it seemed important to do everything well, with no push or strain; it was essential that he maintain just the right rhythm, the simple thoughtless pace appropriate to each moment as it arrived. Evenness. Perfect evenness was needed.

Down Apple Mountain's long main street. Across the wooden bridge at the edge of town. The dirt road, and a turn to the left. Apples in the air, sweet and rotting. An arbor of gnarled branches over the driveway. Slow. Slow through the slush and the puddles. Continue, but slow.

See anything? Just a light. The truck is gone. Stop! Reverse gears. Back up. Slow through the mud puddles, and even slower at the road. Back out of here. Leave the car somewhere.

Why?

No questions now. Put the car away, anywhere. Out of sight. A gray shed, empty and abandoned. Park behind it. Put the lights out, keys in your pocket. Walk back to the

252

house. No hurry. You have half an hour. Maybe more. What will happen at the house?

No questions. One step, one moment at a time. No thinking. Don't spoil it with thinking. Smell the sweetness of the air. See the black earth. All the apples going back into it. The black earth eating the apples, silently sucking in the sweetness. Walk around the puddles. The rainfall helps to rot the apples. And nature thrives on what it kills.

There's a light in the downstairs bedroom. Listen at the window. No sounds. Silence. Are they asleep? Never mind. Go to the back door. Something scurrying about under the house. Field mice. Now wipe your feet. The door is unlocked. Step inside. Quiet. Untie your shoes; take them off. Go softly up the stairs; careful of the bottles on the steps; keep close to the wall and the boards won't creak.

Now you're here. You can do anything.

But what?

Don't think. Thinking makes fear. Turn on the light.

Won't they see it?

Of course not. —There's a bottle under the bed. Go ahead. Why not? Just a couple of swallows. Now the drawer, the bottom drawer. Softly, slowly. No hurry.

Mercury! Hello, Mercury.

Now breathe deep and slow. Relax, drop your shoulders, don't hunch. Don't tighten up. Now open the directory.

Oh, God!

Shut up. Now take it in your hand. It's heavy, and cool. It's wonderful the way they make these things to fit in your hand, just right. Comfortable.

Ugly.

What's ugly? That's a word. That's *thinking*. Don't think. Why not have a cigarette and one more swallow from the bottle. There. Now, better put the bottle under the bed.

If I just pressed my finger against this trigger, if I just squeezed . . .

Shh-hh. One thing at a time.

Turn out that light, you won't need it. Now loosen the bulb. Unscrew it, one full turn. He'll think it's burnt out. Perfect. Now sit down and wait. Don't tighten up and don't think. Just sit.

Maybe if my notebook was here, I could . . .

You don't need it. You can remember it all, every word you've ever written down.

Dearest friend, dearest Bernice, I am afraid you find me at a low ebb as I have been fighting the blues something awful. Isn't it ironical that I have no one to turn to . . .

It's true. I can remember it all. Maybe I won't have to carry it with me, ever again. I'll be free to just . . .

Besides, I am getting curious about Echo O'Brien, the old maid from Toledo that's coming to visit, so why shouldn't I get a look at her first, as there is always time for suicide at a later date.

Will I use this gun? On myself?

Don't be such a fatass phony. You know goddam well what you're going to do with that gun. You think you're some kind of a saint? the only killer in the family is Berry-berry? Swinging his tail around, shoving his meat into any woman he wants? Let the slobs pay the piper. Just smile, move in, screw, *disappearo!* Or maybe stick around for a while, just long enough to slice off her nipples for her.

Then I've come here to kill him. Will I do it?

Take it slow. Wait and see. One moment at a time.

Can a ghost keep a notebook?

Ha.

Dearest Annabel, such beautiful weather here, Echo

254

took me for drive in country Sunday aft, wildflowers all over, I thrive in summer but Echo restless. Gets dolled up and rattles her car keys. But God will find way.

Berry-berry doesn't seem to ever get bothered with these thoughts. He just says, "Isn't it wild?"

So I went to sleep and had this crummy dream about Shirley and her little brother, Willy.

"Ize told once that lavender was my most becomin' color, so I spent an entire Sunday dyeing just about everything I own, even my underwear and my panda."

This is a really crummy dream. Anyway, this person came along and started to climb up the candied-apple tree. He had a real wild look in his eye and you could tell he was the kind of a creep that absolutely despises all little kids. So he started to shake this high branch for all he was worth, and Willy fell out of the tree and got killed. I mean it wasn't any accident.

"Can she bake a cherry pie, Willy boy, Willy boy?
Can she bake a cherry pie, charming Willy?"

I thought about Echo's eyes, how immense they are, and how lonesome, and that day at the airport, the way she kept filling her eyes up with everything she saw, so when it was over she'd have something left. "Berry-berry," I said, "you love her, don't you?" He looked at the picture of Abraham Lincoln. "Yeah, I guess I do."

I mean it wasn't any accident.

"Listen, if I had to put caviar in her crankcase every ten minutes, I wouldn't sell her for a million bucks. I just had such a scrumptious drive comin' down. Made it in just under two hours. I mean, sweetheart, I moved!"

No accident, because there was this stranger in the apple tree that despised all little kids.

255

You don't even have to say his last name. Just say Berry-berry.

If I was to just press my finger against it, if I was to just squeeze . . .

Sh-hh. One thing at a time. Don't think.

My head aches. I want to go home.

It's too late now. Listen.

I want to go home.

It's too late. Here he comes.

Listen.

The sounds of the truck outside, the motor stopping, the slamming of the door. Silence. More silence. Footsteps on the porch. The front door opening. And closing.

Sit still. Wait. It's too late now.

Voices downstairs. Two voices. Berry-berry and a woman. The woman is laughing. Now they're in the kitchen.

THE WOMAN: "I'll come up later, baby; later, I promise."

BERRY-BERRY: "Later'll be too late. Come on."

THE WOMAN: "Honest, baby, I can't. I got to go toi-toi."

BERRY-BERRY: "You just *went* toi-toi. Come on."

THE WOMAN: "Please, sweetie, don't force me. Honestly, you're the best thing, but when you're drunk, I . . . Oh, please, don't, baby, you hurt me bad. I'll do anything you say. I know you don't mean to hurt me, baby, but . . . Let go! *Please!*"

Footsteps on the stairs. A long sustained crashing sound. Bottles falling, bottles breaking.

THE WOMAN: "For Chrisake! Oh, baby, you need a housekeeper!" (Laughter.) "Jesus, this is spooky. Where's the goddam *light?*"

The light! They'll see me!

Don't worry. The bulb is unscrewed. Remember?
What if they tighten it up?
They won't.
I didn't know he'd have a woman with him.
She won't stay long. Easy, breathe easy, breathe through your mouth. Relax, and don't move.
Now they're on the bed.
Listen.

THE WOMAN: "Here, I'll help you."

BERRY-BERRY: "Help me. Help me."

THE WOMAN: "There, baby, now just lay back and rest. Will you do that for mamma?"

BERRY-BERRY: "Don't leave me, don't leave."

THE WOMAN: "I wouldn't leave you, baby. Mamma's here."

BERRY-BERRY: "Lie down with me."

THE WOMAN: "What makes you want to hurt Mamma? Please, sweetheart. You want to put your hand there? All right, baby, put your hand there."

A long silence.

BERRY-BERRY: "Are you Annabel?"

THE WOMAN: "That's right, baby; I'm Annabel."

Annabel? Does he think she's Annabel?
Don't think. Don't think.
But he thinks she's Anna . . .
Don't think! Thoughts make fear, fear makes noise, noise makes trouble. Ss-shh. Listen. Wait.

BERRY-BERRY: "We shouldn't do this. You shouldn't be here."

THE WOMAN: "You want me to go?"

BERRY-BERRY: "No! Stay!"

THE WOMAN: "Let go, baby. I mean it. You're hurtin' me."

Movements on the bed. Violent motion. Heavy breathing. A sudden hard slap. The woman's voice, loud, heavy with anger: "I'll *kill*—you sonofabitch! I swear, I'll kill!" Another impact of fist against flesh, this time harder. Berry-berry groaning with pain.

THE WOMAN: "You sorry sonofabitch. Now lay there and die, will you do that for me? You sorry, sorry bastard?"

The woman stands for a moment at the bedside, breathing heavily, then turns quickly to the door, and goes out, slamming it behind her. Footsteps on the stairs, and on the first floor. The front door opening, closing. Silence. The motor starting, the truck backing up the driveway.

What's wrong with Berry-berry? What did she do to him?

Keep your seat. Listen. Hear him breathing? Quick, hysterical breaths. Now he's sobbing.

And now he's crying.

She made him cry.

Berry-berry?

Crying?

Crying, yes.

Clinton shuddered from head to foot, every inch of him, inside and out. And this sudden violent activity of his body was like a death rattle.

In this instant, with no motion other than this profound spasm, he felt himself transported to some high place, far above the house. This high place was not even a cloud, as one might travel to in imagination or in a dream. Nor was it any place at all: it was simply distance, suspension, a view: and it was terrifying to be there.

Far below, on the ground, in the midst of an orchard so large that it extended all the way to the sides of the earth, sat Berry-berry's tiny and fragile house. In the surround-

258

ing trees of this vast orchard, perched high on all the naked limbs, were tens of thousands of people, all children, and all singing. —All of the people he knew or had ever known were in these branches, and he recognized them, even Annabel and Ralph, but now they were child-people. Each person, of these tens of thousands, sang his individual song, each one separate, different; and it was impossible to make out the words or melodies. Heard from so great a height, all of them together made one sound that was like the wind. But then the wind itself came along, and it made no sound at all. It crept in from all sides, invisible and silent. Clinton knew there was no way to warn anyone of the approach of a menace that could neither be seen nor heard; therefore he had no choice but to witness whatever might take place. So the wind blew, and it blew with such force that all the branches of all the trees, even the highest ones, began to shake so violently that all of the tiny singers were blown away. The branches were bare and silent again and there were no children left in the world.

In the little house, on the top floor, Clinton saw two young men. One of them lay on the bed, fast asleep. The other, seated in a chair, a revolver in his lap, was crying.

Then he himself was back in the room, back into himself. On the bed, Berry-berry was sleeping. Suddenly Clinton knew in an instant all that had taken place. He remembered the scene in the basement on Seminary Street, the terrible telephone call at noon on Sunday, and the nightmare drive to Toledo, the gaping garage doors; and he felt the wetness of his own face and, in his lap, the cold dead weight of the revolver.

Now he could cry. He cried tears that came from the deepest parts of him. It was like a convulsion, a hemorrhage of tears, and the fluids ran from his nose and from his eyes, they rose in him from every corner of his heart. He made no attempt to silence himself, or to stifle this flow. He even encouraged it. He found sorrows hidden deep in the bowels of his memory and of his spirit, agonies he had never known existed. And he dredged them up from all these inside crevices and paraded them before the eye of his mind. Every image that hovered there, even for an instant—not only of Echo, Annabel, Shirley, Bernice, Berry-berry, Ralph, of the invisible little Willy—but of any face he could remember from casual encounters on street-cars, in drugstores, in crowds, even those of dream-people from other ages, other countries—each of them brought forth a new torrent of these profound waters of his sorrow. His lungs pressed against his heart, his stomach twisted and convulsed itself; and the pain became physical as he cried for all the dead children, transmuted, newly become adults, who had flown from the invisible stranger who shook the high branches of all the apple trees in all the orchards of the world.

Now this return to physical pain, this sense of weariness, emptiness, weakness of body, came to him like a sweet breeze to a soul in Purgatory: the gates swayed gently open and he drifted easily into sleep. It was like freedom.

Berry-berry was the first to awaken. In his restless sleep he had moved so close to the edge of the bed that he was virtually hanging there in such precarious imbalance that a sharp sense of falling from some great height brought him with a shock of fear to full wakefulness. He opened his eyes to the daylight that touched the floor. This gave him a momentary sense of physical safety, but it was followed too quickly by a memory of all that had taken place on the previous day. He forced his eyes to close and tried to will himself back to unconsciousness. But his body resisted these efforts: there was a dull pain at the base of his skull, his mouth and throat were unbearably dry. These residual effects of heavy drinking were too familiar to allow him to pretend for long that sleep might, by some miracle, return to him.

In one last futile effort against these odds, he turned to lie flat on his back; it was then that he saw Clinton, slumped awkwardly in the chair, still fast asleep.

He rose quickly to a sitting position on the edge of the bed; and his eyes came in contact with the gun on Clinton's lap. It rested there, between his legs, upside down, the barrel pointed toward the bed. When Berry-berry had looked at the gun for a moment, and back to his brother's face, and suddenly knew the meaning of what he saw, the knowledge affected him like a poisonous gas that caused not only the discomforts of nausea and a deep visceral spasm of pain, but an overwhelming wave of self-hatred as well. The sound that came from him then was not a word; it was more like a sound of vomiting when there is nothing to be emitted but emptiness. And it was followed by a high and interminable moan that he himself could not even hear. He buried his face in his knees and gave way to it; it was like a prayer so dismal that it became a blasphemy.

When this moment had ended, Berry-berry raised his head and looked at the floor, at Clinton's feet. He was almost afraid to look again at the boy's face. But now, in fact, he had no need to, because in an instant he had become totally absorbed in his brother's foot. He kept looking at it, the soiled black gym shoe, the white fragment of sock that showed above it, the bare ivory-colored portion of leg partly covered by a new adolescent growth of hair.

Suddenly he knew that this foot had something to say to him; it clearly held for him some message, perhaps even the secret of some profoundly mysterious riddle. His eyes danced over the shoe, the ankle, the lower calf of the leg, like some crazy moth bent on deciphering the mystery of light.

And then, though he did not move from the bed, Berry-berry saw himself kneeling on the floor and he took the foot in his lap. In his imagination, he saw himself touch, with his hand, gently, the incredible living flesh of his brother's leg; and as he did so, he knew instantly, and in a way that he had never known before, that there is life in other people than himself, blood and spirit, vulnerability, a heartbeat, a pulse; and he experienced as well, at that instant, in that imagined contact with the livingness of another being, a wave of tenderness so profound that he yearned for its continuance. It seemed that all that he had sought to find with his fists and his tongue and his sex had been yielded to him in a moment, with no effort at all. But coming to him, as it did, from the depths of his own sense of sin, he was fearful of the experience, as if it had in it all the cunning of some supreme punishment: it was his only to be withdrawn from him. Clinton had come here to do violence to him, but he had brought instead a knowledge of love, a knowledge that Berry-berry would be forced to relinquish at the moment his brother awakened. And that would be his doom. He would never in the future be able to submerge himself in purely carnal pursuits, because this moment was inscribing in him the indelible knowledge of their limitations. He would be condemned to go along always, all through his life, carrying with him the intolerable memory of what he had surrendered: the power to know and respect and love the living truth of another.

He looked at Clinton's hands, one of them making a fist

in his lap, and the other supporting his head against the side of the chair. He looked at his face, untroubled, resting, the eyelids moist, lips slightly parted, pink as berries not quite ripe, cheeks pale from the strain of suffering, suffering that Berry-berry knew he had inflicted. He saw him there as he was, and as the four-year-old child who had followed him to school when he was in the fifth grade, the nuisance who had asked a thousand questions of him every day, questions he had seldom bothered to answer; he saw him as the peanut-butter thief, caught red-handed with the goods in his bed with him; a child in a household of older persons, hiding behind doorways and furniture to listen to conversations he could not have understood, or could he? and he saw clearly the arrival of the young boy in Key Bonita in the dead of night, inquiring after him in waterfront dives, at the police station, and in the flea-bag hotel, eagerly offering to a whore the gift of his innocence in gratitude for her company, her friendship, and being led by the dirty hand of Ramírez to the bus station without having found what he had come to seek, a hero who did not even exist, himself.

These reflections, the alternating waves of regret, despair, tenderness for his brother, that Berry-berry experienced, had all taken place within so brief a span of time that they occupied a position in his life that can be compared only to a pause, a semicolon of truth in a long memoir of falsehood. In this pause, Clinton had become, for Berry-berry, a mysterious giant possessed of powers that he himself had little hope of attaining.

When Clinton opened his eyes, he found Berry-berry looking at him, examining him with an expression on his face of dumfoundedness, awe. It took him a moment to realize how he had come to be there, in his brother's room, asleep in a chair. And when suddenly he remembered, his first question to himself was: Does he know? Does he know why I came here?

By this time, Berry-berry had averted his eyes. He pretended to be looking for his shoes, and in a tone of casualness so false that his voice cracked under it, he said: "Hi, kid. You sleep good?"

Clinton murmured something that neither of them understood; and then their eyes met and the knowledge hovered there between them, caught like something black and bleeding and awful on an invisible spit. Berry-berry's eyes dropped to Clinton's lap, the revolver between his thighs. Clinton looked at it, too. And then, once again, neither of them able to avoid it, they looked at each other, and at the terrible thing that hovered in the air between them.

Berry-berry was the first to speak; his voice was a soft dry sound produced without air: "Why didn't you do it?"

Clinton could not find the real answer to this question. He knew it must be somewhere in him, but it would not rise to his lips. His mind was too much occupied with what he saw in Berry-berry; or with what he did not see.

For it was as if some devil had committed a serious robbery against him, and left him only a pale and damaged surface, one that clearly showed all the signs of its having been ransacked: eyes like windows in which one saw rooms that were unfurnished, unpeopled. These eyes did not even have Berry-berry in them any more. The robber had taken his brother away with him and left this effigy. But had there ever been a Berry-berry? On the hundreds of occasions when he, Clinton, as a child, had studied his brother's sleeping body, wondering at all the mysteries it concealed, had he beheld an illusion, an invention of his own that had never had any real existence? Or, if he *had* been there, once, and had been robbed of himself, who was the robber? —It was these questions that Clinton answered when he looked at the figure seated on the bed and said:

"I don't know."

Berry-berry drew himself to his feet, and began to comb his hair at the mirror.

"Well," he said, "I can see why you blame me. It's okay. I don't mind. I've always been the sonofabitch of the family. Every place I go, I make trouble. I'm marked. It's okay. I'm used to it. But in this case, I don't happen to be to blame. I don't happen to be to blame for the fact that she drove like a maniac. She *al*ways did. It wasn't anything new, she was bound to get in a wreck sooner or later. —Okay, I know there was something eating her on Saturday, so she took off in the middle of the night. *I* knew she had something bothering her. That's why I went down to talk to her. But she wouldn't say a word."

This activity at the mirror, and the lies he was telling, seemed to have a curiously beneficial effect on Berry-berry's appearance. Clinton witnessed the return of the old illusion: life, vigor, even a kind of beauty. But since he witnessed as well the actual mechanics of deception by which it was animated, the illusion contained for him no more fascination than the sudden appearance of a brace of rabbits holds for the stagehand who has prepared the magician's props.

"All right," Berry-berry went on, "maybe she had some terrific problem. That's not impossible. Christ knows life isn't easy for *any*body. It could have been cancer, or some other terrible disease, and she just couldn't face it."

"Maybe so," Clinton said. He got up and put the gun away, in the bottom drawer of the bureau. For a moment his eyes came in contact with Berry-berry's reflection in the mirror.

"You going?" Berry-berry asked.

"Yeah, I got to. I got to get home."

"You don't want to have a cup of coffee or anything?"

"I better not. Ralph's probably worried already."

"You know," Berry-berry said, "it *could*'ve been just an accident. I mean, there are such things as accidents. Did that ever occur to anybody?"

"I guess we'll just never know," Clinton said, and he walked over to the door.

Berry-berry stepped out of the wrinkled trousers he had slept in, and took a fresh pair from the closet. "Stay. Stay just long enough for coffee, will you?"

"No, I really got to go."

"Okay, go ahead then. Go on. Only, I'd rather you'd just put all those bullets in me than—think what you think."

"You know what I'm really thinking about?"

"What?"

"About being late for work."

"Yeah? Then what were you doin' up here with my gun in your lap?"

Clinton stood at the door for a moment. Then he turned to look at Berry-berry: "You want me to just—*say* it?"

"Yeah, say it."

"'Cause I was out of my goddam head, that's why, and I wanted to kill you."

"Why *me?*" Berry-berry wanted to hear the truth, not for its own sake, but for the pain it would cause him. Suddenly he had become like one of his own whores, begging to be wounded, punished. Clinton sensed this desire in him, but he did not want to take any part in it.

"I don't know." Clinton left the room and started down the stairs. Berry-berry's voice stopped him.

266

"Clint! Why'd you want to kill me?"

"I said I don't know. Maybe I thought you had some disease. And you couldn't face it."

He continued down the stairs, carefully picking his way through the mess of broken glass and bottles. At the bottom of the flight, he was stopped once again by his brother's voice:

"Clint!"

"What do you want?"

"The other night, Saturday night—were you listening?"

Clinton looked at Berry-berry's figure at the top of the stairs. He saw him only in silhouette. Berry-berry stood there perfectly still and in shadow. Clinton felt he had already revealed too much, and that if he did not give some definite answer, Berry-berry would remain there forever, a silhouette at the top of a dark staircase. This was his reasoning, and he did not consider right or wrong; he felt only that he had to lie, as much for himself as for Berry-berry.

"Listening to what?" he said.

"Nothing."

"See you later."

Clinton went out the back door. The sky was clear and there was a cold wind blowing. He started up the driveway at a good pace, not hurrying, but knowing that the sooner he had left this place altogether, the better off they would be, himself and Berry-berry.

[*Clinton's Notebook*]

>Annabel's end of a conversation with Willidene Gibbs; she picked it up on the first ring.

>"Hello? —Merry Christmas to *you*. With whom am

I speaking, please? . . . I'm afraid I don't recognize the voice, I'm sorry. . . . *Will*idene! Do you know I've phoned you four hundred times, you're never home; and I'm just dying to talk for hours, but I've got all these men to feed, and they're clawing at my elbows right this second, how's *Mis*ter Gibbs? . . . Oh. . . . Oh, Willidene, I couldn't feel worse for you. Oh, you poor thing. (Three more "poor things.") . . . Thank you, Willidene, mine are all healthy as mules, but you tell him we'll come and see him during the holidays. . . . No, not Berry-berry, he's in Santa Barbara, California. Oh, yes, keeping very swanky company. Came within inches of getting married this year—but it didn't pan out. . . . Well, it's *plumbing*, as a matter of fact, but on a very high level. *Man*agement. *You* know."

Ralph was sitting in the living room, working the diagramless crossword puzzle from the Sunday paper. When Annabel got to the part about Berry-berry, he looked at me the whole while, and then he went back to work on the puzzle. I write things down right in front of both of them once in a while, and they don't even seem to notice it.

Anyway, I missed some in-between stuff and when the talk came around to me, I got interested again.

"Oh, *that* little snotnose. Willidene, he may surprise us all. Not much in the charm department, but he's *deep*, and that's what counts. . . . Willidene, give me your number again, in case I've been dialing the wrong one all these years. (Pause) Good, I've got it, and I'm going to use it! (She didn't even write it down.) Now, will you forgive me if I fly? It's a soufflé, and you know how *they* are; look cross-eyed

and they fall. Bless you, and a *thous*and Merry Christ-
mases. Goodbye."

She hung up, and then she shuddered and went to
the kitchen and started singing *It's a Long Way to
Tipperary.*

After about ten minutes, when Ralph went to the
bathroom, Annabel and I had the following conversation:

"I don't want to be a nuisance, lover, but I'm going
to have to set that table now. Couldn't you finish at
my desk?"

"Okay."

I moved to the desk. Annabel got out the tablecloth
and put it on. For a while she was quiet, and all of a
sudden she was standing behind me. When I looked
at her, she said:

"I'm *not* reading over your shoulder, Suspicious. I
was just thinking."

"About what?"

"Would you think I was prying?"

"Huh?"

"If I *asked* you something."

"Depends on what you ask."

"Well, thanks. That's encouraging. Just skip it."

She got out the silverware, and started setting the
table. "Would it be too much, do you think, if I put
on the bayberry candles? Not because it's Christmas
Eve *eve* or anything, but they smell like a million
dollars. What d'you think?"

"Sure."

The truth is, Annabel is not going ape this year
about Christmas, and I appreciate it. Naturally she
gave the house a good cleaning this week, did all the
windows and washed the bathroom ceiling. But she's

going pretty easy in the kitchen department, cookies and fruitcake as usual, but in fairly reasonable amounts, and Ralph's not getting too nervous about it. I ordered her a vanity case. They're going to put her initials on it, A.H.W., quite fancy with all the letters overlapping and all.

"They're a little bent," she said, "but I don't think it makes a particle, do you?"

"Nah."

"Clinton, do you ever think of all the people there must be in the world doing the exact same thing you're doing at the exact same second? Women setting tables, or lighting bayberry candles? Are you listening?"

"Sure."

"Because I think it's encouraging. Nice people doing nice things, all over everywhere. Clinton, I'm going to ask you something, the thing I wanted to ask you before. May I?"

"Go ahead."

"Will you answer me truthfully?"

"Okay."

She came over and looked at me. "It's about your notebook."

I didn't say anything.

"You write down things I say, don't you."

"Sometimes."

"Well, when you read it over, do I sound like a silly woman?"

I thought for a minute. Then I said, "No."

She looked like she wanted to come over and kiss me, but there was an embarrassment problem. So I blew one to her and she blew one back. Then she went on setting the table and singing *Tipperary*.

What I was trying to get at before all these inter-ruptions started, I was trying to get at this thing about the dream I had, but it's very complicated to get at.

The point is, I don't think I personally am going to have too many more nightmares about Echo and the wreck and Berry-berry and the tree and all. You have a certain number of them about things like that, and you cry a lot, and then you get to the point where you don't have too many more of them. Naturally I'm no expert but I'm writing all this down from my own experience.

Now, what I'm wondering about is this girl in the dream. We were in this double bed, the two of us, and it was like we were *used* to being in the same bed, as if I was married to her and everything was okay about us sleeping together. That wasn't the point. The point was, this girl was having a nightmare. Not me, but *her*. And she hollered and sort of half woke up. Then I dreamt that I moved over to her side of the bed and turned on the light and held her in my arms.

I said, "Wake up, honey, *I'm* here. Me, Clint." I shook her in a very firm way and then she woke up completely and hugged me and all. She started to tell about this nightmare she was having. What it was, it was my old Willy nightmare about this creep coming along shaking all the kids out of the apple tree. So I explained to her about how it isn't any real person that shakes the branches, it's only the wind that does those things. And I just kept on holding her and telling her everything was okay because of me being right there with her all the time, right next to her. Pretty soon she went to sleep in my arms, and that was the end of the dream.

I think I'd have to be pretty nutty to jump to any

271

conclusions, but I've given this whole thing a lot of thought, and the way I've figured it out is this: I believe I'm through having too many nightmares.

In fact, the kind of a person I believe I am now, is the kind that when somebody *else* has a nightmare, then I wake them up and take care of them—the kind of a person that puts my arms around them and says, "It's okay, honey, everything's going to be okay now. It's only the wind."

The thing I wonder about though is this girl in the dream. I can't remember what her face was like, so I'm none too sure who she's going to turn out to be. Someday I'll probably recognize her all right though.